KU-575-492

His arm moved across to shield her, pulling her in yet closer.

Amelie could have moved away again, but she did not. Nor did she protest when Lord Elyot's hand slid beneath the cape in front of her, settling upon her waist and sending its warmth immediately through the silk. It moved in the lightest of caresses, and she responded, shifting and edging at the infringement, but not knowing whether to stay or flee—wanting to do both, yet feeling herself yield to its heady excitement.

As if he could sense her dilemma, he firmed his hand upon her waist, holding her back, telling her to stay, while his other hand came to rest upon the beautiful curve of her hip, lightly stroking and smoothing where no one could see. And as Amelie continued to call out her goodnights, to smile and make believe that her heart was tranquil, all her awareness was alive to that gentle movement sliding upon the fine fabric of her gown, exploring like a summer breeze over hip, buttock and thigh, as intimate as water…

Juliet Landon's keen interest in art and history, both of which she used to teach, combined with a fertile imagination, make writing historical novels a favourite occupation. She is particularly interested in researching the early medieval period and the problems encountered by women in a man's world. Her heart's home is in her native North Yorkshire, but now she lives happily in a Hampshire village close to her family. Her first books, which were on embroidery and design, were published under her own name of Jan Messent.

A SCANDALOUS MISTRESS features descendants of characters you will have met in ONE NIGHT IN PARADISE.

Recent novels by the same author:

THE WARLORD'S MISTRESS
HIS DUTY, HER DESTINY
THE BOUGHT BRIDE
THE WIDOW'S BARGAIN
ONE NIGHT IN PARADISE

Look for Caterina's story,
the next instalment in Juliet Landon's
Ladies of Paradise Road

Coming soon

A SCANDALOUS MISTRESS

Juliet Landon

DERBYNIWYD/ RECEIVED	23 FEB 2012
CONWY	
GWYNEDD	
MÔN	
COD POST/POST CODE	LL5 1AS

MILLS & BOON®

All the characters in this book have no existence outside the imagination
of the author, and have no relation whatsoever to anyone bearing the
same name or names. They are not even distantly inspired by any
individual known or unknown to the author, and all the incidents are
pure invention.

All Rights Reserved including the right of reproduction in whole or
in part in any form. This edition is published by arrangement with
Harlequin Enterprises II BV/S.à.r.l. The text of this publication or
any part thereof may not be reproduced or transmitted in any form
or by any means, electronic or mechanical, including photocopying,
recording, storage in an information retrieval system, or otherwise,
without the written permission of the publisher.

MILLS & BOON and MILLS & BOON with the Rose Device
are registered trademarks of the publisher.

First published in Great Britain 2006
Large Print edition 2007
Harlequin Mills & Boon Limited,
Eton House, 18-24 Paradise Road, Richmond, Surrey TW9 1SR

© Juliet Landon 2006

ISBN-13: 978 0 263 19395 4

31651984

Set in Times Roman 15¼ on 17 pt.
42-0607-86734

Printed and bound in Great Britain
by Antony Rowe Ltd, Chippenham, Wiltshire

A SCANDALOUS MISTRESS

Chapter One

The steel of the younger man's foil made an arc against the padded waistcoat of his opponent and sprang back into shape, its point lowered to the ground. Laughing at his own failure, the Marquess of Sheen threw up an arm to acknowledge the scattered applause. 'Well done, my boy,' he called, passing his foil to the appreciative fencing master. 'Am I ever going to beat you again, I wonder?'

'Not if I can help it, sir,' said Lord Nicholas Elyot, removing his mask. 'It's taken me long enough to get to this stage.' He shook his father's offered hand, admiring the agility of the fifty-two-year-old body as well as the strength in his fingers, the keen brown eyes, the quick reflexes. As usual, he failed to perceive their similarities in the same way that others did, particularly Mr O'Shaunessy, the proprieter, who could see in Lord Elyot an exact replica of his father at the age of thirty, tall and broad-shouldered, slender-hipped and lithe, with legs like a Greek god. The dark, almost black hair that tousled thickly about the son's handsome face was, on the Marquess, as white as snow and still as dense, and the mouths that broke into sympathetic smiles would have stopped the heart and protests of any woman. As they often had; both of them.

They sat together to watch the next contestants, the Marquess leaning back against the wall, his son leaning forward with arms along thighs. 'Not below par, are you, Father?' said Lord Elyot.

There was a huff of denial. 'Nay, I could claim that as an excuse but it ain't so, m'boy. Never better. Top form. M'mind on too many things at once, I suppose.' The Marquess glanced at his son's strong profile. 'Well, I have to make up some reason, don't I?'

Lord Elyot leaned back. 'Only this once, sir. Where's the problem, Richmond or London?'

'Richmond, Nick. You say you're going back tomorrow?'

'Yes, a few loose ends to tie up here first, then I'll be off. It's been almost five weeks. Time I was attending to things.'

'Petticoat problems, is it? You still seeing that Selina Whatsit?'

'Miss Selena *Whatsit*,' said Nick, 'departed my company weeks ago, Father. You're way out of date.' He began to unbutton his shirt.

'By how many?'

'Oh, I dunno. A few. Thing is, I think it's time our Seton was taken back home before he strays into dun territory. No, don't be alarmed, he ain't there yet, but he soon will be if he stays here in London much longer. There's plenty to keep him occupied in Richmond. He can do the rounds with me and the bailiff and the steward for a start, and get some good air into his lungs. I can find ways of keeping his hands out of his breeches pockets.'

'You might want him to help you with a bit of investigating too, in that case. That may keep him busy.'

'What's to do, sir? Poachers again?'

'No, nothing so simple. Some complaints from the Vestry about interference in parish affairs.'

'By whom?'

'Ah, well, that's the problem, you see. They don't know. Let's go and get changed and I'll tell you about it.'

As with other noblemen who took their role in society seriously, the Marquess of Sheen, whose ancestral home was at Richmond, in the county of Surrey, had several professional obligations, one of which was to King George III to whom he was Assistant Master of Horse, and another to the Bench where he sat as Justice of the Peace. The obligation to his estate at Richmond was administered in his absence by his eldest son, Lord Nicholas Elyot, who would have to perform those same duties sooner or later anyway, so had no objection to taking that particular burden off his father's shoulders. Only a two-hour drive away from London, on a good day, Richmond lay further up the River Thames, and its parish council, the Vestry, was made up of stalwart citizens of good standing, including the church minister, the local schoolmaster, landowners and the squire, who was the Marquess himself. The Vestry's purpose was to deal with matters like street-lighting and the maintenance of roads, fires, crime and poverty. Criminals, who were almost always poor also, were locked into the local pound until they could be sentenced, while other unfortunates were sent to the workhouse, which, although it provided shelter and food, usually did little else for their creature comforts. It was regarded as a last resort.

'Somebody,' said the Marquess, 'is playing a deep game, bribing the workhouse staff to release two young women in the family way who've only just been admitted.'

'And the Vestry don't know who it is?'

'Nope. Mind you, they've been pocketing the blunt fast enough and not asking too many questions, but it's got to be stopped, Nick. Apart from that, one or two debtors and a child have been sneaked out of the pound at night, and nobody knows who's responsible. No law against paying a debtor's debts to get 'em released, as you know, but it has to be done through the proper channels, not by forcing the padlocks or slipping a fistful o' town bronze to the night doorman. It's *got* to stop,' he repeated.

'So you want me to find out who's behind it. Could it be a member of the Vestry, d'ye think? Someone with a grudge?'

'I doubt it. The Vestry have complained to me, so what I'm after is some juicy background information on whoever it is, enough to…er…*persuade* them to go and do their good turns somewhere else. I don't want to raise the hue and cry about it, just a little discreet blackmail will do. A threat of prosecution, if you like. It is an offence, after all.'

'Is it?' Nick smiled.

'Oh, yes. Abduction,' said the Marquess, airily. 'And perverting the course of justice, too.'

'Coming it a bit strong, Father?'

'We…ell, maybe. But I can't have the Vestry upset. They run the show while I'm here, you know. Special headquarters on Paradise Road. They like to be seen to be effective.'

'Which I'm sure they are, sir. I'll look into it immediately. Shouldn't take long. I'll let you know.' Nick shrugged his substantial shoulders into the immaculate dark grey morning coat and allowed the valet to adjust the lapels, the cuffs, the waistcoat and snowy neckcloth with fastidious care. Looking down at his glossy black Hessians, he indicated a speck of dust on one toe. The valet dropped to his knees to attend to it, then stood to hand Lord Elyot a beaver hat, a pair of soft kid gloves and a polished cane with a silver knob.

'Shall we see you at St James's Square for dinner?' said the Marquess.

'I'm not sure, sir. Shall I let you know later?'

'Of course. And don't forget your sister's birthday this month.'

'Heavens! Is it August already?'

'No, m'boy, it's been September these last two days.'

'Really? How old is she?'

'Lord, lad! How should I know? Ask your mother at dinner.'

They parted with a bow and a look that was not nearly as serious as their mutual ignorance of family birthdays would suggest.

Within the shining reflective precincts of Rundell, Bridge and Rundell on Ludgate Hill, the atmosphere was hushed, even churchlike, where white-aproned black-vested assistants spoke in reverential whispers, bowed, smiled and agreed with their well-heeled patrons who could afford not to notice the price of the wares. It would have been of little use to pass the doorman if money was a problem, for Rundell's was the most fashionable goldsmith in London where nothing came cheap and where, if it had, none of their customers would want to buy it.

That much Lady Amelie Chester had gathered from the pages of the *Ladies' Magazine*, and she had made a point of not returning from her first visit to the capital without seeing for herself what all the fuss was about. She had kept her barouche waiting for the best part of an hour while her coachman had driven the length of Ludgate and back several times so as not to keep the horses standing too long, and still there were choices to be made and the wink of a jewel to catch her eye. The ridiculously brief list she had brought had long since been discarded. She smiled at her two companions who hovered nearby, clearly not as enamoured by the Aladdin's Cave as she was.

The plainly dressed one holding a Kashmir shawl over one arm smiled back. 'Miss Chester is getting a bit fidgety, my lady,' she whispered, glancing at the girlish frills and bows disappearing behind a glass cabinet.

Miss Caterina Chester, the bored seventeen-year-old niece of the avid purchaser, had at last seen something she liked, which could best be observed through a display of silver candlesticks and cruets. Two men had stepped into the shop to stand quietly talking long enough for her to see that they were related, that one was perhaps nearing thirty, the other his junior by a few years. Both, without question, were veritable blades of distinction, the best she had seen all day. And she *had* been looking, almost without let-up.

Her practised young eye knew exactly what to expect from a pink of the *ton*; nothing flamboyant, everything perfectly cut, clean, stylish and fitting like a second skin over muscled thighs and slim hips and, although there would be some gathering at the top of the sleeves, there must be no hint of padding or corseting. These two were true nonpareils.

They were a comely pair, too, she told herself, comparing them. The elder one with the more authoritative air would have been in the army, she guessed, while the other, like herself, would be thinking that he could find more interesting things to do than this. Of one fact she was sure, however: neither of them would be in Rundell, Bridge and Rundell's unless they had wealth.

It was inevitable, she knew, that their attention would veer like a weathervane towards her aunt, Lady Amelie Chester, who had turned so many heads that day it was a wonder they had stayed on shoulders. No matter where she went, or did, or didn't do, for that matter, men would stare, nudge and whistle rudely through their teeth at Aunt Amelie. Envious women looked for weaknesses in her appearance and gave up in disgust that the dice could be so heavily loaded in one person's favour.

Watching them carefully, Caterina saw the younger man's lips form a pucker, putting his hand to the quizzing-glass that hung upon his buff waistcoat and dropping it again at the three quiet words from his companion. Then, like cats stalking a kill, they moved nearer.

Lady Chester had come to a decision and, in a state of near euphoria, was oblivious to all else. Having recently rid herself of an old-fashioned teapoy on a leggy stand, she was delighted to have found a small silver caddy made by the Batemans, topped with an acorn finial and handled with ivory. Before the enraptured assistant had finished praising her choice, she spied a beehive-shaped gilt honey pot with a bee on top. Her gloved fingers caressed its ridges. 'This,' she said, 'is perfect.'

'Paul Storr, m'lady,' the assistant smirked. 'We hope to acquire more of his work in the future. It came in only yesterday.'

'Then I'm sure it will be happy in Richmond,' she said. 'Add it to the others, if you please. I'll take it.'

The elder of the two men moved forward. 'Richmond?' he said. 'I thought I knew everyone in Richmond. I beg your pardon, ma'am. We have not been introduced, but pray allow me to take the liberty of performing my own introduction, since there is no one else to do it for me. Nicholas Elyot at your service. And my brother, Seton Rayne.'

The assistant intervened. 'My lords,' he said, bowing.

'Amelie Chester.' Amelie dipped a curtsy of just the correct depth while Caterina moved round the glass case to watch, fascinated and not too proud to learn a thing or two about how Aunt Amelie caused men to vie for her attention. One day, she would do the same. Her aunt neither smiled nor simpered as so many women did to gain a man's interest, Caterina noticed, watching the graceful incline of her head. A soft-brimmed velvet hat covered the rich brown hair escaping in wayward spirals around her ears to accentuate the smooth peachy skin over high cheekbones. Her eyes were bewitchingly dark and almond-shaped, her brows fine and delicately arched, and there was no feature, thought Caterina, that needed the aid of cosmetics.

On the verge of leaving half-mourning behind her, Lady Chester's pelisse was of three-quarter-length pale violet velvet with a swansdown collar worn over a silver-grey silk day dress. The edges of the velvet sleeves were caught together at intervals with covered buttons, and a capacious reticule of matching beaded velvet hung from one arm. The only ornament on the rather masculine hat was a large silver buckle into which was tucked a piece of swansdown, and the effect of all this on the two men, Caterina thought, was as much a sight to behold as her aunt's classic elegance. Surreptitiously, she removed the fussy lace tippet from around her shoulders that she had insisted on wearing and passed it to Lise, her aunt's maid.

The brothers removed their tall hats and bowed in unison. 'You are staying here in London, my lady?' said Lord Elyot.

His voice, she thought, was like dark brown chocolate. 'No, my lord. Only to shop. We must leave soon, now the days are shortening,' she said.

'Indeed. You'll need all the light we have left. Have you been long in Richmond? How could we have missed seeing you there?'

A smile lit up the almond eyes at last with the lift of her brow. 'As to that, sir, anyone could miss us quite easily, even at church. My niece and I have seen little of society since we arrived. May I introduce her to you? Miss Caterina Chester.'

At last, Caterina's moment had arrived. She stepped forward from her vantage point to make the prettiest bob she could devise while she had their entire attention and, though she ought to have kept her eyes demurely lowered, her natural urge to discover what effect she was having got the better of her.

'My lords,' she whispered, allowing her bright golden-brown eyes to reach the younger lord's attentive face for another glimpse of his crisp dark thatch before he replaced his hat. It seemed to fall quite naturally into the correct disorder but his eyes, she noticed, held only a neutral attempt at friendship before focussing once more upon her aunt. Inwardly, she sighed.

Lord Elyot, however, saw that one of his queries had been avoided. 'Is your stay in Richmond permanent, Miss Chester?' he said.

'Oh, yes, my lord. We've been there only five weeks and two days and there's such a lot for us yet to see.' And do, she thought. Again, her gaze turned hopefully in Lord Rayne's direction, but noticed only the quizzical nature of his examination of her over-frilled and beribboned day dress and braided spencer, her flower-bedecked bonnet and the lace gloves that she had believed were all the thing. Until now.

'Oh, you'll need several seasons to see all that London has to offer,' Lord Elyot replied, 'but shopping must come first. My brother and I called in to purchase a gift for our sister's birthday, but we possess neither the flair nor the time to find exactly the right thing. I wonder, my lady…' he returned his attention to Amelie '…if you and your niece could help us out. Your taste,' he continued, glancing at the counter covered with pieces she had bought, 'is obviously of the most sophisticated. Do you have any suggestions as to what would please a sister most?'

'Without knowing her, sir, that would be difficult. Is she single or married? Young or…how old will she be?'

The two men exchanged blank stares until Lord

Rayne offered some statistics he was reasonably sure of. 'Well, she's three years older than me, married with two bra…bairns…er, children.'

'And she's two…no, three years younger than me,' said his brother. 'Does that help?'

Amelie's smile might have grown into a laugh but for her effort to contain it, and Caterina noted again the devastating effect this gentle bubbling had on the two men, for it was genuine yet controlled. 'That is *some* help. Does she have a star sign?' Amelie prompted, twinkling.

The blankness returned.

'The beginning of September? Or the middle?'

'The end,' said Lord Rayne, warming to the theme.

'No, somewhere near the middle,' said Lord Elyot. 'I think. Look, may we leave this with you, if you'd be so kind? Mr Bowyer here will charge the cost to my account and send it to Richmond. We're in a bit of a hurry.'

Smiling broadly, Mr Bowyer assented.

Amelie agreed, wondering at the same time why they had stopped to choose a gift if they were in so much of a hurry. 'Of course,' she said. 'Miss Chester and I will surely find something appropriate in here.'

Lord Elyot bowed. 'You are too kind,' he said, formally. 'I am in your debt, my lady. I hope we shall meet in Richmond.'

There was something about his eyelids, Amelie

thought. He was a man of experience, and he knew how to look at a woman to make her feel as if she were the only person in the room to matter to him. He had spoken to Caterina like that too, and the child had noticed and wished the brother had done the same.

Bows and curtsies were exchanged once more and the meeting was curtailed as Caterina instantly began a search for something that would fritter away someone else's money. The men made for the door, their voices carrying easily across the subdued interior.

'I didn't know we were in so much of a hurry, Nick.'

'Well, we are. We need to return to Richmond tonight. A problem to sort out for Father. Rather urgent.'

'What kind of a problem?'

Lord Elyot tucked his cane beneath one arm and picked up a silver snuff-box, turning it over to examine the base. 'Oh, just some loose screw or other springing young nob-thatchers and bairns from the local workhouse,' the deep voice drawled softly, distinctly bored. 'Anybody who thinks that a bit o'skirt with a bun in the oven is worth rescuing must be an addle-pate, don't you agree, young Rayne? But the Vestry want it stopped. It's only a twenty-four-hour job, but we have to make a start before we get a new plague of vagabonds. You can help, if you like.' He replaced the snuff-box. 'Come on. It won't take all that long, then we can go and look at some new cattle, eh?'

'Stupid do-gooders! Ought to be locked up themselves. If only they knew the trouble they cause.'

They passed out of the shop into the sudden clamour of Ludgate Hill, where the street-criers and rattle of wheels drowned the rest of their conversation, and Amelie was left doing what her niece had done earlier through salt-cellars and candlesticks. She watched them pause as her own barouche drew to a standstill outside the shop and the footman leapt down to hold the horses' heads. Her heart hammered with sudden fear.

Loose screw…springing young nob-thatchers and bairns from the local workhouse…bit o'skirt with a bun in the oven…do-gooders…

It was not so much the vulgar cant that raised Amelie's hackles, for the men were entitled to say what they wished when they were alone; it was the revelation that they had a particular problem to solve for their father, whoever he was, which was apparently upsetting both him and the Vestry. And without a shadow of a doubt they were, without knowing it, speaking of her, Lady Amelie Chester, for she was the 'do-gooder' in question whose deep commitment to the plight of unfortunate women would never be understood by toffs of their kind who didn't know the date of their sister's birthday, or even how old she was. She felt the surge of fury, resentment and disappointment like a pain as she heard their mocking voices again. She watched them linger outside to examine her new coffee-coloured barouche with its cream-and-brown striped upholstery, its Italian lamps, the dapple-grey horses, the eight-caped coachman and liveried footman in brown and pale grey as neat as could be. They would not find any cattle to beat that showy pair, she thought, turning away with a frown. It had all ended on a very sour note, for she had liked their manner until then. She would find it even more difficult to fulfil her promise now she had seen the kind of men she had agreed to oblige. 'Caterina dear, have you seen anything suitable?' she said.

Wallowing almost knee-deep in expensive metalware, her niece had suddenly become animated and was eyeing a pair of very pretty silver chinoiserie cake-baskets that Amelie would not have minded owning.

'Mm…m,' Amelie said. 'Pretty, but…'

'Well, then, what about a large salver? They're always useful. One cannot have too many salvers, can one?'

The catalyst was the word 'useful'. If there was anything a woman disliked being given for her birthday, it came into the 'useful' category unless, of course, she had asked for it. Like a carriage and a pair of horses. Eagerly, she looked around for the largest, the most tasteless and most expensive 'useful' item on display, though it was Caterina who spotted it first, a massive silver and gilt tea urn with three busty sphinxes holding up the bowl on their wings and a tap that swung away like a cobra about to strike. Standing on an ugly triangular base, it was a monstrous reminder of Lord Nelson's recent victory in Egypt.

'What if she doesn't drink tea, though?' whispered Caterina, without knowing how she and her aunt were working at cross-purposes. 'It looks *very* expensive.'

All the better. 'Oh, she's sure to, dear.'

'Is it in good taste?' Caterina queried, having doubts.

Amelie was careful here. 'It will depend,' she said, cautiously, 'on what their sister's preferences are, I suppose. If she has a growing family and plenty of visitors, then a large urn will be just the thing.' And it would go some way, she thought, towards mollifying her resentment at the insensitive, not to say *inhuman*, attitude of the two brothers who, she hoped, would not follow up their introduction with anything more presumptuous.

But although the purchase of the vastly overpriced and vulgar gift had evened the score for Amelie in one direction, there was yet a more serious one to consider, calling for a return home at a faster pace than their earlier ride into London. There was now no time to lose. 'Lise, go and tell the footman we're ready to go home,' she said.

The stares of admiration directed at the beautiful coffee-coloured barouche and the Dalmatian running behind were only vaguely heeded on the return journey to Richmond, for the event that concluded their shopping spree weighed heavily on Amelie's mind, making her realise yet again that, however good it was to be an independent woman, she was still vulnerable without the comforting support of her husband.

Sir Josiah Chester had been taken from her with a frightening suddenness two years ago, a most unusual two years that left her with few relatives close enough to assist her through the worst months, the problems of inheritance and estate. The only one of their number whose help had been constant and ungrudging was Sir Josiah's younger brother Stephen, himself a widower with a young family, of whom Caterina was the eldest.

It had been to thank Stephen for his generous support that she had agreed to take Caterina with her when she moved down to Richmond. Had it not been for that debt which she owed him, for his plea, and for Caterina's motherless state, she would have made the move alone, which had been her first intention. She had no wish to stay in the Derbyshire town of Buxton for, although she had been happy enough there for her first twenty-two years, the two years after that had pointed out with brutal reality who she could depend on for true friendship.

Caterina's joy at being taken to live with her, though flattering, was not what Amelie had wanted, and the inevitable conflict of interests had not been satisfactorily resolved in their first few weeks. Caterina had expected to make a new set of friends and to be received almost instantly into high society. Amelie had not the heart to explain either to Caterina or to her grateful father, that the fickleness of high society was something she would rather have shunned than sought, and that the reason she had chosen Richmond was for its proximity to Kew Gardens, to Hampton Court Palace, to the famed Chelsea Physic Garden and to Royal Academy exhibitions. The day's shopping in London, though necessary, had been more the result of a guilty conscience than for Amelie's own pleasure, not having tried as hard as she might to make contact with the local leading families, as Caterina had expected her to. The young lady's very inadequate wardrobe had dictated the pattern of their shopping, and now the maid Lise sat beside a mountain of brown paper parcels that threatened to topple and bury her at each bounce of the carriage. Fortunately, there had not been room for the controversial tea urn, or Lise might have been critically injured.

The reason for Amelie's accelerated haste to reach home was neither asked nor explained, as the clouding September sky was supposed by Caterina to be the cause. The truth, however, was more to do with Lord Elyot's stated intention to attend directly to the problem of which the Vestry had complained.

Homeless mothers-to-be were often hustled over the boundary of one parish into the next, even during labour, to avoid the responsibility of more mouths to feed. Naturally, these women could not be let loose to give birth under hedges: untidy activities of that nature did not look well where refined citizens could be shocked by such sights. As a last resort, they had to be rounded up until it was all over, by which time the problem was often solved more permanently.

Sir Josiah Chester had not retained his vast wealth by giving it away to charitable causes, but by saving it; whether it was the powerful combination of childlessness, bereavement and wealth that gave rise to Amelie's concern for waifs, strays and hopeless debtors, she had never tried to analyse, but the fact was that her acceptance of her new state had been smoothed by the help she had given to others less endowed and more distressed by far. She could be distressed in comfort, while they could not.

With a name as well known in Buxton as Sir Josiah's, it had been relatively easy for Amelie, as a widow, to pay the debts of poor families threatened by imprisonment and worse and to find employment for petty criminals. She had given shelter and aid, sometimes in her own home, to pregnant homeless

women and had found suitable places for them afterwards, had persuaded farmers' wives to take in
starving children and had poured money into improving the local workhouse facilities. The legacy
she had received from her own wealthy parents had
been exceptionally generous, and all that giving had
made a greater difference to her sense of worth and
general well-being than it had to her reserve of funds.

As long as she was actively helping the Vestry in
Buxton to deal with their problems, no one had stood
in her way, though nothing could stop the gossip of
society women concerning the status of a young,
wealthy and beautiful widow and the attentions of
her brother-in-law, of supposed lovers and supposed
rivals. The whisperings of scandal. It had been time
for her to leave.

But in Richmond, the advantages associated with
the name of Sir Josiah Chester had not opened the
same doors as they had before, and all the help she
had given so freely in Buxton now had to be done
rather differently. In the dark. Anonymously. By
bribery and deception and, if need be, by the useful
burglary skills of a servant in her employ. It went
without saying that she had far too many servants,
most of them without references.

Last night, she had promised a distraught and
heavily pregnant young woman, via the woman's
equally distressed companion, that she would help

to release her from the workhouse where she was about to be taken. Amelie fully intended to go there that very night, and the last thing she needed was an extra guard on the gate put there by the interfering Lord Elyot. What on earth could have possessed her to agree to an introduction?

She heard the aristocratic drawl again, smoother than northern tones, more languid, deep and perfectly enunciated. His teeth were good too, and she recalled how something inside her had lurched a little at the way his eyes had held hers, gently but with devastating assurance. They had not raked over her as so many other men's did, trespassing and too familiar. No, they had almost smiled, telling her that there were things to be shared, given the opportunity.

Well, my fine lord, she thought, grinding her teeth, there will be no opportunity. I shall know how to steer well clear of you and any family who believe charity to be a waste of time. Hateful, arrogant people.

What colour were his eyes?

Pulling herself up sharply, she redirected her thoughts to the three over-endowed sphinxes and their hideous cobra companion, drawing the Kashmir shawl closer about her at the sudden chill.

After a later-than-usual dinner, after the unwrapping of every single purchase and an examination of each item, after umpteen reviews on the perfection of Lord Rayne's neckcloth, his hair, his noble features, Caterina was at last persuaded to retire to bed with *The Mysteries of Udolpho*, which she had longed to read but had not been allowed to, for fear her younger sister Sara should want to do the same. Such were the joys of leaving one's siblings behind.

Immediately, Amelie began a transformation from lady of fashion to dowdy old woman who might, in the dark, pass for a servant or an itinerant fruitpicker looking for work. She had seen the plight of the one to be rescued the day before, waiting, weeping outside the impressive Vestry Hall on Paradise Road, a grandiose Roman-style building that would have intimidated anyone by its sheer size alone. Amelie's house was only a few doors away, and she and Caterina, passing on their way home from the apothecary's shop, had been arrested by the pitying group of women who stood to sympathise and scold that the woman in question was being expected to walk all the way up to the workhouse on Hill Common. The woman's companion, probably an aunt or her mother, had been shouldered aside by the beadle, but Amelie had managed to find out from her what was happening and to assure her, in a moment of extreme compassion, that she could rely on her help the very next night, one way or another.

Previous rescues had been undertaken by those of Amelie's devoted servants who were themselves of a similar background to the women and, so far, she'd had no need to risk her own discovery, nor would they have allowed her to if she had proposed it. This time, she had kept her plans to herself, knowing that the woman's companion would need to recognise her.

It was a fair hike up to Hill Common and a carriage would easily be identified so, instead of walking, she rode her donkey Isabelle. It was appropriate, she thought, confidently rejoicing that she was well ahead of that obnoxious man and his abortive schemes. What a pity it was that she would not see his reaction to the latest 'springing of a young nob-thatcher'. What disgusting jargon men used.

The road was uphill, rough, and well beyond the street lights, and the rain that had threatened all afternoon had begun to fall heavily, turning the stony way into a river and soaking the thick shawl over Amelie's head. At last she came to the great iron gates and the gatekeeper's box from which the dim glow of a candle could be seen wavering in the draught. Sliding thankfully off Isabelle's back, she saw the dark figure of a woman approach and could hardly contain her relief that she would not have to wait long on such a night. Soon, they would all three be safe and comfortable, and the new life would be welcomed instead of being someone's burden.

'Well met,' she said, peering hard into the blackness and easing her reticule off her wrist. 'Have you heard how your…sister…is? Or is she your daughter? Do forgive me, I didn't see you too well.'

'Aye, she's well,' the woman croaked. 'No babe yet, though.'

'And have you spoken to the gateman? He'll cooperate, will he? Do we have to bribe the doorman, too?'

'Oh, aye, each one as we pass through. How much did you bring, m'lady? If you'll pardon me asking.'

'Let's get out of this downpour…over here under the tree.'

The steady roar took on a different note as Amelie pulled the donkey behind her, then took the reticule out from beneath the folds of dripping wetness, turning her back on the woman to rest its weight on the saddle. It was in that brief moment of heedlessness when Amelie should have been holding all her wits on a knife-edge that the woman's hand darted like a weasel towards the bag of money, pulling it off the saddle and out of Amelie's hands, swinging it away into an indistinct flurry of blackness.

Bumping into Isabelle's large head, Amelie threw herself after the woman and made a wild grab at her clothes, feeling the resistance and the ensuing twist as her fingers closed over the rough wet fabric. Unable to see, the two of them grappled and pulled, suffering the frantic grasp of fingers on head, hair, shoulders and throat, their feet slithering and tripping over tree roots. But the woman was stronger and older than her opponent and trained to every trick of the seasoned thief, and Amelie was taken by the hair, spun round and pushed so hard that she fell sprawling upon her front in one great lung-crushing thud that pressed her face into the wet ground with a squeak of expelled breath.

The fight was over; the sound of fumbling, then of running feet on the track becoming fainter, and the unrelenting rain pattering noisily on the leaves above, throbbing like a pain, humiliating and raw. She had promised to help a woman in need and been robbed of the chance. *Failure.*

'Isabelle…Isabelle?' she called.

She heard the jingle of the harness and a man's voice urging the creature to come on and be quick about it, then a soft thwack on the animal's wet rump.

'Who…where are you?' Amelie called. 'Who is it?' She struggled to gain a footing, but her boots were tangled in folds of wet skirts and she was unable to rise before a dark shape bent down to help her.

'Forgive me, ma'am,' he said, politely. 'Allow me to help you up. Hold your hands out…no…this way.'

'Where? How do I know you're a friend?'

'Well, you don't, ma'am. But you can't stay down there all night, can you? See, here's your donkey. Come, let me help you. Are you hurt?'

'Not much. I don't know. That woman's nowhere to be seen, I suppose?'

'Gone, I'm afraid. Has she robbed you, ma'am? Did she take…?'

'My reticule. Yes, it's gone. Tch! Serves me right.'

The stranger eased her up, releasing her arm immediately to look, as well as he was able, at the patch of ground round about. 'No reticule, ma'am. It looks as if she must have taken it. I'd never have thought there'd be game-pullets like her out on a night like this, I must say. Shall I get hold of the gatekeeper for you?'

'Er…no, not now,' said Amelie, quickly. 'I'd better go back and try again tomorrow. Thank you for your help, Mr…?'

'Todd, ma'am. No trouble at all. Would you like me to escort you?'

'Oh, no, thank you, Mr Todd. I'm most grateful to you, but I have not far to go and Isabelle will carry me.'

'Well, if you're sure. I'll hold her while you climb aboard. There now. Good night to you, ma'am. I didn't catch your name?'

'Ginny,' she said, realising at once that her voice was not in accord with her appearance. 'Ginny Hodge. Good night to you, Mr Todd.' She fumbled for the reins and kicked Isabelle into action, swaying and tipping over the puddles as her body, already aching with bruises, tried to stay upright. Once or twice she felt compelled to turn and look over her shoulder into the solid blackness and driving rain, though mostly her troubled thoughts were for the woman she had let down who would now believe the worst of her sort of people, as others apparently did. Perhaps she should have been a little less bountiful with her promises, a little more suspicious of people's need to be helped. She had learned to be more philosophical over the last few years, but the disappointments of the day were felt more keenly than her bruises during the uncomfortable journey home and well into the small hours. It was at such times that she missed Josiah's fatherly counselling most of all.

Sheen Court, Richmond, Home of the Marquess of Sheen

A guarded tap on the door of the study was answered by a gruff monosyllable and the lowering of a pen on to the leather-covered desk. A single candle guttered in the draught as the door opened and closed.

'Any luck?' was the quiet greeting.

The visitor allowed himself a half-smile. 'Yes, my lord. I believe we may have something.' He held up a wet embroidered reticule, the drawstrings of which had been pulled wide open. 'It was not so fortunate for the woman, a certain Ginny Hodge, mind you. She got herself mugged by a thieving old dowd at the workhouse gates and lost the contents of this.' He laid the bag on the desk before his lordship and watched as the long fingers drew out the remaining objects one by one: a blue glass perfume bottle with a silver stopper, a damp lace-edged handkerchief of very superior quality, and a tortoiseshell and silver filigree card-case, which opened to reveal one single card.

This was removed and studied in silence for what seemed to the visitor like an extraordinarily long time before his lordship shook his head with a grunt of disbelief in his throat. 'Well…well!' he whispered. 'Was this…Ginny Hodge…hurt by the mugging?'

'I think not too seriously, sir. I followed her home to Paradise Road. One of the big newish houses. She went in by the back way, but she didn't sound like a servant to me, sir.'

Raising himself from his chair, his lordship went over to the side table, poured a glass of whisky and handed it to his informant. 'Drink that,' he said, 'and get into something dry. You've done well.'

'Thank you, my lord. Shall you need the coach in the morning?'

'No, the crane-neck phaeton. Good night, Todd.'

'Good night, my lord. Thank you.' The empty glass was exchanged for a silver coin, and the door was closed as quietly as it had been opened. But it was much later when the candle was at last extinguished and Lord Nicholas Elyot, swinging the reticule like a trophy, ascended the staircase at Sheen Court.

Chapter Two

By breakfast, Lord Elyot's surprise had mellowed and a plan of action had already begun to form in his mind about how best to proceed, given that his father's instructions would require some readjustment. To the genteel rattle of newspapers and the clatter of cutlery on plates, he had consulted his brother about the day ahead, though his suggestion had not been received as favourably as he'd hoped.

'Nick,' said Lord Rayne, laying down his knife, 'if I'd known you'd hauled me back to Richmond to be wet-nurse to a green chit, I'd have stayed in London. You know I'd do anything for you, but this is a fudge if ever I saw one.' He laid down his crisp white napkin with rather more force than was necessary and sat back, still chewing. 'She's only just out of the schoolroom, dammit!'

'It's not a fudge,' said Lord Elyot. 'I mean it. And

I'm not asking you to *marry* the child, only that you keep her happy while I—'

'While *you* keep Lady Chester happy. Thank you, but I have a better idea. You take the frilly one and I'll take the diamond. How's that?'

Lord Elyot reached for the marmalade-pot and heaped a spoonful of it on to his toast. 'Two good reasons. One is that you're not her type. Second is that you don't have the time. You'll be a member of His Majesty's fighting force soon, don't forget.'

'Not her type? And you are, I suppose?'

'Yes.' The bite into the toast was decisive.

Reluctantly, Lord Rayne was obliged to admit that his elder brother would succeed with Lady Chester if any man could, for it would take a cold woman to be unaffected by his darkly brooding good looks and the singular manner of his total concentration upon what she had to say. Which was not the usual way of things. As to the time he would need, Nick was right about that, too. The lady's response to him had been polite, but far from enthusiastic, and he would need both time and help to gain a more lasting interest. 'What's it worth to you?' he said.

Lord Elyot's pained expression was partly for his brother's mercenary train of thought and partly for the messy nature of toast and marmalade. 'I'm doing you a *favour*, sapskull,' he snapped. 'The child's a pert little thing, not a dimwit. Pretty eyes, rough round the edges, but you could have the pleasure of working on that. She'd not resent it. She'll be a little cracker by the end of the season and then you can leave her to somebody else. A built-in escape route. What more d'ye want, lad?'

'Cattle. I shall need three or four good mounts to take with me.'

'What happened to your allowance?'

'You know what happened to it or I'd not be on a repairing-lease in the country, would I?'

'All right. Four good mounts it is. For your help, Seton.'

'For my full…unstinting…liberal and generous help. When can we go and look at them?'

'We'll look at the *women* today. This morning. We'll take my new crane-neck phaeton out. You can drive.' Lord Elyot leaned back, satisfied.

'Just one detail, Nick. How d'ye know there isn't a husband there somewhere?'

'I made enquiries.'

'You don't waste much time, do you? And what about this urgent business for Father? Where does that come in?'

'That's in hand, too,' he said, 'but I want you to keep that very much to yourself, Seton, if you will. A word about that in the wrong ear can send them up like pheasants.'

* * *

The particular pheasant Lord Elyot had in mind was already flying at a steady pace along the edge of Richmond Park in a coffee-and-cream phaeton. The driver of this neat little turn-out had evasion in mind, but her passenger was on the lookout for the merest sign of the two men who, since their meeting yesterday, had satisfied her every criteria for what makes the perfect Corinthian. Believing that she had won the argument about a need for fresh early-morning air, Caterina had resisted all her aunt's recommendations that she should wear a shawl over her spencer and pale blue walking-dress, and now she wished that the stiff breeze would abate a little. Holding the long ribbons of her blue ruched bonnet with one hand, she clung to the side of the phaeton with the other as they bounced on elliptical springs through a deep puddle.

'Aunt Amelie,' she said, half-turning to see if the tiger was still on his seat behind them, 'do you think…we could…slow down a little? There's a… phaeton over there…in the…distance…oops! I can't quite…see. Please?'

Amelie's hands tightened on the reins. It had been her intention to speed with all haste to Kew Gardens with Caterina in order to avoid the visit that she feared might result from their introduction to Lord Elyot and his brother, who she knew to be returning to Richmond yesterday. Conversely, sending a message to the door to say that they were not at home would not please Caterina one bit, nor would it help to fulfil her assurances to Caterina's father.

Yet after last night's bitter disappointment and her poor night's sleep, the thought of being even civil to the unfeeling pair was more than she could bear, and Caterina's pleas to go out driving instead of revelling in her new dress-lengths had seemed to Amelie like a chance to please herself while appearing to please her niece. Now it looked as if her strategy had been identified, as the vehicle in question had swung round in a dangerously tight half circle to head in their direction.

It would have been folly for her to go any faster, as she would like to have done, with the small body of the phaeton suspended above the lightweight undercarriage and the greys being so eager, but Amelie saw no reason to slow down either. The road ahead was clear except for the approach of an open landau, and it was the tiger's warning as he stood up to peer between their heads that decided the pace after all. 'Watch out, m'lady!' he called. 'Them two are 'avin a bit of a frisk, by the look o' things. Better pull up till they've passed. Aye, I thought as much. It's the Oglethorpes' new pair. That's it, m'lady. Keep 'em on the rein till I've got their heads.' He leapt down off his rear perch and ran to the bridles, and Amelie had no choice but to wait for the two fretting horses to pass, receiving the coachman's thanks but only the briefest of acknowledgements from the two female passengers.

Amelie would have been surprised if it had been otherwise; only the men in Richmond had ever offered any warmer salutation in the last five weeks and, as yet, no lady had left her calling-card. Before they could move off again, the towering crane-neck phaeton had caught them up, making their lower version look sedate by comparison. Sensing Caterina's *frisson* of excitement, Amelie glanced at her and saw how nervous fingers smoothed the blue muslin over her knees, saw the alertness in her posture like a soldier on parade. So soon she was in love, and all a-flutter. Within her own breast, she felt again that uncomfortable kick against her lungs and put it down either to the affray of last night or having eaten her breakfast muffin too quickly.

'Lady Chester, Miss Chester,' said Lord Elyot, tipping his hat. 'What a happy coincidence. You are out early. Do you go to see and be seen up on the Hill?'

Richmond Hill was a favourite parade-ground for showing off one's horse or carriage, which Amelie had so far avoided. 'No, my lord,' she said, aware of the looks being exchanged between Caterina and Lord Rayne, 'we're on our way to see the newest blooms at Kew. I'm teaching my niece to depict them.' She wished instantly that she had not made it sound so school-marmish, but her large canvas bag lay at their feet, bulging with sketchbooks and paint-boxes, and the men would surely have seen it from their height.

Lord Rayne leaned forward the better to see Caterina. 'The study of blooms,' he said, 'would seem to be a glaring omission from my education, my lady. Would you allow us, just this once, to ac-company you to see how it's done?'

Caterina was about to enthuse, but Amelie used an elbow to nudge her into silence. There was no question of her showing them or anyone else except her niece how to draw blooms, and the mock-interest Lord Rayne was showing annoyed her by its face-tiousness. 'I cannot prevent you going where you will, Lord Rayne,' she replied, 'but we are not inclined to demonstrate. I beg you to excuse us.'

Her indignation swelled once more as she recalled for the hundredth time those hurtful words the two men had used only yesterday: 'Loose screw...do-gooders...addle-pate...ought to be locked up...' Buxton people had thanked her and called her stout-hearted: here, they called it interference and would put a stop to it, if they could. Not even for Caterina's sake could she forget or even try to find an allowance for their heartlessness, nor could she shake off the thought of the miserable childbearing woman she had failed last night. At that moment the two events were linked in her mind, and any goodwill she might have pretended for the sake of Caterina's burgeoning emotions was still-born.

Sitting nearest to Amelie as his brother's passenger, Lord Elyot was better able to see the coolness as well as the anger behind her dark eyes and, though they were now turned towards the horses' ears, not to him, he was determined to get more out of this meeting than an excuse when it was obvious that the niece was setting so much store by it.

'Of course,' he said. 'We have no wish to intrude, Lady Chester. But will you explain something to me, before you leave us?'

'Certainly, if I can.'

'I noticed that Mrs and Miss Oglethorpe could hardly raise an acknowledgement between them just now. Not that it matters, of course, but I wondered if there was a particular reason for their rudeness. Have they not been introduced to you?'

He was right. It did not matter, but he may as well know now as later, and it may as well come from her, to set the facts straight. 'Yes, they were, at church.' He would want to know more, she was sure.

'Yet no smiles and hardly a bow? Was she attempting to cut you, by any chance?'

She sighed, then looked slowly at him and his handsome brother. 'I think you and Lord Rayne will soon discover,' she said, 'that you do yourselves no favours by being seen speaking to Miss Chester and me. In London where we can be more anonymous, perhaps, but not here in Richmond. We are not quite the thing, you know.'

'Is that so?' said Lord Elyot. 'How very intriguing. Well, I suppose we could drive on at a smart pace, but I am inclined to beg for more details. I'm sure my brother is of the same mind. Do tell us. You are highwaymen in disguise? Escaped Muscovy princesses?'

Though his eyes were shaded, Amelie recalled how they had looked at her in the shop, and she could not meet them again. 'Nothing quite as dramatic,' she replied. 'We are *northerners*, sir. Worse still, my family has connections with industry. To put it bluntly, my lord, *trade*. There, I've said the awful word. Now I shall go and rinse my mouth with water and vinegar and you will put some distance between us as fast as you can. We shall not hold it against you. I bid you both a very good day.'

'Wait!' Lord Elyot's gloved hand could not reach Amelie's phaeton, but his command was enough to hold her back. 'Please?' he added, squeakily.

When she sneaked a look upwards, she saw that he and his brother were grinning broadly. 'You may smile, Lord Elyot,' she said, 'but the good people of Richmond take such things very seriously, you must know. Or had you forgotten? We might display any number of harmless eccentricities like sketching blooms at Kew Gardens, but *trade* is unforgivable, sir. Somebody has obviously got wind of it. And the *north*…well, nothing there but mills and clogs and smoke and strange dialects. Miss Chester and I own only one head each, but some have two, or even *three*! Can you imagine it?'

To keep her straw hat firmly in place in the blustering wind, Amelie had tied a long gauze scarf over it, swathing her neck and making it difficult for him to see her face without craning forward. But her sarcasm had produced an angry flush and a sparkle to her superb eyes that Lord Elyot could only guess at until his brother moved the horses forward a step. Then he was better able to judge the passion behind her droll revelations and to see that she was not quite the amenable obliging creature he had met the day before, nor was she the misguided woman whose reticule he now possessed.

Equally significant was the expression of dismay on the pretty niece's face at the scuppering of her hopes. So this was the reason why they had kept out of the social scene for five weeks and why the young lass was so keen to make contact with the first half-decent beau to speak to her. His laughter had stopped well before Amelie had finished her explanation.

'With difficulty,' he said, in answer to her question. 'But am I to understand that Richmond approval is what you desire, my lady?'

Her voice lost its flinty edge. 'Not for myself, my lord. I did not come here to seek high society and there is no one's approval I need. I have more interesting matters to keep me occupied. I bid you both good day, my lords.'

Giving them no time to recover or to say a proper farewell, she called out to Riley to let the horses go, cracked the whip above their heads with astonishing precision, and set them off so fast that the poor tiger had to take a flying leap at the back of the perch as it passed.

'Whew! You in an 'urry, m'lady?' he gasped.

'Yes. How do we get out of this place?'

'Thought you was going to Kew, m'lady.'

'Well, I've changed my mind. Left or right... *quick*, man!'

'Left! Steady, for pity's sake, or we'll all be in the ditch.'

'Rubbish! If you can't stay aboard, get off and walk.'

Riley grinned. 'Yes, m'lady.' He would rather have been seen dead.

Amelie's sudden reversal, however, was heartily disapproved of, and had done more than bring a mild disappointment to the young breast at her side, for now there were tear-filled lashes and a voice husky with broken dreams. Turning round after taking a last lingering look at the classy phaeton's driver, Caterina rummaged in her reticule for a handkerchief and dabbed, reserving her questions for the privacy of the breakfast parlour at Number 18 Paradise Road. Travelling at Amelie's speed, it did not take long.

Caterina was a vivacious but not unreasonable young lady, even at times like this when her desires had been thwarted, and such was her admiration for her aunt that the explanation and assurances she was given were accepted without argument. If Aunt Amelie said that the men would not be put off, then she must wait and hope it would not take too long, though privately she could not see why they should have been so positively rejected in the first place if they were expected to try again. Did Aunt Amelie *hope* they would?

The rest of the day was not wasted, for Caterina's weekly singing lesson with Signor Cantoni used up an hour after noon, then there was piano practice to be done followed by a thorough search through back copies of the *Ladies' Magazine* to find some day dresses for the mantua-maker to reproduce. After which she read all the advertisements for cosmetics, hair colourants, rouge for lips and cheeks, mouth fresheners, skin softeners, soaps, pills and whalebone. Amelie protested. 'You need no stays, my dear,' she said. 'You have a beautiful youthful figure that needs not even the shortest corset. Nor does your hair need extra colour.' It was no flattery—Caterina was

exceedingly pretty and trim, and Amelie was convinced that, with an overhaul of her somewhat
childish wardrobe and some practice of womanly
ways, she would soon be a beauty. Her naturally
curly red-gold hair would respond well to the dishevelled look, so they set about experimenting,
there and then, with the Grecian style, with bandeaux,
plumes, combs and knots, twists and coils. The next
time Lord Rayne saw her, Amelie predicted, he
would be astonished by the transformation.

Next morning, the mantua-maker and her young assistant arrived to measure Caterina for new gowns. It
had rained heavily again during the night and well
into the morning, damping the dressmaker and
chilling her helper to such an extent that, although one
of her roles was to model some of the gowns they had
brought with them, her emaciated and shivering body
stuck through the sheer fabrics like a grasshopper's
knees. Amelie resolved to mend that problem before
the coming autumn sent the child to an early grave.

While they were merrily draping themselves with
new muslins and silks, Henry the footman came to
announce that Lord Elyot and Lord Rayne were
below, hoping to be allowed to see them.

'Oh, *please*, Aunt,' Caterina said, clutching at her
unstable toga. '*Do* say we're at home. Don't send
them away.'

If she wondered, fleetingly, how far Lord Elyot's enquiries had led him into the workhouse affair, Amelie concealed it well; she had no heart to disappoint her niece again so soon, even though she felt herself to be wading in rather deep waters.

'The morning room,' she said to Henry. 'Leave your hair just as it is, Caterina. It looks most becoming like that, and they must take us as they find us, mustn't they?' Nevertheless, the advice was amended in her own favour as she passed the long cheval mirror brought downstairs for the fitting, and the darkly tumbling curls bound with lilac ribbons were tweaked into place. As a married woman she would have worn something over them, but any inclination towards convention had grown less attractive after Josiah's death. Yet at the back of her mind was a nugget of satisfaction that there was someone in this town who, in full possession of the facts, had not been so easily put off. Indeed, a timely show of her very comfortable life without Richmond's friendship might be no bad thing. Even now they would be looking around with some interest at the fine white and gilded entrance hall and the Axminster carpet, while in the morning room were two views of Venice by Canaletto that would impress them more.

The visitors were shown into the room only moments after Amelie had seated herself at the rosewood pianoforte with Caterina standing by her side, a sheet of music in her hand. Despite herself, it was an impression she wished to convey, though she could not have explained why.

'Lady Chester. Miss Chester.' The men bowed as the door closed behind them, their reflections disappearing into the shining oak floor.

Caterina smiled, but Amelie chose not to while resisting the temptation to continue her former irony. 'You are welcome, my lords. May I enquire how you knew our address?' She stood to meet them, inclining her head gracefully.

'From the man who delivered the heroic silver tea urn from Rundell's this morning,' said Lord Elyot. 'I made a point of asking him so we could offer you our thanks in person.'

'Ah…I see.' Amelie sat on a chair newly upholstered with her own embroidery and saw how Lord Rayne sat near enough to Caterina to admire the glossy red curls he had not seen before. Against the simple gown of white muslin, the sight seemed to hold his attention most satisfactorily.

Lord Elyot went to sit in a corner of the sofa, his arm thrown across the scrolled end, his long legs crossed as if the creasing of his tight buckskins was of no consequence, and it was this relaxed manner and his study of her face that made Amelie suspect that her choice of gift for his sister had been recognised for what it was, for now he must have caught a flavour, at least, of her excellent taste in all things domestic. Other than the tea urn, that is.

There was something more to be seen in his steady regard, however, that kept Amelie's eyes upon his face longer than at any time since that first meeting. She noted how the dark hair down the side of each cheek reached the level of his earlobes and how the starched points of his white shirt touched each dark column. Now she was able to see the colour of his eyes away from the shadows, grey and dark-rimmed like the clouds, and very intent upon her. She gulped as the sly thud against her lungs forced her to take an extra breath, then the silent exchange ended as she looked away, conscious that this was not at all what she had expected to feel. She did not like or approve of these men's carelessness of others' misfortunes, but they were noblemen who could open doors for Caterina and, for that reason alone, she would have to stifle her reservations and show them some civility.

'I hope you approve of our choice, Lord Elyot,' she said. 'Miss Chester and I thought that, if your sister enjoys taking tea as much as we do, then an urn would be just the thing. Especially as she has a family.'

'My sister's family is still very young,' he said, 'but taking tea is one of her delights. I'm sure she'll be…er…'

'Dismayed?'

'Oh, no, indeed. She'll be gratified that we even

remembered. We're not very good at that kind of thing, you see.'

'I would never have guessed it, sir. Does she live nearby?'

'At Mortlake, just across the park. May I congratulate you on such a beautiful room, my lady?'

The long sash windows looked eastwards out over the kitchen garden where the light was bright and new, bouncing off pale yellow walls and white ceiling, pinpointing the delicate gilded moulding, the silver pieces, the rosewood and satin surfaces, the sumptuous sofa striped with white, gold and apple-green, matching the chair seats. Inside the pierced brass fender stood a large white jug holding late blooms and berries, and before the white marble chimney-piece lay a pale rug.

Lord Elyot's scrutiny paused at the views of Venice then lingered over a beautiful still life with yellow-and-white flowers. 'I recognise Canaletto,' he said, 'but not this one. This is very fine. Are you a collector?' He stood up to examine it in silence and then, leaning a little closer, read out the signature. 'A. Carr? That's a painter I'm not familiar with.'

'My maiden name,' said Amelie.

He turned to look at her, and because he was too well-bred to show his astonishment, he came back to sit on the sofa at the end nearest to her. 'You *were* on your way to paint blooms,' he said, quietly.

'You doubted it?'

'Not exactly, though I did think it an odd excuse. I hope you'll forgive me. You are obviously no amateur. And a collector, too. Have you attended any of the exhibitions in London yet?'

'One or two. I bought a set of Thomas Bewick engravings while we were there, but Caterina doesn't share my interest, and there have been others things to attend to since our arrival.'

'From the north,' he smiled, reminding her of the dire warnings. 'I am not put off in the slightest, by the way.'

'If that includes Lord Rayne, sir, my niece will be happy to hear it.' They glanced at the two, talking animatedly like old friends.

'And you, my lady?'

'I hoped I had made that clear, my lord. My concern is for her, not for myself. She left her friends behind, sadly.'

'You are brutally honest. But the name Carr carries some considerable weight in the north, I know. Are you by any chance a descendant of the Manchester Carrs?'

'My father was Robert Carr, the Manchester industrialist, one of the cotton-printing Carr dynasty, sir.'

'Is that so? And the name Chester?'

'Was my late husband's, Sir Josiah. A merchant banker. Miss Chester is his brother's eldest daughter.'

His firm lips had begun to form an 'oh' before being readjusted into an expression of admiration and approval, which Amelie misinterpreted as the usual interest at the sound of substantial assets. She was not disappointed—it would be an exceptional man indeed who failed to respond to the scent of wealth.

'So you lived in Manchester, my lady?'

'In both Manchester and Buxton, in Derbyshire. Among other places. I didn't want to stay there.' She realised that this had an unfortunate ring to it. 'Buxton has always been my real home, Lord Elyot. It's a lovely place. People go there to take the healing waters, you know. But it's a small town, smaller than Richmond even, and there is gossip and snobbery, which I cannot abide, and so many restrictions for people like myself. It was time for a change. I chose Richmond for its nearness to…oh, well, never mind that. I don't wish to be tedious.'

'You are far from becoming tedious, Lady Chester, I assure you. But you were saying at our last meeting how your neighbours have not so far taken the trouble to leave their cards. I find that sad, but not particularly surprising, given that they're far too cautious for their own good round here. But there are exceptions.'

'Oh? Who?'

'Myself. And my brother. The Marchioness of Sheen is the leading society hostess here, but she's in London and I dare say everyone is waiting for her approval before they know whether they're allowed to like you or not. But that doesn't apply to us.'

'I really do not care for her approval, sir. She sounds like a very disagreeable woman, and I've had my fill of such people for the moment.'

Lord Elyot smiled at that. 'May I ask how long you were married, my lady?'

'Two years, sir. Why do you ask?'

'You must have been a very young bride.'

'But not a foolish one. I am well able to take care of myself.'

'And of your niece too? You say you are concerned for her.'

Amelie's shawl had slipped, exposing the peachy skin of one arm where a row of dark bruises had begun to show. Unhurriedly, she drew the shawl up over her shoulder while her glance passed lightly over Caterina and came to rest upon the rain-spattered window. 'I cannot deny that I have an obligation to my niece and her father. You must have noticed how she longs for the company of other people, but we arrived too late for the season and, in any case, next year looks to be the same as this if things don't improve. I had not forseen that making contacts would be quite so fraught with difficulties. Perhaps I should have done. Perhaps I should have made more of an effort.'

'You brought no letters of introduction?'

'No, my lord. There was no one I wanted to ask.'

'I see. So you have not attended the local assemblies yet?'

She blinked. 'Assemblies? I haven't heard about any.'

'There is one tonight at the Castle Inn. It's our local hop, you know, but always well-attended and respectable. We have a very good Master of Ceremonies who doesn't allow anyone in without a ticket. My brother and I have season tickets. If you think Miss Chester would care for it, and if you would permit it, we'd be delighted if you would be our guests.' The last sentence was directed towards Caterina, whose ears were tuned to the sound of her name.

Its effect on her was predictable; her conversation with Lord Rayne stopped to make way for a pleading that Amelie thought was excessive, even after her previous refusal of company. 'Aunt...please, oh, *please*, may we?'

Amelie was not the only one to think so, for she caught the lift of an eyebrow from Lord Rayne to his elder brother before he took Caterina's part. 'There would be no lack of partners for Miss Chester,' he said, 'or for yourself, and you may be assured that my brother and I make the sturdiest of escorts. We can call for you and deliver you safely home again, and we shall not wear boots, I promise.'

Caterina giggled, but Amelie felt the waters deepening around her as she thought of the poor woman to whom she had promised freedom and failed. She had fully intended to go with one of her manservants to make another bid for her freedom, and now those plans would have to be revised again, or abandoned.

Her face must have reflected some doubt, for when they met Lord Elyot's for the expected answer, it was he who looked back steadily at her as if they had already formed some kind of embryo understanding. 'It's all right,' he said, very quietly. 'Miss Chester will be quite safe with us.'

And you? she wanted to say. *Will I be as safe with you, who have instructions to investigate me? Will you find me out? Will your friendship turn cold, then, and leave Caterina bereft? Will that be the end of a brief fling with Richmond society?*

There were other concerns also, to which she hardly dare allot any thought for fear of making them more real. His voice. His perceptively intimate way of looking at her. His devastatingly good looks. They would dance together. He would hold her hand, and more. She would be lost. He would be well used to this game and she was sadly out of practice, and vulnerable.

'Yes,' she whispered. 'I'm sure she will, my lord.'

'At eight, then? They always have a decent supper.'

'We shall be ready. Thank you.'

Fortunately, Caterina managed to contain her squealing hug of excitement until the two visitors had been shown out. 'Only *think*,' she laughed. 'their father is a

marquess and they live up at Sheen Court. We passed
the gates on one of our drives. Do you remember wondering who could live at such a grand place? Well, *they*
do. Oh, what am I going to wear, Aunt?'

'A marquess? Then their mother is…?'

'Yes, the Marchioness of Sheen.' Caterina
whirled away in a solo dance, already imagining a
queue of beaux.

'The leader of society.'

'I beg your pardon, Aunt?'

'Oh, dear,' murmured Amelie.

Beneath the hood of the two-seater curricle, the
two men were quietly confident, if not self-satisfied,
on their return to Sheen Court. 'I think that went
rather well this time,' said Lord Rayne. 'Progress,
would you say?'

'An improvement, certainly. But still as wary as
a wildcat.'

'Well, we'll see how they perform this evening.'

'Yes, but try to avoid any mention of Father and
Mother, will you?'

'Sorry, old chap. Already have. She asked me.'

'Oh, well. Too bad.'

'I'll warn Todd we'll need the town coach for
tonight, shall I?'

'No, it'll have to be one of the others. I'm sending
Todd up north for a few days to make some enquir-

ies for me. Tell me, why would neighbours in a small town gossip about a wealthy young widow so much that she feels bound to move away?'

'Scandal, I suppose. That's the usual gossip fodder, isn't it?'

'That's what I thought. Now we shall have to wait and see.'

'Ah, so that's why Todd's going up north. Enquiring into her background? You're *that* serious, then?'

'Certainly I am.'

'So why can't you just *ask* her what it is you need to know?' The look he received from his brother apparently answered him, and there were no further questions on that subject. 'You said we'd be calling at the workhouse on the way home. Are you still of that mind?'

'It's our duty, Seton, you know that. And I think it's time you took another look. There's a package under the seat. Infant wrappers from Mother and Dorna's sewing-group. We're to take that in with us.' Then, because there was something on his mind that would not take a back seat, his remark came out of the blue. 'I must say though, brother, she's the most out-and-out stunner I've ever seen in my life.'

With years of youthful hope behind her, Caterina could still not have predicted the impact she was to make upon her standoffish Richmond neighbours that evening or the bliss she would feel at being sought for every one of the twenty or so dances. Attired with studied simplicity in a bead-embroidered white gown of her aunt's and quickly altered to fit, the young lady shed her blue velvet cape and waited with her hand tucked into Lord Rayne's arm, slightly behind Aunt Amelie and Lord Elyot. And from that moment on, when all heads turned in their direction, the steady stream of young men to her side increased, for one had only to watch her beauty and vivacity to see that here was a new star in the ascendant.

Naturally, she could not have been expected to pay more than a passing attention to her aunt's enjoyment except to note, whenever she happened to look, that she was dancing, or had disappeared, or was just returning from the supper room. But the press of people, mostly men, around her aunt would have made more than the briefest contact difficult. Altogether, it was a most satisfactory beginning, especially in view of Lord Rayne's care of her. He was the most perfect escort.

They had been taken up in Lord Elyot's coach, although the new assembly rooms at the Castle Inn on Hill Street were only walking distance away from Paradise Road. But the roads were still muddy, and to be helped up into a coach with a man's hand beneath one's elbow was vastly more romantic than a moonlit walk swinging a shoe-bag and holding one's skirts up over the puddles.

The jest about not wearing boots might, Caterina thought, have been a hint for them to dress up rather than down, for both men wore pale knee-breeches and white stockings with their long dark-blue tail-coats and, if she had not already been half in love with his brother, she would have fallen for Lord Elyot, even if he did not smile as readily at her aunt as he did at her. Indeed, his expression was quite severe at times.

'Is your brother displeased with my aunt's appear-ance, my lord?' she whispered as they waited to be greeted by Mr Newbrook, the Master of Ceremonies. 'He rarely smiles.'

Patting Caterina's fingers in the crook of his arm, Lord Rayne reassured her. 'You will find, Miss Chester, as you gain experience, that men's smiles are not always an indication of approval, just as a straight face does not always mean the opposite. I can assure you that my brother's regard for Lady Chester could hardly be higher.'

Caterina thought his lesson rather patronising but, from then on, her observation of men's expressions became rather more acute. Amelie, on the other hand, with or without Lord Elyot's smiles, was dealing with the kind of approval she had missed since the death of Sir Josiah, having recognised in her escort's appraising glances a darkly disturbing yet controlled desire to make their short coach-drive last for hours, alone. His lingering support down the two steps confirmed it and, to her own astonishment, her body responded, if only fleetingly. It was just as quickly cautioned. This man, she reminded herself, would never be one she could allow herself to warm to.

Mr Newbrook was gratified to welcome such illustrious members of Richmond society. A rare visit, he said it was, and how honoured. They had arrived just in time for the opening minuet, and would Lady Chester and Lord Elyot be pleased to take the lead for the first figure? Splendid.

It had been over two years since Amelie had danced, but no one would have guessed it as she swept gracefully into her first curtsy, then into the slow and languid movements of the minuet. Feeling all eyes upon her and her equally elegant partner, she was confident that the white gauze-covered silk with its simple classic lines had been the right choice. Instead of a lace cap or turban, she had defied convention by binding her glossy curls into coils threaded with ropes of pearls and, apart from one very large diamond surrounded by small pearls on a chain around her neck, these were her only adornments. The pendant, however, was enhanced by the glorious expanse of peachy skin inside the low-cut neckline, her beautiful breasts crossed with satin ribbons over fine pleats, the long sleeves clinging to the point of each shoulder, tied with ribbons at intervals. Lord Elyot, she was pleased to see, did not take his eyes off her once during their duet until the others came to join them.

This, my lord, is what you will never get to know, however much you may discover about my inconvenient do-gooding, damn you.

The minuet ended and, to the accompaniment of glances, open looks and more outright stares, Amelie was led off the floor to a corner where, before she could be surrounded by potential partners, Lord Elyot made his own claim upon her quite clear. 'You will go into supper with me, my lady,' he said, watching carefully for her reaction, 'and you will save the next and the last dance for me too.'

'My lord, that sounds remarkably like a command. And you know what will be said if I dance more than twice with you.'

'It *is* a command,' he said. 'And people may say whatever they wish. They are talking already, I dare say.'

She looked. Yes, heads were bent behind fans, plumes nodding. It was as she had half-expected, and although most of her new acqaintances were men introduced to her by Lord Elyot, only a few were their wives and daughters who may or may not have been told that they must be introduced to her, like it or not.

Lady Sergeant and *her* daughter obviously had,

otherwise their greetings would have come sooner and been delivered with more sincerity. 'Well Nicholas,' said Lady Sergeant, squinting through a waterfall of heavy blond lace and greying curls, 'you've picked up another handsome gel, and no mistake, though you could hardly miss her on your own doorstep, could you? Eh?' She tapped Lord Elyot's arm while looking Amelie up and down several times. 'Heard your husband was in the metal trade…what was it…lead?'

Amelie's policy had always been to make no response to outright rudeness, which was quickly fielded by Lord Elyot. 'Lady Chester's late husband was in gold,' he said, 'not lead. He was a banker, Lady Sergeant. Now, if you and your daughter will excuse us, this is my dance and I don't intend to miss it.' Taking Amelie firmly by the hand, he drew her away, transferring his palm to the small of her back on purpose, Amelie thought, to give the obnoxious woman something else to talk about.

'Lead mines,' she said to him in a low voice.

Across the set, he faced her, mouthing the words, 'Lead mines?'

They met in the middle. 'In Derbyshire.'

'Good grief!' he murmured, retiring.

'I knew it,' she said as they met again.

He took her hands. 'What?'

'I should have worn my other two heads.' She turned with him and retired, smiling to herself.

His response, when it came, made her blush. 'That, my lady, would be to gild the lily.'

The glow was still in place when they next met to go down the set, hand in hand. 'No,' she said. 'It would shock you as much as the rest of them.'

'I am learning enough about you to be neither shocked nor surprised.' Ducking under the arch of hands, they parted to return to the top of the set, and his meaning was not made clear to her, as the dance steps forbade anything more than the odd word in passing. Then it became more than a holding of hands and a linking of arms, but a series of more recent dance moves where she was entwined and turned by him, where arms were placed across waists with hands clasped above, where there was a closer contact than ever with him looking down at her as if they were alone, and this but a prelude to something even more intimate.

She felt the firm pressure of his hands upon her shoulders and knew that her own hands were resting on hard muscle that could have lifted her clean off the floor with little effort, and that dance was what epitomised the manly qualities of self-confidence, support and…yes, captivation. What use was there in denying it?

Taking her hand again, he led her away. 'I shall re-

introduce Mrs Oglethorpe and her mousey daughter
to you,' he said. 'She may not leave her card until you
do, so now I shall remove both your excuses.'

'I'd much rather you did not,' Amelie said, releasing herself. 'I prefer to choose my own friends.'

'You must know you cannot do that in this
business, my lady.'

'In what business, sir?'

'In society. For your niece's sake, you need all the
contacts you can get, as long as they're respectable.
It won't cost anything to know who they are.'

But there he was mistaken, for it cost Amelie not
a little in hurtful remarks that she felt could not
possibly be unintentional, some to her face, others
overheard. 'Ah, from the north,' said the hard-faced
Mrs Oglethorpe, not knowing Derbyshire from the
Outer Hebrides. 'Is that not where they fix the heads
of stags all round the halls? And do they still use the
furs on their beds?'

'You seem to know more about that than I do, Mrs
Ogelthorpe,' said Amelie, tiring of such nonsense.
'Did your coachman manage to get your horses
under control, by the way? I always send my men to
Tattersalls, you know. Costs are higher, but I prefer
that to local dealers. Don't you?'

Then there was the barely concealed remark concerning Lord Elyot, which, for different reasons,
Amelie would rather not have heard. 'Well, my dear,

with a reputation like *his*, you know where *she*'ll be heading, don't you? Heartbreak, almost certainly. Two mistresses that *I* know of and plenty more that I don't. His brother is just as bad, I believe.'

Amelie concluded her dance with a charming red-coated army officer who returned her to Lord Elyot, who knew him. 'Where is Caterina?' she said. 'Perhaps we should be thinking of leaving soon.'

'What is it?' he said.

'Oh…nothing. But it's time we—'

'You've heard something. I can see by your face.'

'No…really…I…' she looked round for Caterina, but now there was a general movement towards the supper room and there she was, with Lord Rayne and a group of young people heading for the refreshments, chattering and laughing, oblivious to her aunt's concern.

'She's perfectly safe,' said Lord Elyot. 'You surely cannot take her away from that because of some idle gossip, can you? Isn't this what you wanted for her? Is it not worth a little discomfort? Here, come with me.' Threading her hand through his arm, he led her through large glass doors that opened on to a long verandah on the northern side of the inn that looked out over a large torchlit garden. Steps led down to wide terraces, the lowest one to the Thames where boats were tied, rocking on dark-mirrored water. Couples sauntered round huge stone flower-filled pedestals or sat on benches drinking and eating, and on one of these he bade her sit and wait while he went to find food.

In admiration, she watched his tall lithe figure stride away, stopping to speak to two officers who had partnered her. As if they had been waiting for permission, they kept her company with their gallantry until he returned with a servant then, bowing politely, left her alone with him.

'If you hope to get through the evening at the same pace, my lady, you're going to have to eat something. The tea may be lukewarm, but—'

'It's very good. Thank you.'

'You're not still thinking of leaving, surely? You will disappoint a great many admirers if you do.'

Notes of high-pitched laughter floated through the darkness, followed by the deeper men's tones. 'Is she…?'

'Miss Chester is in safe hands. Why? What is it you've heard?'

'Oh, the usual kind of thing. I suppose there must be some truth in it, my lord.'

'About Seton, or me?'

'Both.'

'Well, then, it's probably true unless you've heard that we eat live eels, or some such thing. That's not true. But one would hardly expect two men of our age to have lived a celibate existence, surely?' He waited for a response, then asked, 'Does it matter to you?'

She might have returned some flippant and meaningless answer, but again his eyes demanded that she stop to think before she spoke. It *did* matter to her, so much so that she felt something rage inside her at the thought of him being intimate with other women, speaking tenderly to them, looking at them the way he'd looked at her all evening. Watching him dance while trying not to be observed, she had scolded herself for her prying unnatural curiosity. Now, he was asking her if she cared, and if it mattered that she cared.

'Does it?' he insisted, gently.

'No…no, of course not,' she said, looking away. 'Why should it?'

'Look at me and say that.'

Nettled, she kept her face averted, unable to lie so blatantly. 'I made a mistake about Lady Sheen…the Marchioness…I'm afraid I may have…well, put my foot in it. Please accept my apologies, my lord.'

'None are necessary. She'll never hear of it. She's still in town or I suppose she'd have been here tonight. But perhaps it's as well that she's not or we'd not be dancing Irish jigs and Scottish reels, I can tell you. She's a stickler for propriety.'

'Are you saying she would not approve of me, my lord?'

'I have never been influenced by my parents' approval or disapproval of my friends, Lady Chester. Nor has Seton.'

'Thank you. That is a great comfort to me.'

Tipping his head sideways, he studied her expression in the dim light. 'I could make myself much plainer, if you wish it.'

'No, sir. I think you will find that our friendship will die a natural death quite soon without any help from the family.'

'You suggested something similar once before. Are there more skeletons in the cupboard, then?'

Her smile was rueful. 'Yes,' she said. 'Shall we go in? I can hear the musicians tuning up. Do you have a partner for "The Shrewsbury Lasses"?'

'No. I shall be watching you instead.'

Climbing the damp stone steps towards a blaze of chandeliers whilst holding up a long gown caused more than one lady to slip and others to cling like crabs to their partners. Amelie did neither. Laying her arm along Lord Elyot's, she experienced the rock-solid hardness and the firm grasp of his fingers under hers, receiving smiles for the first time as she entered the ballroom, some of them from women.

Not quite believing that he would watch her dance, she glanced every now and again to see if he meant what he had said. And since he did, every one of her looks was intercepted. But now she made a point of observing Caterina and Lord Rayne more closely, for although there would always be talk about the morals of handsome men, her thoughts on the matter were less than charitable where these two were concerned. Still, she had found a certain comfort in learning that their mother, at least, had high standards.

Several times she met him in the dances that followed as they crossed the set, turning to smile. She danced twice with Lord Rayne and found him as good as his brother, and as attentive. Speaking to Caterina several times, the latter could hardly finish a sentence for laughter and breathlessness, and even Lord Rayne admitted that Caterina was like quicksilver, meaning it as a compliment. Lord Elyot danced two dances with the young lady, thus making the score infuriatingly even for those who were counting until the last dance, which tipped the balance and caused tongues to click more furiously than ever.

That, however, was not the only effect it had, for there was a repeated movement where partners stood face to face, holding hands and taking turns to draw each other forward, stately, provocatively and, if one were in the mood, significantly. One, two, three, he stepped forward and she stepped back as if to tease him; one, two, three, he drew her towards him with unyielding hands and eyes that said, 'You will come to me, woman.' His message was clear, and she was too tired to misunderstand it, and they were both particularly silent as they left the floor for the last time, hand on hand.

Their departure was more delayed than their arrival by the good nights and the finding of cloaks, hats and shoes. Bundling her velvet evening cape over one arm, Amelie was able at last to smile and bid adieu to many of her neighbours with Caterina by her side making last-minute introductions. Then they had to wait for the coach to move up the queue outside, while she warmed her back on Lord Elyot's solid chest and watched the glitter of diadems and flushed faces.

His arm moved across to shield her from the doddery footwork of an elderly gentleman, pulling her in yet closer. She could have moved away again as he passed, but she did not, nor did she protest when Lord Elyot's hand slid beneath the cape in front of her, settling upon her waist and sending its warmth immediately through the silk. Then it moved in the lightest of caresses, and she responded, shifting and edging at the infringement, but not knowing whether to stay or flee, wanting to do both yet feeling herself yield to its heady excitement and by the events of the evening.

As if he could sense her dilemma, he firmed his hand upon her waist, holding her back, telling her to stay while his other hand came to rest upon the beautiful curve of her hip, lightly stroking and smoothing where no one could see. And as Amelie continued to call out her good nights, to smile and make believe that her heart was tranquil, all her awareness was alive to that gentle movement sliding upon the fine fabric of her gown, exploring like a summer breeze over hip, buttock and thigh, as intimate as water.

Vaguely, she tried to excuse her own deplorable behaviour with references to her exhaustion, her elation, and the years of solitary mourning, the newness of the company, her success and the lateness of the hour. But she could find no truly acceptable reason for allowing such a thing to happen, knowing what she did of the man.

He had stopped of his own accord when the crowd began to move, had placed the cape around her shoulders and, in doing so, had obliged her to look at him with neither reproach nor approval in her dark confused eyes, but to accept the mastery in his. It was, without question, the most outrageous and unacceptable behaviour towards a lady, which could never be condoned, but the aching fires deep within her body were a new experience that held any sense of insult or shame well out of her reach.

In the coach, the two men sat beside their partners and, as Caterina bubbled over with chatter to Lord Rayne's happy prompting, Amelie sat in silence close to Lord Elyot, linking hands beneath the folds of her cape, feeling the gentle brushing of his thumb over her skin and thinking of nothing except that she was in imminent danger of losing her wits along with her closely guarded principles.

Chapter Three

The crash back to earth came as soon as the door had closed upon the departing escorts and their cries of farewell. Caterina was halfway up the staircase as the sound of a door into the hall made Amelie turn in surprise. She had forgotten about Fenn, her gardener, until that moment.

'Ah, Fenn,' she said, pulling her thoughts back into reality. 'You waited up for me? What time *is* it?'

''Bout two o'clock, m'lady. No matter.'

'And what news? Did they come back with you? Where are they?'

'No, m'lady.' Fenn stifled a yawn and rubbed his nose. 'I went up to the workhouse as you bade me. I offered them the purse, but they sent it back.'

'With what message?' Hardly able to believe it, she leaned against the wrought-iron banister, suddenly overcome by tiredness and impending disappointment after such an evening. It would be too much for her to bear, she was sure of it.

'You all right, m'lady?'

'Yes, just tell me what happened. *Why* have they not come?'

'I don't really know. It was like she didn't want to. They told me she was well enough and that the babe was well too, and that she'd chosen to stay where she was, thank you very much. And that's all.'

'And you didn't get to see her or the child?'

'Lord, no, m'lady. I didn't get no sight of them.'

'So you don't know whether this is the truth, or whether she's being prevented from leaving?'

'Well, no.' He looked at the door, then back at her. 'But she's had her bairn and they said she's all right, so perhaps it's for the best. I dunno.' He fished into one baggy pocket and brought out a leather purse weighted with coins. 'They wouldn't take it,' he said, passing it to her and watching how her hand sunk a little.

'They actually...sent it *back*? Well, that's a first.' She sighed and shook her head. 'Thank you, Fenn. You did your best. Did they tell you...?'

'Tell me what, m'lady?'

A hand crept to her breast. 'Did they say... whether it was...?'

Fenn understood. 'Oh, aye. It were a little lass. Night, m'lady.'

'Good night, Fenn. And thank you. You did your best.'

The mother would rather stay where she was, in that dreadful place, with a new babe? Yes, and I'd like to know who gave the orders to turn all bene-factors away at whatever cost to the unfortunate inmates. Was it you, my fine lord? Could it have been you, by any chance? You, with your lack of compassion and your wandering, knowing hands? Damn you...damn you...

If anything more had been necessary to persuade Amelie that this so-called friendship must cool, this was it. Not only had she made a complete fool of herself in allowing a most indecent intimacy, but now he would believe her to be no better than a low woman ready for anyone's favours. All her earlier protestations about caring nothing for her own social contacts would be worthless, for she had shown herself to be desperate and ready to drop the hand-kerchief at the first man to show an interest. Well, she had warned him that their friendship would not last. Now, he had better believe her.

Wriggling deeper into her warm bath, she scrubbed vigorously at the parts where his hands had smoothed. 'Like a horse...a mare...' she growled.

'Beg your pardon, m'lady?' said Lise.

'My hair. Is the shampoo ready?'

She could never have grown to like him, anyway, a man with so little pity in his heart that he could actually forbid a woman's release from a squalid workhouse to the safety of a caring employer. He must know that there was no likelihood of exploitation or abuse in such circumstances. And he was a womaniser, too. Never was there smoke without fire, nor had he bothered to deny it.

One more thing was certain. Caterina must be better protected from men like Lord Rayne. Perhaps she ought never to have allowed the introduction in the first place. Yes, it had been a mistake. Both friendships must be slowed, before it was too late.

Accordingly, Caterina's breezy request to go driving in the park and to leave cards at the homes of her new friends met with a puzzling refusal that put an end to any chance of meeting Lord Rayne, which was what she had intended. Instead, she was taken through the aspects of housekeeping and accounting using Mr John Greig's *The Young Ladies' New Guide to Arithmetic*, which did little to banish her yawns or her frustration.

Later that morning, the mantua-maker arrived for a fitting of Caterina's new gowns, though her young assistant had gone down with something and had not arrived for work. Amelie suspected that the child was close to starvation.

* * *

After a light luncheon, they went into the garden to practise the sketching they had missed at Kew, and there Henry came to say that Lord Elyot and Lord Rayne were in the hall asking if they were at home.

Caterina was already on her feet, drawing-pad and pencils discarded.

'No, Henry,' said Amelie. 'Tell their lordships we're not at home today. Caterina, come back if you please and finish your study.'

'Very good, m'lady,' said Henry.

'Aunt Amelie!' Caterina squealed. 'How can you say that? You *must* know how I want to see him. Please…*please*, let me go. He'll want to—'

'Not this time, my dear. Take my advice on this. It doesn't do to show too much interest at this stage, you see. Make him wait a while. In any case…' She bit her lip, regretting the necessary deviousness.

'In any case what? Don't you like him?'

'Of course, I cannot say that he's not a charming companion, but such men are not innocents, you know. They tend to…well…change partners rather too frequently for most women's comfort. Such men break hearts, I'm afraid.'

'Well, I'*m* not afraid of *that*,' said Caterina, knuckling away a tell-tale tear. 'I haven't given him my heart, so he can't break it, can he?'

'You'd be surprised what men can do, my dear.'

Although her aunt's enigmatic remark did very little to inspire a recognisable drawing of an artichoke head, it provided food for thought in other ways, one of them being the exact nature of Lord Rayne's interest. Being less experienced than her aunt in such matters, Caterina was by no means sure that he would care as much as she did about her being unavailable. All this waiting was a huge risk, at seventeen years old.

Her fears were allayed next day when Lord Seton Rayne arrived after breakfast in his brother's perch-phaeton to ask if Miss Chester would be allowed to take a turn with him round the park and up the hill. Amelie was speaking to her housekeeper, Mrs Braithwaite, in the hall when Lord Rayne was shown in, so it was well-nigh impossible for her to refuse the invitation with anything like a convincing excuse. Realising that this would do nothing to cool matters between the two of them, she could only beg Lord Rayne to be careful with her niece, to return her in exactly two hours and not to allow her to drive, no matter how much she might wish it. If Caterina had not yet given him her heart, she had certainly loaned it to him.

Expecting that Lord Elyot might follow his brother's example and hoping he would not, Amelie went up to her workroom where she had already begun a painting of her artichoke in an interesting state of decay. The tap on the door and the arrival of the footman caused her heart to leap uncomfortably, but it was only to deliver a letter, the handwriting of which she didn't recognise, nor did it have the assured flourish of an aristocrat's hand.

Laying her fine sable pencil aside, she broke the wafer and opened the sheet of paper, puzzled by the unfamiliar scrawl. Then, before reading it, she searched for the signature at the bottom and found the words that drained the blood from her face. *I remain your most obedient and loyal servant, Ruben Hurst.*

A sickness churned inside her, and she held her mouth to prevent a cry escaping. This was a man she hoped had vanished from her life forever and, although she had never seen his handwriting before, she had seen enough of him to wish him perpetually at the ends of the earth. Which is where she believed he had gone.

Her hand shook as she read:

Dearest and Most Honourable Lady,
My recent return to Buxton has made me aware of your removal from that town, which saddens me, for I had hoped to speak with you about our future sooner than this. However, while staying at St Anne's Hotel, I discovered that enquiries were being made about you other than my own, these from a manservant in the employ of the Marquess

of Sheen, a magistrate of Richmond in Surrey, where I understand you to be residing. Without revealing my own interest, I tried to ascertain the nature of this man's enquiries and the reason thereof, but all he would say was that it was a personal matter. Nevertheless, from the escutcheon on his carriage door, I discovered that it belongs to the Marquess's eldest son, Lord Nicholas Elyot. Which begins to sound, my Dearest Lady, as if your past is about to follow you whether you will it or no, as the man has taken the liberty of interviewing your erstwhile neighbours. I believe he is soon to be on the road to Manchester, whereas I am to leave Buxton at my leisure by post-chaise tomorrow. I shall send this news to you by mail, for you to receive it soonest.

Assuring you of my Highest Esteem and Devotion at all times, I remain your most obedient...

Lowering the unwelcome letter to the table, Amelie propped her forehead with one hand and stared at the words which, more than any she could think of, were the most disagreeable to her. Furious that her privacy should be so invaded, she felt in turn the raging forces of fear, resentment and indignation, followed by a desire to pack her belongings and move on again before the troubles of the past could reach her.

Ruben Hurst was the ghost of her past who had wedged himself between her and her beloved husband. He was a man who lost control of his affairs to such a degree that he could ruin the lives of others. He had ruined *her* life quite deliberately, and eventually she'd had to move away. And so had he. Now he had found out where she was and, of all the times when she needed the protection of a husband most, Josiah was not there to do it.

What made this news even more unacceptable was that Lord Elyot, the man from whom she was hiding her other self, the 'do-gooding' as he would see it, had somehow known of it from the start, otherwise why would he want to investigate her so thoroughly? Was he muck-raking? And she had even had him in her home, let him escort her to a ball, had danced with him and…oh…the shame of it! What a deceiver the man was.

Once again the footman knocked and put a toe inside the room. 'Lord Elyot, m'lady, asks if you'd be pleased—'

'No, Henry! I will *not* be pleased to see him. I'm not at home.'

'Er, yes, m'lady. Though he may find that hard to believe.'

'He's not *supposed* to believe it, Henry.'

'Very good, m'lady.' The door closed.

Within moments, he was back. 'Lord Elyot says to

tell you, m'lady, that he'll call tomorrow afternoon and hopes you'll receive him.'

'Order the phaeton for tomorrow afternoon, Henry.'

Henry grinned, beginning to enjoy himself. 'Very good, m'lady. Anything else?'

'Yes. Get Lise to come and make some tea.'

Having bought tickets for a local charity concert for that evening, Amelie decided that there were more pressing matters to be attended to. The idea that Lord Elyot and his brother might also be there was only a passing thought in her mind that had nothing to do with her decision, she told herself.

That afternoon, she sent her housekeeper and maid to the house of the mantua-maker's young assistant to ask if a contribution of food would be acceptable to the family. Furthermore, would Millie, when she was sufficiently recovered, care to come and work for Lady Chester as a seamstress and to live in at Paradise Road? The grateful reply came within the hour, a small victory that soothed much that was disturbed in Amelie's mind. It had occurred to her more than once that it might not have been the most diplomatic method of solving Millie's problem, but she feared that the mantua-maker would do her utmost to delay the matter of the girl's welfare, and delay was unacceptable in cases of dire need.

* * *

A very disturbed night's sleep found Amelie unready for Caterina's company the next morning, and she was not able to find any good reason why Lord Rayne should not whisk her away to visit his sister at Mortlake, which seemed a safe enough way to spend an hour or two.

But no sooner had she settled down to her painting when Henry came up to say that a gentleman had called and hoped to be allowed to see her. Amelie stared at the footman. If it had been Lord Elyot, she knew he would have said so. Could it be someone she had met at the dance?

'Did he give his name, Henry?'

'Yes, m'lady. Mr Ruben Hurst. You all right, m'lady? I can send him away? Tell 'im you're not at home? He said you'd want to see him.'

If Henry had been one of her Buxton servants, he would have known how far from the truth that was. But he was not, and now Hurst was here, in her house, and there was no one to protect her as there used to be. To have him thrown out, shrieking his protests, would attract exactly the kind of attention she wished to avoid, yet to be civil to the dreadful man after all the damage he had done was more than most women could cope with. While she had the chance, she must know what else he had discovered about Lord Elyot's man, which of her old neighbours he had spoken to, what she might expect from their loyalty, or lack of it. If she wanted to control her future, it was best to be prepared in every way possible.

'Show him up, Henry, but wait outside the door. Don't go away. Do you understand?'

'Perfectly, m'lady.'

She heard Hurst take the stairs two at a time and was reminded of the fitness that had once stood him in good stead. He had changed little since their last meeting over two years ago when he had suddenly ceased to be the devoted friend he claimed to be. His bow was as correct as ever, his figure as tall and well proportioned, his clothes as unremarkable but clean, a brown morning coat and buff pantaloons setting off the curling sandy hair like a crisp autumn leaf just blown in. Yes, he was very much the same except that the blue eyes were a shade more wary and watchful, marred by pouches beneath, which one would hardly have expected from a man of only twenty-eight years.

'My *dear* Lady Chester,' he said, having the grace not to smile.

Amelie remained seated at her work table. 'It would have been more fitting if you had given me some warning of your visit,' she said. 'That is the usual way of things.'

'Ah, a warning. Now that's something you might have gleaned from my letter, then you could have had…' his eyes swivelled melodramatically '…an escort. Would that have been too inhibiting? You did receive my letter, I suppose?' His faint Lancashire burr sounded strange here in Richmond.

Rinsing her paintbrush in the water-pot, Amelie took her time to wipe it into a sharp point before laying it down, then she rose from her chair and picked up her shawl to drape it around her shoulders. Her morning dress was a brief pale-green muslin over which she wore a deeper green sleeveless pelisse, and she did not want his stares at her bosom any more than she wanted his stupid insinuations.

'I did receive it, sir, and I think you are as much of a fool as ever you were to make contact with me, whether by letter or in person.' *And if I did not want desperately to find out more of another matter, you are the last person to whom I would ever give house room.* 'What have you come here for, exactly, and why on earth did you return to England?'

He was about to lay his hat and gloves beside her paintbox, but was stopped. 'Not on my work table, if you please.'

He tried again on the demi-lune by the wall. 'Why did I come out of hiding? Well, you know, I thought I'd take a gamble on seeing you again. The stakes are high, but I cannot stay out of society for the rest of my life, can I? And two years without a sight of your lovely face is too long for any man.'

'You might have suffered a far worse fate, Mr Hurst.

Indeed, you *should* have done. Don't expect any help from me, sir.' Even as she spoke, she heard the emptiness of her refusal, for she knew full well that he had come as much for money as to see something of her, and that to keep him quiet she would, eventually, give him some. What alternative was there?

'Ah, yes,' he said. 'One law for the toffs and another for the rest of us, eh?'

Amelie was committed to redressing that imbalance, but she would not discuss that with such a man. 'And what *have* you come for, sir, apart from delivering the mealy-mouthed flattery?'

For an instant, Hurst's eyes narrowed at her rebuke. 'You were always cruel, Amelie,' he said, quietly.

'*I loved my husband,*' she replied.

'And he's left you even more comfortable than you were before,' he said, looking around him at the beautiful feminine green-and-whiteness. 'Well, then, perhaps you might consider sharing it with me for a few days since I'm looking for somewhere to lay my head.'

'Here? Don't be ridiculous, man. You must know you can't stay here. What would…?'

'What would the neighbours say? They wouldn't see me.'

She felt the fear crawl inside her, standing the hairs up along her arms, and she summoned all her grit to hold on to her apparent coolness.

'Oh, I understand why you had to move on,' he

continued, picking up a pencil sketch of a toadstool and studying it. 'You've not lost your knack, I see. You must have known you'd not escape while I'm still alive, but the gossip…well, that's equally tricky to shake off, isn't it? And there's Miss Caterina too. She'll not get far in society once *your* affairs get an airing, will she? And you're not going to blow the whistle on me or you'd have to be a witness at my trial, and then the whole nasty business will be there for everybody to pick over. Newspaper reports, cold shoulders. Very embarrassing. No, my lady, surely you didn't think moving down here would solve everything, did you?'

'You've thought it all out, haven't you? And put that down.'

'I've had two years to think it out, my dear Amelie, and only the memory of your beauty to keep me sane. Oh, yes, I've thought it out all right, so now you can start with a generous subscription to my funds. Then you can send for Mrs Braithwaite. See, I still remember your housekeeper's name. I'll take one of the best rooms. Next to yours?'

'Get out! Get out of here and crawl back into the gutter.'

'Tch! Still like ice, dear Amelie. Did that old husband of yours never—?'

'Get *out*!' She reached for the hand bell on her work table, but Hurst's hand was quick to grasp her wrist, holding her arm in midair as if he was about to assault her.

She had known him during the two years of her marriage, and indeed there had been a time when she had thought him likeable, charming and clever. He and Amelie's husband had gambled together regularly, but whereas Sir Josiah knew exactly when to stop, Hurst never did, nor when to stop drinking, or borrowing money, or making promises he couldn't keep. Perhaps if Amelie had never shown him any of the kindliness she extended to all Josiah's friends, this man might never have deluded himself about her. But self-discipline was not a strong point with Hurst as it was with her husband, and there had come a time when all his weaknesses came together. Now he was a man to be feared, for the pity she had once borne him had been purged forever, and he had become a menace.

'Let go of my arm, Mr Hurst,' she said calmly, though she quaked inside with every shade of insult and anger. 'You have forgotten yourself, I believe. I can lend you some money and then I shall expect you to go and find somewhere to stay. You can *not* stay here. It's not as safe as you think. I have some rather influential friends, you see.' It was a long shot, but it might work.

Releasing her, he watched as she moved away well beyond his reach while his eyes widened at her boast.

It was unlike her. 'You surely don't mean the Marquess and his son? Him, too? What's his name…Elyot? So you know the man who's been scouring Buxton for gossip about you, then?'

'He was not *scouring Buxton for gossip*, Mr Hurst,' she said, fabricating the beginning of an outrageous piece of fiction in the hope that he might swallow it. 'He was simply clearing up some questions to do with Sir Josiah's property. The man you spoke to was Lord Elyot's lawyer. Naturally he wouldn't disclose his client's business to a complete stranger, would he? The neighbours he visited are those whose names I gave him, personal friends, and loyal. There was no need for your dramatic conclusion, Mr Hurst. It's all quite innocent. He should be back from Manchester any day now, I dare say.'

Hurst sat down rather suddenly, gripping the arms of the chair until his knuckles were white. 'What? You *know* this Lord Elyot and his father? The magistrate? Is it true?'

'Of course I know them,' she said, derisively, warming to the theme. 'What do you suppose I've been doing for the past five weeks, living like a recluse? Miss Chester is at this moment out driving with Lord Elyot's brother, visiting his sister.'

The arrogance drained from his face as he sifted through this surprising development, hoping to find a flaw in it. He tried scepticism. 'Hah! You're not telling me he sent a man up to Buxton to prepare the ground for some kind of...*understanding*...between you, are you? After only five weeks?'

'He's settling a few legal matters for me, visiting my solicitor. He has the means. It's quite the usual way to proceed, I'm told.'

'That's not what I asked you,' he said, nastily. 'Do you have an understanding with this man?'

'Yes, of sorts.' The plunge into such a fathomless untruth was like a douche of icy water, so absurd was the idea. She had never told such a whopper before, but nor had she needed the protection of a man's name more than she did now, her excuse being that Lord Elyot would never know how she had used him, of all unlikely people. 'You really do ask the most indelicate questions, Mr Hurst. It is not common knowledge, yet.'

Hurst leaned back in the chair, eyeing her with some disbelief. If a man could win her in five weeks, he must have something no one else had. Even Chester with all his wealth had taken longer than that, but then she had been only twenty and as green as grass. 'Not common knowledge, eh? That sounds to me remarkably like saying that Lord Elyot doesn't know of it either.'

'Then you'll be able to ask him yourself, won't you? I'm expecting him to call any time now.' That, she thought, should see the back of him.

To her joy, her clever ruse began to work. Hurst rose slowly from the chair and strolled over to pick up his hat and gloves, apparently taking seriously the possibility that he might at any moment bump into the influential son of the local magistrate. This time, he suspected that the odds were definitely stacked against him. 'Money,' he said. 'There's a small matter of a contribution, if you would be so kind. Then I shall leave you to your lover. Are we talking of wives, or mistresses?'

Amelie paled with the effort of controlling her fury. 'We are not talking at all, sir. The sooner you go, the better. Here, take this and get out of my house. It's all I have available.' She took the weighty bag of coins that had been returned from the workhouse and threw it in his direction, but because she was thoroughly unnerved by his insult and by her own indiscretion, and because he was not expecting that particular mode of conveyance, the bag landed on the floor with a heavy thud some way from his left heel.

At that precise moment, Henry threw open the door, but was unable to announce the visitor's name before he strode in, pulled up sharply, and stood there with that unshakeable poise which was one of his most attractive qualities.

Amelie could have screamed at him that he was not expected until the afternoon, and that he was not to speak to Mr Hurst under any circumstances. Her plan was destined to come unstuck, however, teaching her never to lie like that again. 'Lord Elyot,' she said, breathlessly, 'your timing is perfect, as ever. My guest is just about to leave.'

'I hope you will introduce us,' he said coolly, taking in the complete picture including the money-bag on the floor, Hurst's eagerness to be gone, and the angry red blotches upon Amelie's neck and cheeks.

'Ruben Hurst. Lord Elyot,' she said.

The two men bowed, and Hurst would have made for the door except that Lord Elyot stood in his way and looked unlikely to move.

'Mr Hurst is an old friend of the family,' Amelie said, 'on his way to London.'

'Is that so? And you're staying here in Richmond?' said Lord Elyot, still not moving.

Hurst seemed to cringe a little. 'Well, my lord, I am suffering a slight embarrassment. I came down by post-chaise from Buxton and discovered at the first stop that my luggage has been left behind… mixed up, somehow…stupid porters…you know how it is…well, no, you probably don't. And now I find myself without my belongings or my money. It was in my trunk, you see, safe from highwaymen. So annoying. I had wondered whether *dear* Lady Chester would be in a position to offer an old friend a night's hospitality, but perhaps that's not a good idea after all.'

'There are some good inns in Richmond, Mr Hurst,' said Lord Elyot with a remarkable lack of sympathy.

'Ah…yes, of course. Lady Chester has kindly offered to lend me some funds to pay for accommodation until my own arrives. We have been close friends for a good many years, you see, as I'm sure she has sometimes mentioned to you. *Very* close.'

'No, I don't believe Lady Chester has ever mentioned you.'

'Oh…er, that *does* surprise me, my lord. She has confided in me something of the nature of *your* personal relationship…your *understanding*, that is, though of course I shall keep it to myself until it's announced. May I offer you my felicitations, my lord? You are fortunate indeed, as I'm sure Lady Chester is also.'

Amelie closed her eyes and held her breath.

'Thank you for your felicitations, Mr Hurst. Yes, I am indeed a very fortunate man,' came Lord Elyot's unwavering response. 'And as a *very* good friend of the family, you will be kept informed of our progress. However, I am sure you will appreciate that our negotiations are still at a rather delicate stage, and I must point out to you that Lady Chester's circumstances are changing, even as we speak. So the funds she has so kindly offered to lend you are frozen for the time being. Unfortunately, she is no longer in a position to lend you anything, Mr Hurst. Not until everything is finalised, you understand. Then we shall review the situation.'

Amelie opened her eyes and slowly began to breathe again.

Hurst took a step backwards, glancing at the money-bag on the floor with a grimace between a frown and a forced smile of defeat. 'Yes, indeed, my lord. Yes…er…I had not thought, and naturally Lady Chester did not say as much to me.'

'No, she wouldn't.' Lord Elyot smiled at her. 'She is the most kind-hearted lady.'

'Quite, my lord. You see, she lent me money in the past for which I have never ceased to be grateful. *Most* grateful.'

'Really? What was that for, Mr Hurst? More luggage problems?'

'No, it was for my beloved sister, my lord. A predicament. These things happen,' he whispered, sadly. 'Lady Chester was *infinitely* generous.' He turned a look upon her that Garrick could have boasted of, full of devotion, adoration, and a sickening intimacy that almost turned Amelie's stomach.

At that, she caught Lord Elyot's eye for the first time and, without the slightest effort, conveyed to him all the fury and humiliation of the past half hour. Relieved beyond words to have had his support at this most disturbing interview that had satisfied none of her intended queries, she also felt the repercussions of her grotesque lie banking up behind her like the thunderclouds of doom in some Gothic novel, with the supernatural calm that comes before the storm.

'I could not agree more, Mr Hurst,' said Lord Elyot smoothly. 'Lady Chester's warmth and generosity are the first things that attracted me to her. Now, my good fellow, I can recommend some excellent inns in Richmond: the Red Lyon and the Feathers are opposite each other, the Greyhound, the Talbot…oh, any number of them. On the other hand, the mail coach leaves for London from the King Street posting-office three times daily. You may wish to take advantage of that as soon as your baggage catches you up. I see you understand me well, sir.'

As he spoke, Lord Elyot reached behind him to open the door where the faithful Henry was waiting for just such a moment.

From beneath his gathered brows, Hurst glowered with deep distrust at his audience, but carefully avoided looking at the money he was forbidden to retrieve. He bowed. 'Your servant…my lady…my lord.' Then he was gone.

In spite of her new predicament, Amelie's relief and gratitude robbed her of words and, if she had been of a weepy frame of mind, she would almost certainly have burst into tears and thrown herself bodily into the arms of her rescuer. But since her rescuer was bound to be expecting some convincing explanations very shortly, she stood with both hands enclosing the entire lower half of her face as if she were praying. Which, in a sense, she was. She was also wondering how on earth to explain herself, not to mention Ruben Hurst.

She realised she was in for a rough ride as soon as Lord Elyot approached her with that maddeningly cryptic expression he favoured, and said, 'Well, my dear Lady Chester, there's a dirty dish if ever I saw one. You really do have the oddest friends. I fear I may have to forbid you to see him again once our engagement is formally announced. He won't do, my dear. Really he won't. Not up to the mark at all.'

'You were not expected until this afternoon,' Amelie mumbled through her fingers.

'Yes, and you'd have been out, wouldn't you? Hardly the way to behave towards your intended husband.'

'Please…stop it! You must have realised that was a last resort.'

'Thank you. I cannot recall when I was last known as a last resort. Must have been in my schooldays, I suppose.'

'That's not what I meant.'

'Then what did you mean? And who was that jackanapes with his bag of moonshine?'

Inside her hands, she shook her head, closing her eyes.

'You'll do better like this,' he said, taking her wrists. 'It releases the mouth, I find. There now. Come and sit over here.' Leading her to the chair vacated by Hurst, he lowered her into it. Then, pouring her a glass of some mulberry-coloured liquid from a decanter, he passed it to her. 'I don't know what this stuff is, but take a sip.'

'Blackcurrant juice. Thank you.' Obediently, she sipped.

A pained expression fled across his eyes. 'Is that what I'm going to have to put up with? Heaven help me.'

'Lord Elyot, I owe you an explanation, I know, and an apology for making use of your name. I didn't think you would ever find out, and that's the truth of it and, at that particular moment, I desperately needed that dreadful man to believe I had influential friends here.'

'Well, that's an improvement on being a last resort, I suppose. But if you didn't think I'd find out, what d'ye suppose he'll be doing in the nearest tap-room at this very moment but telling everyone within range that Lady Chester, his *very* close friend, has an understanding with Sheen's eldest son? I'm really quite gratified to discover who my next partner is to be before the rest of Richmond does. You must understand my relief, I hope?'

That was a possibility she had not taken time to consider. 'Would he do that?' she asked, weakly.

'Well, I would if I were him. He needs all the clout he can get. Who is he?'

'A gambler and prime scandalmonger from Buxton. I'm afraid this so-called affection he professes is all in his mind. He *was* a family friend, my lord, but not any more.'

'So why let him in?'

'If I'd thought he would come here to Richmond, I would have told Henry to keep him out, but since he was in, I thought it was best to know exactly what he was up to. Better the devil you know than the devil you don't know, as they say. I suspected he'd ask for money. He always needs money. So I gave him some, hoping he'd go away and leave me in peace.'

'Most people would call that blackmail, Lady Chester. You really are *not* the most worldy-wise of women, are you? A charming naïvety, I suppose some would call it.' He glanced at the money bag still on the floor.

Stung by the criticism, even though it was accurate enough, she threw him a glance not intended to alter the rhythm of his heart, which it did. 'I had a good husband,' she snapped, 'who was worldly-wise enough for both of us and I have not acquired the knack of it yet.'

'Then it's time you had a replacement, my lady.

Indeed, you've already set the machinery in motion all on your own. I find your reading of my mind quite uncanny.'

Amelie leapt to her feet, slamming the glass down upon her table so hard that the juice slopped on to her toadstool sketch. 'I'd rather not stay in here with you any longer, my lord. This is my favourite room, not to be shadowed by argumentative men with silly talk. Two in one morning is more than I can bear.'

Glancing around him again, Lord Elyot could well understand her feelings on the matter, even if the expression of them came close to a set-down. The room was obviously special to her, for not only was her work table spread with paints, papers and sketches, but by his side stood a large oak folio stand holding her unframed watercolour paintings, very like the one he had admired on his first visit. He would much rather have given his sister one of those. Leatherbound volumes lined the walls, botanical journals, poetry, and novels in French and Italian. A portrait of a middle-aged businessman holding a roll of parchment looked down from above the marble chimneypiece. Her father, perhaps? Whoever he was, this conversation would be better continued, he thought, out of the man's hearing.

'I agree,' he said. 'I have a better idea.' Before she could object to any plan, he hitched the shawl up around her shoulders and threw the long end over to the back. 'There's a decided chill in the air. Come with me.'

Without a murmur of protest she went with him downstairs and out through a back door into the garden, boxed into sections by waist-high hedges and paved pathways. Rose-covered columns supported wooden beams across which blowsy roses drooped their wet rusting petals and, at the far end in the shelter of a tall yew hedge, a curved stone bench waited for them, warmed by the sun.

With some foreboding, Amelie wondered if she would be able to fend off his imminent and no doubt relentless questions, for it was clear he was not going to leave things as they were. Brushing the dust off the bench, he waited for her to sit before taking his place at her side, and she could not hold back a comparison of his tight white breeches with Hurst's buff pantaloons, a world apart.

He saw what was in her mind. 'Memories?' he said, softly.

Beneath the shawl, heat flooded into her neck and she looked away quickly to conceal the reply in her eyes. 'I *have* apologised, my lord,' she said, stiffly. 'Pray do not retaliate by reminding me of... things...I would rather forget. You cannot know how deeply shamed I am.'

'So shamed that you thought it a good idea to

attach your name to mine? That doesn't sound like shame to me, my lady.'

'A temporary device. I've tried to explain. What more can I do?'

'Oh, that's easily solved,' he said, smiling. 'But we'll discuss those details later, shall we? What I'd like to know is why you were—'

'Naïve?'

'...*generous* enough to lend money to Hurst in the past. I suspect he was lying when he said it was for his sister. Didn't you?'

'The story does me no credit, my lord. It happened when I was newly married and very trusting of men. I know better now. He told me his sister was being evicted because she was...well... in a difficult situation. She needed money desperately. I let him have some and he swore he'd repay me. He never did. It was not until after my husband's death that I discovered Hurst had no sister, that the money was to pay a gambling debt. To Josiah. And since you are about to ask the obvious question, no, Josiah did not know of my loan to Hurst.'

'Or he would have been angry with you?'

'For trying to help a woman in distress? No, not for that, though he might have been surprised by the amount I was asked for.'

'But Hurst can be prosecuted for such a thing.

That's theft, you know. Obtaining money by false pretences. Fraud.'

'It's too late for all that. Water under the bridge.'

'No, it isn't. You have friends who know the truth of the matter, surely? They'd testify at a trial. And your word is worth something.'

'His word against mine. I told no one about the loan because the reason for it was confidential. Afterwards, I was not likely to tell anyone how I had been duped by a man like that. I hoped to learn by it, that's all.'

'But you haven't, have you?'

This was getting too close. She must seem not to understand him. 'Oh, I think I have, my lord. I've learnt that it's best to stay clear of men, for the time being, at least. It's my niece who needs to get to know them, not I.'

'You wish to protect Hurst, then?'

'I wish him to stay well out of my life, sir.'

'Then the best place for him is behind bars or, believe me, he'll keep on coming back for more. Unless you can rely on the timely intervention of your future husband, that is.'

'Please…can we forget that now? I shall manage well enough, I thank you, and I'd be most grateful if you would think no more about the device I used. It was an emergency and I shall never do it again.'

'You won't have to. It'll be all over Richmond by this time tomorrow.'

With any other man of so short an acquaintance, especially one whose compassion was so underdeveloped, she would have asked him to leave her to sort out her problems alone. But having used Lord Elyot's good name and linked it so firmly with her own, she could not now tell him it was nothing to do with him when it so patently was. And unfortunately he was right about Hurst spilling the news. She'd had enough evidence of the power of his malicious tongue to know that the damage would spread like oil on water. Why this had not occurred to her at the time she would never know, her only excuse being that she was taken unawares.

'No, you're mistaken,' she said, rising. 'I know him. He'll leave.'

But the other matter had not been resolved to Lord Elyot's satisfaction, and he was determined she should not escape so lightly. He stood before her just one step too close for comfort, his dark head inclined towards her. 'For a lady who thinks it best to steer clear of men, I'd say you were not making a very convincing job of it, wouldn't you? Could it be that you're sending out the wrong signals? Eh?'

'No, my lord. I think it more likely that they're being wilfully misinterpreted, if indeed there are any signals to be seen.'

'Really. But to adopt a man's name for such an intimate relationship for whatever reason seems to me more like a miscalculation on your part, for if you believe I shall simply ignore a signal like *that*, which is what you suggest, then you *have* miscalculated, my lady. I take such an appeal for help very seriously.'

'You were not meant to know. If you had not turned up—'

'If I'd not turned up when I did, you'd have had that wretch in your house for the next few weeks. You're too generous for your own good, and far too impulsive to be let loose on your own in a place like this. You must admit that you've not made a very impressive beginning, have you?'

'I've hardly had time in five weeks, but thank you for the vote of confidence.' She made as if to turn and walk away, but he anticipated her, facing her into a curve of the high yew hedge where she could not turn without standing almost on his toes.

She felt again the solid and potent bulk of him at her back, his warmth through her clothes, the unaccustomed and mysterious electric charge that had a strange effect on the softness deep inside her, and it was as she had been at the dance, too tired and exhilarated to feel anything except an inexplicable urge to surrender herself without protest. It seemed then not to matter that she couldn't approve of a man who took mistresses instead of marrying, who used his power to restrict the freedom of others, and the unacceptable elements faded into nothing as he moved closer and placed his arms across her, pulling her against him until, this time, his mouth was against her ear, whispering, beguiling.

'Hush, my beauty. You need a man's protection, if ever a woman did.'

Oh, yes...yes...I need your protection...no other...

She kept her head turned as he stopped her from twisting away, but his warm breath was upon her neck, emptying her lungs of air with a sudden shudder of delight. 'My lord,' she said, willing herself to concentrate, 'I am not...th...things are not as they seem...please...let me go. What happened that evening was a terrible mistake...and today also...and I deeply regret...' But his arms held her fast while one hand eased her face upwards and, before she could say more about how wrong he had got it, her protests were tenderly extinguished under his lips, holding her mind in a limbo between excitement and fear.

If she had thought that this might be a quick peck meant to tease her, the idea dissolved within seconds as his mouth moved expertly over hers, unhurried and assertive like that of a man who knows how to change a woman's protest to wanting. Yet Amelie knew almost nothing of kissing. It was not something she and her late husband had ever practised, and now it was her complete lack of proficiency that became obvious to Lord Elyot, who knew from years of experience the difference between a novice and an unwilling woman.

Though surprised, he was unable to resist letting her know of it. 'At last, my lady,' he whispered, lapping at her lips, 'I have discovered an art at which you are not so accomplished. A little more tutoring, perhaps?'

She was not ready for the taunt, nor could she pretend not to know exactly what he meant. Angrily, she pushed herself out of his arms and, if he had not held her, she would have fallen into the hedge. 'Let go of me!' she snarled. 'I should have expected a man like you to take advantage of a lady in such a manner, Lord Elyot. Please leave me.'

He did, but not without having the last word. 'I think, my lady, that you should not be the one to be complaining about taking advantage. That was to even the score, nothing more. Your servant, ma'am.'

She had little choice but to watch him march briskly away towards the house, knowing that he would find his way out as easily as he'd found his way in.

Planting tulip bulbs was as good a way as any of dissipating anger, though this time it was only partly effective, even after Amelie had lectured the polished copper bulbs on being fortunate enough to have everything they needed, that they had nothing to complain of, not even a lack of companionship. It was the missing element in her own life that no talking-to would be able to reverse.

Signifying everything she had lacked in her marriage, Lord Elyot's kiss had brought home to her for the second time how little attention she paid to her own physical needs, perhaps deliberately. His hands on her body, his desirous eyes, his deeply moving voice, his authoritative manner that both riled and fascinated her. Josiah had had other sterling qualities, but this was the first time a man had aroused in her such intensely disturbing emotions, combining dislike and fear with a yearning to be near him. He would never know, she told the fecund bulbs, what his kiss had meant to her and, though he had detected a lack of practice, he would surely put it down to her two years of widowhood without taking into account the two bleak years that had gone before. Her despair was for what she had missed, for what she had just been allowed to see, and for what she would never taste again, for by now his enquiries must be nearing some kind of conclusion.

It would mean little to him, of course, one way or the other. His sort made a game of such minor diversions, of teasing respectable women before leaving them to pick up the broken pieces. Twisting the old dry roots from the base of a bulb, she allowed indignation to take the place of sorrow. 'Well, not *me*, my lord,' she growled. 'I know exactly what to expect from *you* any day now.'

* * *

That same day, Amelie's obliging young footman, Henry, carried a note to a certain Mr Ruben Hurst at Number 9 King Street from where the mail-coach departed for London three times daily. So intent on his mission was Henry that he failed to notice Lord Seton Rayne resting there on his way home from delivering Miss Chester safely back at Paradise Road. Nor did Henry notice that he was being overheard asking for Mr Hurst, or being told that Mr Hurst had already taken the mail-coach half an hour earlier. Tucking the note back into his waistcoat pocket, Henry was observed leaving the posting-office, whistling.

As Lord Rayne had been asked by his brother, Lord Elyot, to keep his eyes peeled for anything havey-cavey, he thought the incident worth reporting, though this he was unable to do until after his brother's long consultation with Todd, the coachman who had just returned to Sheen Court from his visit to the north.

Chapter Four

After helping to plant tulips without noticing her aunt's unusual preoccupation with the task, Caterina went to her room to write her weekly epistle to her father and brother in Buxton. She followed this with a more chatty account of her doings to Sara, her younger sister.

Dearest Sara,
It has been such a week I cannot begin to tell you, but you recall saying how I must find someone with a perch phaeton and that nothing less will do? Well, I have, dear sister. Yes, just imagine your dear Cat bouncing along beside the handsomest gallant with shining top-boots and an hauteur such as you never saw. A marqess's son, no less. We went to see his sister and her darling puppies today. She has children too. And we've been to a dance, a local affair where the men

didn't wear gloves, but good fun with more militia than one could dance with. So very dashing. My escort? Well, yes, I suppose I may be falling in love, which I could not tell to Father. Oh, how I wish you could be here. Write to me soon. I have my French lesson next. Aunt Amelie lets me read to her from the Journal des Dames et de Modes and I am also reading The Mysteries of Udolpho at last and I have a new bonnet with strawberries on, and Aunt Amelie is getting a new seamstress called Millie. I am to learn how to ride side-saddle tomorrow.

Your ever loving sister who misses you. Cat.

Post Script, take good care of Father and Harry, won't you? Aunt Amelie's house is prettier than ours, but smaller. I'm learning to play the harp.

Lady Chester's new house on Paradise Road was known only as Number Eighteen. Found for her by her agent, then extended and renovated to conform to Amelie's requirements before her move, it had been on the same site in one form or another for close on three hundred years, growing and evolving through each new style, now more like a mansion than the original timbered cottage. From the road, the white stone façade was elegantly four-storied, the front door with a beautiful fanlight above and accessed by a paved bridge across the basement yard known as 'the area'.

Through the large double gates along the adjoining wall, the land surrounding the house was more extensive than one might think. Here was not only a sizeable formal garden, a hothouse, kitchen gardens and an orchard, but also a square courtyard surrounded by the kitchen buildings, the servants' quarters, offices and stores and, beyond all that, the coach house and stables.

In the Peak District of Derbyshire, Amelie's previous existence had been countrified on a larger scale than this, her entertaining both lavish and frequent in accordance with her husband's status. At Chester Hall she had tended the preserving of plums and the drying of apple rings, she had pickled walnuts and helped to lay down spare eggs in ash, store the pears, pot the beef and concoct lemon wine using brandy smuggled through Scarborough and Whitby. She had fish on her table from her own ponds and streams, her own ducks and geese, vegetables and fruit enough to send up to the Manchester house and, best of all, she had her own blooms to draw and paint. There was very little that Sir Josiah had denied her—intended, they both knew, to make up for what she could not have.

Being offered her niece's company for the next phase of her life had required some consideration, but whereas it meant accepting a responsibility she had not anticipated, the diversions had so far been entertaining, even satisfying. Caterina was good company, eager to learn, intelligent, well-mannered and, thank heaven, possesssed of a natural grace that was easy to clothe. The new riding habit she had worn that morning fitted her shapely young figure like a dream, already attracting some admiration from the men and envy from the women.

They had gone riding in the park well before breakfast to avoid meeting certain acquaintances, and a party of young officers from the local militia at Kew had hung around them to stare and to vie for her attention. But Caterina had acquitted herself well and had even managed a comfortable trot attached to the head groom's leading rein. Fortunately, they had not met anyone disagreeable to Amelie, who had already begun to reap the benefits of having attended the ball, for now there were several waves and smiles and calls of, 'Good morning to you, Lady Chester.'

Clattering into the stable yard two hours later, however, was like a sneaky winter breeze to cool Amelie's warm praise of her niece, for there, being walked up and down by a groom in Lord Elyot's grey livery was a very large and glossy dark bay with a double-bridle. On a marble table in the front hall of the house lay a beaver hat, a pair of leather gloves and a riding whip, with a rather concerned Henry standing by to tell his mistress that Lord Elyot felt sure she would not mind him waiting.

Biting back the very obvious reply, she asked instead, 'Where?'

'In the morning room, m'lady.'

'Very well, Henry. Caterina, go up and change, dear. Then go and take a little breakfast, then perhaps a little practice on the pianoforte. The new Haydn sonata we bought the other day—you might take a look at it.' She would have given much to go with her instead of to the council of war in the morning room. The staircase seemed twice as high, for she knew why he had come at this early hour and why he had insisted on waiting.

Pausing only to remove her gloves, hat and veil, Amelie half-expected to see her visitor standing on the hearth with hands clasped behind his back, as her late husband had often done to hear an account of her activities. But Lord Elyot was reading the newspaper over by the window and did not hear Amelie's quiet entry through the rattle of the paper as he fought with a wayward page.

She caught sight of herself in the round ornate mirror over the mantelshelf, like a miniature fashion plate of a high-waisted habit of soft violet velvet with a mandarin collar open at the neck to show the delicate ruffle of lace on her habit-shirt. Her brown curls, however, were in a mess. No matter, she thought. Who was there to impress? She closed the door with a loud click, taking pleasure in the crash of paper as he turned, quickly.

'Ah, Lady Chester. Do forgive me.' He laid the crumpled heap of newspaper upon the table, then stood to perform an elegant bow.

'You've waited all this time to apologise, my lord? Well, then, I shall accept it on condition that it never happens again. Which I think is a safe bet in the circumstances. Don't you?'

His smile was full of admiration. 'On the contrary, my lady, I think it an extremely dodgy one. In any case, I never apologise for kissing a woman. So very hypocritical.'

Refusing to be drawn further along that line, Amelie went to pick up the crumpled newspaper and, carrying it between her finger and thumb to the door, dropped it outside. 'Then I think,' she said, moving to the striped sofa, 'that you had no need to wait so long.' She waved a hand towards the nearest chair, trying to appear calm and in command of the situation. 'If you do not mean to apologise, then what can be the purpose of your visit?'

'Given your record of being out when I call, even when you're in, I thought it wiser to be in first, while you were out, so that we could stand a fair chance of being *in* together. Eventually.'

'Ah, to be of such importance,' she sighed, gazing at the top of the sash window. 'Can you bear to get to the point, I wonder?'

Slipping one hand into the front of his deep blue morning-coat, Lord Elyot pulled out a velvet reticule and passed it to her, dangling it by its long drawstrings. 'Yours, I believe? Or that of a certain Ginny Hodge?' he said.

Amelie's heart pounded. This was horribly unexpected. Frowning, she took it. 'Who? Why would you think this was mine, my lord?'

He leaned back into the chair, making a steeple with his fingers. 'For two reasons—one is that it had one of your visiting cards inside.'

'Which this…Ginny person…could have stolen. How did you come by it?'

'The man who picked it up after you had been mugged on the night you went up to the workhouse followed you home again. You were riding a donkey named Isabelle.'

'Todd!' The name escaped before she could prevent it.

'Exactly. My coachman.'

So, he must have known of this for quite some time.

Her heart still hammered under the strain of staying calm. 'And does this prove something, my lord? Apart from being robbed, is it a crime to ride one's donkey at night?'

'It *is* a crime to bribe His Majesty's servants to release people in their custody,' he said, quietly. 'You did not quite manage it that time, but you have done it several times before through your servants, I understand. Those who live at the workhouse have been sent there by the authorities, my lady. By the Vestry, in other words. Any release must be done through the proper channels, not by stealth or bribery, or without permission. You sent a man up there to try again while you were with me at the Castle. Am I correct?'

'So it *was* you who prevented—' Unbidden, the words tripped out.

'Prevented?'

'Prevented that poor woman from giving birth to her child in decent surroundings,' she snapped. 'It *was* you, wasn't it? You told them to keep her there at all costs because your father is the local magistrate who heads the Vestry who put her there in the first place. And no matter how inhumane, how stigmatising, how downright *dangerous* it is for a child to be born in a workhouse, your father's interests must come first. Think how he would look if the poor unfortunates were cared for properly,' she went on, striding across to the window. 'Would he ever hold his head up in Richmond again?'

'So you admit—'

'What good would it do me to deny it?' she said,

sifting through the untidy pile of music sheets on top of the pianoforte. The Haydn sonata caught her eye as she hit the edges with a clack on the rosewood surface. She slammed them down. 'Do your worst, my lord. There must be more serious crimes a woman can commit than trying to help those less prosperous than herself. If that's so wrong, then it's time the law was changed.'

'It isn't a crime when it's done openly and above board. By your method, any gypsy or conman could bribe his way in and take his pick of anyone there, even a child, and whisk it away in the dark, never to be seen again. The rules are there to safeguard—'

'I would have *cared* for them,' she croaked, on the verge of tears. 'I would have…oh, you would not understand. People like me are loose screws and addle-pates, are we not? And the women in that predicament not worth rescuing.'

'Women who get themselves into *that* kind of predicament—'

She rounded on him, furiously. 'Tell me, how does a woman do that, my lord? Any woman who gets *herself* with child will be the talk of the century, surely. Don't talk such nonsense. And in any case, I am not a gypsy or a conman. I am Lady Chester and I know what women need.'

'Then why could you not have gone to the Vestry with your suggestions?'

Sending him a withering look of scorn, she replied, 'Because there was no time for all that. Do you think a woman can wait a week or two while the Vestry makes its mind up?'

'So what about the men released from the pound since you came to Richmond? That was your doing too? And the child?'

'Yes, and I'm proud of my success. The men were desperate. They had families to feed. The child had stolen a carrot. Yes, my lord, a *carrot*. There now, you can tell the noble Marquess how diligent you've been, and then I can remind you how accurate my prediction was, can't I?'

'About the end of our friendship? Well, yes, that's quite a collection of skeletons you have in your closet. It must be quite a large closet, for there are still more to come, I believe.'

'Let me help you out, my lord, to spare you the effort. You have my card with my old Buxton address on it, so you sent your man up there to rake up all the tittle-tattle he could find about Sir Josiah and Lady Chester. And how do I know? Because your Mr Todd bumped into Ruben Hurst, who warned me. You see, I've known for days, like you. And now you know all, and if I'm not arrested for perverting the course of justice, then I shall certainly make no progress whatever in society. Poor Caterina.'

Poor Caterina entered on cue just in time to hear

the sentiment. Standing with one hand on the brass door-handle, she looked from one to the other, hoping for an explanation.

Lord Elyot came promptly to his feet. 'Miss Chester,' he said.

'Caterina,' said Amelie. 'I was saying what a pity it was that you'd have to come looking for the Haydn. Here it is, my dear. Use the other pianoforte, will you?' She handed over the bundle of music sheets with a smile.

'Yes, Aunt. Thank you.'

'Miss Chester,' said Lord Elyot, 'I believe that in a matter of...' he took a gold fob-watch from his waistcoat pocket, flicked open the cover and glanced at it '...about ten minutes, my brother will be calling upon you. He's a great admirer of Mr Haydn.'

Caterina's sweet face lit up with a smile. 'Is he really, my lord? Oh!' The door closed again, leaving the two opponents to face each other for the next bout. Lord Elyot resumed his seat. 'Tell me,' he said, 'about the duel, if you will. Would it pain you too much?'

Amelie had sensed it coming and had to turn away to hide her face from him. Now she must control the anguish that came every time she thought about it. 'Oh,' she said, taking a slow deep breath, 'I expect you must have heard. People are usually ever ready to give their own version of events.'

'That's why I'd like to hear yours, my lady. I heard that Hurst was responsible for your husband's death. You should have allowed me to have him arrested while there was still a chance, instead of warning him to flee. I take it that's what your message to him contained?'

Her curls bounced as she whipped round to glare angrily at him. 'You have spies posted at every corner, do you? You must live a depressingly dull life to go to such lengths. Yes, if you must know, I did warn him to flee, but he'd already gone.'

'But why warn him? Because you desire his safety? Your amazing generosity is sometimes hard to understand, my lady.'

'Not from where I stand, it isn't. Surely you can see that for Hurst to face trial would mean a public airing of events I need to forget, sir. He would say whatever he liked about me to try to lay the blame elsewhere. My name would be blackened, and Caterina's chances of…well, you know the rest.'

'Yes, I can imagine. So Hurst quarrelled with your late husband, I take it? Gambling, was it?'

Reluctantly, Amelie recounted the story while roaming from one piece of furniture to the next, touching and tracing the outlines as if to keep herself safely grounded. 'They played hazard together with a group of friends. It was Josiah's relaxation. Nothing serious. But Hurst became a nuisance. He craved my attention, and it was noticed. The men laughed it off, but the women didn't.'

'And your husband?'

'Josiah was twenty-three years my senior. I would not have done anything to hurt him…a younger man hanging around his wife…you can imagine what that would have meant to him if he'd believed it. I suggested excluding Hurst, but Josiah saw only that he lost too regularly and drank rather too much. He did everything too much. Rumours began to circulate about his…well…obsession, I suppose one might call it.

'Then one evening at their club, Hurst lost far more than he could afford to Josiah, and he became abusive. He shouted that I was…no, I cannot say it…' Her voice broke up, and for some time she stood quaking, clinging to the curve of the large harp that stood in one corner, fingering its gilded scrolls. Eventually, as Lord Elyot waited in silence, she found the strength to continue in a voice husky with emotion. 'He told Josiah that he was my lover and that he should tend his wife better if he wanted to keep me. It was shocking… So shocking.'

'Did your husband believe that?'

'No, my lord, he didn't. He knew I would never, *never* have…. But the insult was too near the bone, too wounding to both of us, and he challenged Hurst to a duel. Josiah's brother tried to reconcile them, but Hurst would not apologise and Josiah would not withdraw the challenge. They met in the woodland early the next morning, but Josiah was no shot and Hurst knew it. He was much older, was Josiah, and he died in his brother Stephen's arms. Caterina's father.'

'I'm sorry. And Hurst?'

'Well, you must know how the law stands on such matters,' said Amelie, staring out into the garden. 'A nobleman may be allowed to get away with it as a matter of honour, but not a man like Hurst. He knew he'd be brought to trial and condemned, so he fled to Ireland and I believed he would stay there for good.' She came at last to the sofa where she sank down with her back to the light, fighting the tears. 'You can imagine the rest, I'm sure. The inevitable gossip, the jealousy of what some seemed to think were my favoured circumstances. It would have been easier for them to bear if I'd been penniless, I suppose, as a result. They could have forgiven me that. Some found it hard to understand why a wealthy woman of twenty-two could be so distressed by the murder of her forty-five-year-old husband, or why she should be so grateful to his widowed younger brother and his family who, as it happened, was one of the few to offer me real help and support. The others were all too afraid of their wives, I suppose, and their wives were too concerned about the rumours to believe totally in my innocence. One quickly learns about true friendship at such times, my lord. The moral of the story is never to challenge anyone to a duel unless you are prepared to lose more than your honour.'

'Well, your advice comes too late for me, my lady. But then, I always make a point of winning, you see.'

Glancing at him, she noted once more the impressive length of his muscled leg as he lounged into the chair, the width of his shoulder, the deep chest and strong hands. At ease, he was a darkly brooding god, and she could imagine only too well how proficient he would be at any physical activity. She had seen his dancing, so unlike Josiah whose keen brain was his most active part. He had provided for her well, however, and he was no stranger to compassion, as some men were.

'Your parents,' said Lord Elyot. 'I understand they were lost to you only the year before. Was that as sudden?'

'A coaching accident in Switzerland. Had they still been alive, I would probably have gone back to live with them immediately. But the Carr estate was entailed to my cousin, and his wife couldn't wait to claim it as soon as it became vacant. Fortunately, when my husband died, his brother Stephen allowed me to stay in my own home until I bought this one, instead of claiming it for himself and his family as he was entitled to do. He moved in after I left, but I suppose you must know that.' She shot a resentful

glance at him, but he received it with no more than
a slow blink. There had been gossip about the mutual
support of the brother and sister-in-law which, in
many people's eyes, could not have been platonic.

'According to my information,' said Lord Elyot,
'you were highly regarded by Buxton people.'

'Really,' said Amelie, twisting the wedding ring on
her finger. 'What a pity all those charitable people
who were glad to accept my husband's hospitality for
so long could not have maintained the same charity
for his widow when she most needed it. It comes a
little late, wouldn't you say?'

'I can offer you *my* help, my lady, if you will
accept it. The situation is certainly grave, but not
irredeemable.'

Suddenly fearful of the soothing tone, Amelie leapt
to her feet. 'Oh, come now, my lord. Don't tell me
you came here to *help*. Why not be truthful and admit
that, armed with all you know of my past and present
life, you cannot wait to hound me out of here? An
upstart northerner with trade connections in
Richmond? We'll soon get rid of *her*. I can almost
hear your parents in chorus, sir. Well, now I'm in
trouble with both of them, am I not? Which one will
you tell first, or have you already done so?'

'Calm down,' he said, rising to his feet. He strolled
to the chimneypiece and lay an arm along its edge,
resting the sole of his shining Hessian boot along the

brass fender. He took some time to study her graceful but guarded bearing, the angry challenging tilt of her head upon the long neck, the dark moist flash of her sun-flecked eyes. 'I have not told either of them, and Todd knows better than to speak without my permission. But my father *is* expecting some kind of result and so are the Vestry and, yes, you could certainly be in serious trouble if word got out about your involvement in their affairs. And the scandal wouldn't do much to help, either.'

'Not to mention the do-gooding,' she snapped over her shoulder.

'That might have done very well for Buxton where you were known, but creeping around at night with a reticule full of bribing-brass is not the way it's done here,' he snapped back. 'Anyone knows that, but *your* brains appear to be governed by your woman's instincts, and look where that's got you!'

'What choice did I have?' she cried, furiously. 'I've told you, it would have taken too long. Why, by the time those bumbling old fools had got together, you'd have had more corpses on your hands. Is *that* the way it's done round here, my lord? It certainly saves on food, but *my* way saves lives. Don't expect me to apologise for *that*. As for the scandal—well, it will soon be common knowledge now, won't it? So you had better warn your Haydn-loving brother to have no more to do with my niece. She'll do better in Buxton, after all.'

'You're forgetting something.'

'What?'

'That your past is not yet known hereabouts, but what *has* become common knowledge is what your loud-mouthed little friend Hurst blabbed to the entire posting-office before he left for London yesterday. This morning I've received two invitations for myself and my lady. Not to put too fine a point on it, for *you*. And if you think,' he continued before her open mouth could let out a squeak, 'that I'm going to have my future wife's name linked to a local court case *and* to my mother's scalding disapproval of *that* kind of scandal, you can think again. I'm not!'

'You said you were never influenced by your parents' approval.'

'*I'm* not. But that doesn't stop her telling the rest of society what to think. Once she's done that, Miss Chester's future will be even less assured than it is now, that's for certain. Mother has resigned herself to having sons who keep mistresses, but neither she nor my father would welcome a daughter-in-law with a criminal record.'

Amelie shook her head, trying to clear it, wondering what she was supposed to make of this tangle. 'Then remind me, will you? You think I should go and explain? Is that what the Vestry will expect? An apology? I've told you, I *won't* apologise.' She flounced away, slapping at the reticule as she passed it.

He moved just as fast. 'Will you hold your peace, woman?' he barked. 'Saints alive, but it's time somebody took you in hand before you fly off at another fence you can't clear. Come back here!' In two strides, he had cut short her quick march towards the door and, rather than subject her to an undignified tussle, he bent, placed an arm under her knees and swung her up against him before she could escape. Carrying her to the sofa in three more strides, he set her firmly back against the round tasselled pillow and held her by the wrists, sitting to face her so closely that his previously mysterious statement about offering her some help now began to take on a new meaning.

'No!' she said, growling and spitting with rage. 'No…no!'

There was more she would have said, but although she was beginning to guess at his intentions, the ensuing struggle took all her concentration. Then it was too late, and a cry was all she could manage before his mouth silenced her, blotting out all memory of words and protocol. Dominated by the weight of his chest upon hers, his hand in her hair, and his arm around her back, she was held captive by his searching mouth. She felt the change in him from the previous gentle occasion, a new urgency, as if to reinforce the message that someone should take her in hand. All the half-formed sensations that had

filtered into her mind like moonbeams since yesterday suddenly faded, unable to compare in any way
with the fire that flared through some deep untouched
place inside her, seeping an ache into her thighs.

One of her arms was trapped under his, her hand
idle upon his warm broad back, her lips teased into
a response where she could not remain passive
beneath the tormenting invasion. Heady and upset by
the emotional wrangling of the last half hour, and
confused, her voices of conscience ceased to protest,
then wavered and collapsed beneath the expertise of
a master, and at last her lips moved and parted, tasting
and curious, waiting for more, perilously close to
surrender. His kiss deepened and her nostrils filled
with the intoxicating and elusive scent of his virility,
luring her even deeper into his complete control.

But all the pent-up fears of a lifetime were even
greater, surging over her like a giant wave that pushed
back the needs of her body, lending strength to her
arms. It was neither propriety nor reticence, but raw
fear of some unspeakable consequence that held him
away at last, tearing her lips from his. 'Stop…no…
stop! I cannot do this,' she panted. 'Let me go, my
lord. If this is what you wanted from me, you should
have given me warning, then I could have told you…
to spare yourself…the effort.'

However, if she had expected that he would leave
her immediately, full of contrition, she had mis-

understood his purpose, for he was not the kind of man to apologise for kissing a woman, as he had said, and his purpose was as resolute as ever. So, although he eased back enough to allow her to recover, he caught her pummelling hands by the wrists and held them close to his chest.

'Let me go, my lord. You must leave immediately. *Please.*'

'All right...all right...I've ruffled your feathers, my beauty, but I'm not leaving till we have this business sorted out.'

'To your advantage, of course.'

'Of course. Well—' he almost smiled '—to both our advantages. You are in a bit of a mess, there's no getting away from that, is there? And I can offer you a way out of it, if you've a mind to listen.'

'I don't need to listen. You've already shown me what's in your mind, and I'm astonished you should take me for *that* kind of woman. I have received some serious offers, sir, but no one has ever taken such outrageous liberties, and I—'

'Shall I kiss you again?'

'No!'

'Then be quiet, or I will. There. Now calm down and listen to what I have to say. And don't pretend you didn't enjoy that, just a little, because I know otherwise.' He watched the colour flush her cheeks again, adding an angry sparkle to her eyes where a single tear hung like a pearl. 'And talking of outrageous liberties, have you forgotten already how Hurst has set Richmond ears buzzing and how he'll be doing the same in every gaming-den in town? So who was it first took liberties with the name of Elyot, my lady? Remember?'

'I told you, it was an emergency. I thought you understood that.'

'Oh, I do understand. But this whole situation is an emergency, isn't it? And I'm not inclined to deny that I have an understanding with the lady who accompanied me to the local assembly when to do so would look as if one of us has had second thoughts. And no one in their right mind would believe it was *me*, would they? Unless, of course, they knew about your illegal deeds of charity and your exceedingly interesting past. Oh, I agree *that* was not through any fault of yours,' he went on as she tried to protest, 'but nevertheless, it's there, and the only way you can keep it all quiet is by keeping *me* quiet. Do you understand me?'

Her lovely face, usually so serene, was a mask of anger as every word took her further into a situation that both offended and enticed her, for she had not recovered from the effects of his lovemaking, and her body still trembled and responded to his shocking closeness. 'You are…a…*demon*!' she cried. 'An unprincipled—'

'There's not a lot wrong with my principles.'

'Let go of me!'

He released her wrists, but the sudden blaze of rage in her eyes gave him all the warning he needed, and he blocked her arm in midair as it swung towards his head, hurting her with its terrible hardness.

The pain infuriated her, and she tried again and again to inflict some kind of damage, astonishing herself by the release of a physical rage she had never known before, blaming everything and everybody in the process, herself in particular, Lord Elyot and his parents, Hurst, the Vestry, and society in general. But for that one crazy moment of weakness after the ball, he would never have known of her vulnerability, and now he had identified her needs far more accurately than she herself had done. Like a swordsman, he had dived straight under her guard, and the only way she could escape was to damage herself in the process.

If the damage had been limited only to her, the dilemma would have been simpler to manage. She would have lived without the approval of society and been content to do so, for society had not shown itself to be worthy of her patronage. But Caterina's future could not be jeopardised with a clear conscience, for the young woman had everything in her favour except an impeccably aristocratic lineage and the right connections. It would take far more than

Amelie could do on her own to launch Caterina into an approving world. She had been foolish to believe otherwise and even more foolish to put everything at risk in order to ease the tender place in her heart that responded too keenly to the needs of others.

There was yet another side to his dubious proposal that cut even deeper into Amelie's objections, a fear that he had made real to her from their very first meeting concerning his attitude to certain unfortunate women. Where would she stand then, she wondered? In the gutter?

Against his superior strength, her attempts to wound him failed miserably as she was caught and held hard against his chest, panting with anger. 'No,' she whispered, hoarsely, 'you ask too much of me. I've told you, I'm not that kind of woman. How could you ever have thought so?'

'Shh…shh,' he said, rocking her. 'Hush, lass. I know you're not *that* kind of woman, but since your name is now linked with mine, whether you like it or not, all you have to do is to be seen with me on a regular basis and to agree to our engagement.' Tenderly, he brushed his thumb along the line of her jaw.

'Only *seen* with you?'

'Er, no. There will be times when I'm sure we shall not be seen, but there will be other times when I shall wish to be accompanied by my future wife to various functions. It makes life less complicated if I can rely on a woman of your calibre to play hostess to my host. All those dreadful mothers and daughters. Ugh!'

Stiffly, she drew away from him and wiped a finger across one eyelid, giving herself time to recover. He waited until she was ready, then he rose and eased her to her feet, handing her a slipper that had fallen off and watching how her dark curls fell untidily at odds with her attempts to pull herself together. In his eyes, the tousled hair and her recovering composure seemed to typify this complicated woman with her conflicting social needs, her passionate yet fearful nature, her astounding stylishness and amazing generosity of spirit that was leading her into untold trouble. Hearing at first hand of her last four years, he could see how lesser women would have become hardened and embittered by the strain far more than she, though her cynicism had already made her distrustful of men, shunning their company. He could also sense the struggle taking place inside her and how, although she had responded to him, she was still on the point of refusing his offer. She would take more persuading than this. He took her by the elbows, turning her to face him.

'My lord,' she said, 'I realise how you are trying to make this suggested arrangement sound equally advantageous to us both, but it isn't, is it? For instance, did you ever make any provision for your lovers when they reached an interesting condition? Did you send unwanted infants to the Foundling Hospital? Did you pack the mothers off to the work-house to get on with it alone? They do, after all, get *themselves* into that awkward situation, don't they?'

'Tch! Tch!' He shook his head at her. 'My, but you're a fierce one, my beauty. Like a dog with a fa-vourite bone. What is it that set you on this path, I wonder? Could we not agree to deal with that problem if and when it arises?'

'That would do well enough for a man, I'm sure. But I know of a better way of dealing with the problem, my lord. From a woman's point of view.'

'Which is?'

'Surely you can guess. This talk of engagements and understandings is merely a cover for something else, isn't it? To all intents and purposes, I would be your mistress and you would leave it so, if it were not for my resistance to the idea. You see, I am not such a fool that I cannot see what *you* want from this relationship, but what would you say, I wonder, if we left *that* part out of the bargain altogether?'

His head tipped slightly, and Amelie found that she was being scrutinised until a ripple of colour stole around her neck like a scarf.

'That,' he said, 'sounds to me almost like a con-tradiction in terms, my lady.'

'Yes, I can see that it would. Still, who's to know?'

'I would. And you would.'

'Does that matter?'

She knew what his reply would be, for he had already demonstrated to her how important it was. 'Lady Chester,' he said, 'listen to me a while. Your fears about the intimate side of things are groundless…no…don't protest. I can see that you have concerns, but you need not. I shall take into account your period of widowhood and, before that, your marriage to an older husband which, I take it, must have been more your parents' choice than yours. Am I correct?'

'Yes.'

'And you had no children?'

She shook her head.

'Well, then. But I think you may be overlooking some of the benefits to you in this. There is the matter of Miss Chester, isn't there? Together, you and I can take her into the heart of society and, with the protection of my name, doors will be opened to her. Isn't that worth something to you?'

'You know it is, my lord. In fact, my niece's welfare is my only reason for even considering your proposal which, I should tell you, offends every code of decency I've ever been taught.'

'Coming from one who flouts the law when it suits her purposes, my dear lady, that is a load of moonshine that doesn't wash with me. If there was ever a way out of the tricky situation *you* got us both into, this is it. Can you not see that? It may be that people will wonder at it. Well, I have never offered for a woman before, but we are both old enough to make our own decisions, and I am not likely to leave you in an embarrassing situation, my lady. I can promise you that, if you should find yourself so, as a result of our relationship, I shall not abandon you. There, how does that sound?'

'It sounds like a typical man trying to make light of his responsibilities, my lord, if you must know.'

He drew her slowly towards him until her face was under his. 'And this evasive idea of yours about being mine in name only sounds to me like a woman doing exactly the same. So now I shall make a decision for both of us, and if you think it's weighted in my favour, that's because *you* were the one to cause the problem in the first place. You have yourself to thank for it.'

'You are ungallant, and a *fiend*!'

'And you cannot afford to refuse my offer, can you?'

Before he could kiss her again, which she knew he was about to do, she lifted his arms away and stepped sideways out of reach. She felt trapped and angry, yet now there was a kind of excitement, an anticipation, a new dimension in her life to take her into the future, beckoning even while warning her of the risks and of the fearfully intimate part of the deal which she would somehow have to delay. He had not been duped by the 'name only' idea.

'This is not going to look good, my lord,' she said, picking up the sadly abused reticule. 'A widow of only two years engaging herself so soon. I left Buxton to escape the gossip only to plunge myself into a different sort. I cannot imagine what my brother-in-law is going to say. Or Caterina, for that matter.'

She would have expected him to offer some dismissive reply to that. After all, had she not already been seen in his company, been visited, and had he not made his interest in her quite obvious to Richmond's prying eyes? Who would be *really* surprised to learn of their deepening friendship, and who would be upset by the news except those dreadful mothers and daughters he had mentioned? And his parents. But to her annoyance, he simply rested his behind on the scrolled end of the sofa, sprawled out his long legs, folded his arms and waited for the rest of her objections.

Disconcerted, she tried another tack. 'How long does it usually take you to win a woman's consent to be your mistress, my lord? Hours, is it? Days… weeks?'

'Never much longer than that.'

'So you've never had to work too hard at it, then?'

'I've been fortunate, I suppose. I find it best playing it by ear.'

'Forgive the indelicacy. I need to know, you see, because you are apparently expecting a commitment from me in a matter of minutes, which surely must be some kind of record. I would not call that "playing it by ear", my lord, I would call it *molto allegro con brio* more like. Wouldn't you?'

His laughter was so prolonged that it was some moments before he could speak. 'Lady,' he said, still gasping a little, 'you have shown up a problem that had not occurred to me, I have to admit. Blame it on my keenness. If it will make you easier, I will woo you, take time to win you, seduce you. I don't want to rush my fences, believe me.'

Blinking a little at the change of metaphor, she felt another surge of heat flood into her throat as the thought skipped into her mind that it might not take her as long to submit to him as she was indicating, and that she had already begun the journey, to her shame. 'I have not been likened to a fence since I don't know when,' she murmured, moving away from him.

But his reach was long and she was scooped up against him and held fast while he looked down into her troubled eyes, all signs of his former levity gone. 'Steady, my beauty,' he said, quietly. 'You are an exception. I would have pursued you anyway, with or without the complications, but they give me a hold over you that I will not let go of. I need to be sure of you; you with your prickly defences. I suspect

you've never been truly wooed before, have you? It's
not only the Hurst ordeal that's cooled you towards
men, is it? It's fear, too. I can feel it in your kisses.
Well, we'll take it slowly, eh? And you'll not find me
difficult to please, or too demanding.'

His kiss did nothing to convince her of that and, at
the back of her mind, Amelie wondered once again
how long she would be able to keep him waiting for
her full involvement in the art of being a lover.

Breathless and reeling, she held herself away. 'I
cannot approve of this arrangement, my lord, except
that it appears to solve my major problems. But I beg
one thing of you before I am obliged to accept it.
Please do not *ever* offer me money, for then I shall
be no better than a kept woman. A whore, to put it
plainly. I value my independence, you see.'

His face revealed nothing of his reaction to that,
and Amelie thought that perhaps this time her out-
spokenness had gone too far. Indeed, she doubted she
had ever spoken that word out loud before.

'I shall not offer you anything, my lady, that you
have no need of. Does that reassure you?' he said.

It was a cleverly crafted, if ambiguous, reply that
made her feel ungracious. Instead of warning him,
she could have thanked him for helping her out of
more than one very damaging predicament which, if
it created others of a different kind, would surely be
of a more manageable order. But for the life of her

the only difference she could see between the black-
mailing methods of Ruben Hurst and Lord Elyot
was that one man was a vile and treacherous
murderer and the other an attractive but heartless
rake whose offer had perhaps not insulted her as
much as it ought to have done.

As for not offering her what she had no need of, he
would probably never appreciate the full significance
of that or how it created the greatest of all her fears,
which he had thought too remote to be worth discussing. In which case she must ensure that his promise
of a slow seduction was performed *ralentando*.

'Yes,' she said, 'that does reassure me. Thank you.
Now, we must not trespass upon your brother's
patience any longer. I cannot hear any sounds of
Haydn. Do you think…?'

'That's probably because they're both out there,'
he said. Looking over the top of her head towards the
garden, he had caught sight of Miss Chester leading
his brother towards the summer house in the far
corner of a lawn. 'Shall we follow?'

The french windows opened on to a large verandah
with steps leading down to pathways, plots and
lawns. Further along the verandah another pair of
french windows were open, too. 'My workroom,'
she said, seeing him look, 'where I am presently
trying to incorporate a blackcurrant stain into a
painting of a toadstool.' She took the arm he offered,

thinking it a particularly comforting gesture after what had just transpired. 'What of your father?' she said. 'He will be expecting some kind of result from your investigations, surely?'

'As long as the matter is cleared up, he will accept my findings. There will be no proceedings.'

'Thank you. Will he accept your choice of mistress...er...wife?'

The arm clasped hers tightly to his side as they reached the bottom of the steps. 'What a beautiful garden,' he said. 'Your design, of course?'

This was all very well, Amelie thought, walking by his side, but what is to happen when he wearies of the pretence or finds someone to love, someone he *really* wants to marry? Would she then be obliged to quietly fade away into a demi-monde like Mrs FitzHerbert, the Prince of Wales's 'wife'? Would the two of them have any kind of future together, her with her unacceptable northern industrial connections and him with his noble mistresses, while there in the background was the possibility of a pregnancy, which he preferred to believe would not happen after a childless two-year marriage. *Not so, my lord. Not so. You do not know the truth of it.*

'My design,' she said. 'But still immature, as you see.'

Chapter Five

The needs of Miss Caterina Chester were of an immediate kind upon which good breeding and example from her elders would have not the slightest effect, and when she might have benefited from her aunt's advice, that dear lady was talking privately with Lord Elyot.

Lord Rayne's professed enthusiasm for the music of Mr Haydn appeared to have deserted him and, despite Caterina's invitation to sit close to her, he neither helped her to interpret the score nor did he take advantage of their closeness, which Caterina thought a great waste. There was not even a hand-touching. Not even a long gaze into her eyes. Nothing except a murmured enquiry about her aunt's horses.

In Buxton, she and her sister had commanded a faithful following of male and female friends who had taken the art of flirting just a little way beyond the boundaries proscribed by their governess. But

Lord Rayne was in a class all his own—a man, the very first attractive man who had shown her some interest, and she was falling more deeply in love with him each day. If she was not allowed to show it, how would he ever know? Was she supposed to wait for ever?

'Will you tell me something, Lord Rayne?' she said. 'Without thinking me too presumptuous?'

'Probably, my dear Miss Chester,' he drawled, stifling a yawn.

'Probably what? You'll think I'm being presumptuous?'

'Er…oh, no. Of course not. What is it?'

'Then may I ask you your age?'

'That's easy enough. Twenty-four. Why?'

'Seven years older than me. That's quite a lot.' Caterina sighed, gathered the music sheets together and took them over to the table. 'So am I the youngest of your lady friends?' She glanced down to appreciate the smooth curves inside the white muslin, which could hardly have failed to impress him.

'Oh, by far,' he said, knowing exactly where this was leading.

'And am I…? But, no, that's unfair, isn't it?'

'Is it?'

'Yes. I was about to ask if I'm the prettiest, but you would be bound to say yes out of politeness.'

'No, I assure you I wouldn't.'

'Wouldn't what?'

'Say yes out of politeness.'

'Oh. Then what *would* you say?' She turned to stare at him, feeling that her innocent enquiries had suddenly turned into a challenge.

'I would say, Miss Chester, that you were angling for compliments, and that I never compare my lady friends with each other for their delight. Bad form, you know.'

'But I was not angling for compliments. I simply wanted to know what kind of lady attracts you. I'm sure you must have known dozens.'

Lord Rayne strolled over to the window, wondering how long his brother would take to win the prickly widow to his side. 'Yes,' he said. 'Dozens.' It was some time before he noticed that the questions had stopped. 'Well…er…not exactly *dozens*, but a fair few, anyway. Look,' he said, realising that something was going amiss, 'shall we go down into the garden? Is that a summer house over there?'

It was a mistake. He knew it as soon as Caterina's face softened into a flirtatious smile with a well-rehearsed nibble at her bottom lip.

'Yes,' she said, suddenly demure again. 'I'll show it to you, shall I?'

Summoning all his past experiences of summer houses, Lord Rayne wondered whether she would employ the squeeze-through-the-door technique, the cobweb-in-the-hair, or the it's-quite-cold-in-here method. As it turned out, she tried the one where the top of her sleeve gets caught on something, but he was saved from the predictable consequences of that by the timely arrival of his brother and Lady Chester, who appeared to be gently arguing. Then, after a summary of the view across Richmond, they were off again, the men to their horses and Lady Chester to a late breakfast.

For Caterina, it was to do some soul-searching about the ingredients lacking in her usually irresistible flirting. 'What more can I do?' she asked, almost in tears.

'Less,' said Aunt Amelie, 'not more. Rarely more, my dear.' Impolitely, she licked the last smear of porridge off the back of her spoon and placed it at an exact half-past position in her empty bowl so as not to spoil the symmetry of the design. 'Will you take chocolate?'

'Yes, please. If I did any less, he'd fall asleep.'

'That's not what I meant. Pass your cup. What I mean is that you appear to be taking the lead, Caterina. That doesn't give a man much to do, you see.' Amelie handed back the cup of chocolate, reading the affliction in her niece's eyes. 'It's also a question of age difference, and the best way to deal with that problem, since you cannot catch him up, is to emphasise it. Pretend he's too old for you, not that you're too young.'

'How?'

'Easy. Start by ignoring him more. Show less interest in him. Look at him less, and pretend not to hear, sometimes, when he addresses you. That kind of thing. Smile and be animated, but not for his benefit. You're far too concerned by what he thinks of you at the moment and he knows it. It's not good for him. Don't show him your heart. Keep some secrets.'

'You don't mean that I should cut him, surely?'

'No…oh, no…nothing as drastic. Just pretend he's a minor character instead of the main one. Men hate to be ignored, love. It really puts them in a quake, especially when they're supposed to be escorting you. You saw how all those young officers buzzed round you this morning? Well, take advantage of their interest. There was that dashing Captain Flavell at the ball. He was interesting. And the one they called Bessie?'

'Captain Tom Bessingham.'

'Another captain? Well, my dear.' Amelie sat back, smiling.

'What happens when Lord Rayne offers to take me driving?'

'You don't *have* to accept him, my dear. Anyway, we're riding this afternoon, so when he offers to assist you, show him politely that you don't need him. It's just as much fun, you know.'

Caterina was smiling again. 'Yes,' she said, 'oh,

yes. I think I could have some fun with that. Where shall we be going?'

'I really haven't been able to find that out yet.' She stood up, catching sight of a newly ironed newspaper draped over one of the chairs.

Lord Elyot had been annoyingly mysterious, and Amelie's trust in his motives had now taken such a pounding that the idea of a mystery tour held no appeal for her. Although she was trying her hardest to conceal it, the events of that morning had turned her careful plans upside-down along with her personal code, which was to keep men at a distance and, as far as possible, out of her life completely. To progress from that to being little better than a nobleman's mistress in a matter of days went against all her intentions, for which she blamed Hurst for his baseness, and herself for allowing her heart to rule her head. Lord Elyot was right about her being unworldly, and now her chat to Caterina about how to deal with men had left her feeling distinctly hypocritical and by no means as sure as she sounded about the outcome. Perhaps she ought to take the plunge by taking Caterina into her confidence, but the young lady was having enough trouble understanding her own situation without trying to make sense of her aunt's also. And there was a limit to Caterina's knowledge of the Buxton scandal.

* * *

'You've *what*?' said Lord Rayne to his brother. A deep crease drew his dark brows closer together like a thundercloud, his mouth forming a narrow line that heralded some caustic remark regarding the cool announcement. 'You've formed an alliance already? I know you work fast, Nick, but this is almost indecent.'

'Lord, brother, you sound more like Father every day,' Lord Elyot muttered.

'No, I don't. Father would remind you that you don't form that kind of alliance without first consulting him so that he can tell you why it won't work. Is that why you've given him the slip?' He grinned, mischievously.

Approaching the heavy wrought-iron gates of Sheen Court, Nick waited until they were on the long driveway before answering. 'It was not the way it appears. I've had to move rather faster than usual, that's all. Well…no, that's not quite all. This one is different, Sete.'

Seton's frown returned as he stole a sideways glance to judge his brother's seriousness and saw, by the total absence of the usual triumphant grin, that it was indeed quite a different matter, this time. He drew gently upon his reins. 'Well slow down and tell me, then. Are you saying you've *offered* for her? Why couldn't you come to the same informal arrangement you usually do?'

'Take her as my mistress, you mean? That suggestion would not have gone down very well, but the problem is that word has already got out that Lady Chester and I have an understanding. Don't ask me how it happened, because I'm not at liberty to explain, but it's there, and rather than have to deny it at every end and turn, which would take some doing, it suits my purpose to go along with it. But it looks as if Father and Mother may hear our names linked before I can inform them of my intentions.'

'Which they will not like one bit. Send them a letter, Nick.'

'Yes, I shall send Todd up to St James's Square this afternoon with some other information. That's the best I can do. Don't look like that, lad. They've been nagging me for years to find a wife, so I may well get round to it, eventually.'

Seton picked up on the tone. 'That sounds as if you're not too sure of her, in spite of the understanding. Is she not willing, after all?'

'The story's a bit complicated, Sete. I'll tell you one day, but I wanted you to know that she's accepted me partly because it will help to get Miss Chester launched into the auction ring, which she's having trouble with down here.'

'Only partly? What's the other part?' When his brother's reply was slow to emerge, Seton made it for him. 'Ah,' he said, 'so you've got something on her.

She's not willing, but she has to accept you to keep you quiet. Eh? Well, that's not your usual style. And how long is this…engagement…going to last, may I ask, until you snare another bird, or until she…?'

'No, there will be no other, Sete. It's this one, or nothing.'

'Oh, really. And does *she* believe that?'

'It's the last thing she wants to hear at this point. She would not believe a word of it, I'm afraid.'

The hooves clattered across the stableyard cobbles where grooms came running to hold the bridles and to wait for the men to dismount. With a last look at the swishing tails, the brothers turned towards the house.

'Sounds to me,' said Seton, unhelpfully frank, 'as if you're nicked in the pipkin, old chap. Taking on a prime Ace of Spades and a niece can spell nothing but a fistful o' trouble, 'specially if it's not much to her liking. Still, you usually know what you're doing. You can rely on my discretion, you know that.'

'Yes, I do know, Sete. Thanks. The story so far, in case our sister wants to know, is that Lady Chester's affairs are being examined to see what's what. Meanwhile we shall be seen out and about together before any announcement is made. That should give the parents time to see that I'm serious.'

'But Father's bound to think she's Apartments to Let, Nick.'

'Maybe at first, until he can see for himself that it's

not so. She's as able to flash the screens as any
widow in London, and more than most. You've seen
for yourself what would drive a man to make a bid
for her, haven't you?'

The long slow breath expelled from between
Seton's lips was followed by a deeply envious
growl. 'I wish that pert little miss had half her aunt's
style. She's a nice enough little thing, and I don't
mind helping you out while I have nothing much
else to do, but there are times when I'd like to put
her across my knee.'

'Then you're being too kind to her,' said his
brother, tersely, passing his hat, gloves and riding
whip to a waiting footman.

'You told me to be kind, dammit.'

'Use your loaf, Sete. If the chit needs a firm hand,
then use one. She'll not break in half.'

'You don't suppose she'll go crying to Aunt
Amelie, then?'

Lord Elyot allowed himself a huff of amusement
at last, though it was for the name, not the potential
crisis. 'No!' he said. 'She might cry into her pillow,
but she'd not admit to losing the upper hand. I expect
she's had her father wrapped round her little finger
since her mama died, so now's the time to break the
habit before she kicks the door down.'

Seton's whip slapped hard against the side of his
top-boot before he handed it over. 'Oh, good lord,

Nick, why should I care what bad habits she gets? She's not a filly of my choosing.'

'Then have yourself a bit of fun,' said Lord Elyot, callously. 'It's only for the short term, after all. You've broken in fillies before.'

'Not two-legged ones.' The frown returned. 'You're not suggesting I seduce her, are you?'

'Of course I'm not, halfwit. I'm not suggesting anything as irrevocable as that. But if you want her to grow up, you must school her. You've had it too easy, Sete. See what you can make of her.'

'Hmph!' Seton grunted.

It soon became evident, that afternoon, that the promised ride was to lead them up the stony road to Hill Common, the road Amelie had last travelled on a donkey in driving rain and darkness. By daylight, it gave them astonishing views across the river, across Richmond town and the royal parkland beyond. But it was the workhouse itself that surprised her most, having never seen it except in her imagination where she expected it to resemble all the others she knew of, stark, uninviting, with high walls and barred windows, silent, forbidding, a desolate last resort.

In reality, the only common factor with those she had seen was its size: in every other respect the Richmond workhouse was revolutionary in its attitude to care and clean accommodation, in variety of useful occupation and teaching, in food and self-sufficiency, in everything but the luxury of family, which many of them had never had, anyway. Amelie and Caterina learnt that it had its own infirmary and maternity ward, which is where Lord Elyot guessed they would stay longest.

While the men visited the leather workshop, the weavers, the gardens and the blacksmith, the two women were escorted by the friendly white-aproned matron into a bright clean dormitory that smelled of babies and soap and woodsmoke from the fire. Between curtains, beds and cots were arranged along each wall and round the central pillars and, although privacy was not a priority, mother and childcare was of a kind that Amelie had thought quite impossible in a place which, by tradition, had such a low regard for human comforts.

They visited every mother and her infant, of whom at least six could have been the one she had attempted to rescue on that rainy night a week ago. And by the time Amelie had held the last soft helpless bundle against her shoulder, nuzzled its downy head and breathed in the sweet milky aroma, the tears she had been fighting were running freely down her face and dripping off her chin, and the mothers to whom she had come to offer pity were, without exception, pitying her.

The last sleepy little mite was prised gently out of

her arms and put to her mother's breast. 'Her name?' Amelie asked, still weeping.

'She ain't named yet, m'lady. What's yours?'

'Amelie.'

'Then that's what I'll call her. Emily. She'll be called Emily.'

'Thank you. It's a lovely gown she wears.'

The mother smiled while the matron explained, 'The Marchioness and her daughter run sewing groups,' she said. 'They make most of the baby gowns, and very nice they are too. Lord Elyot and Lord Rayne brought a bundle of them up only a day or two ago. They're very caring, that family.' She opened the door and waited for her guests to pass. 'Always have been. Very involved they are, bless 'em. People come here from all over the country, you know, to see how we manage things, and there's never a month goes by without Lord Elyot coming to see us, never emptyhanded.'

The full significance of the matron's revelation made less than its full impact upon Amelie then, although she recalled feelings of both confusion and contradiction. But outside the door, Caterina took her aunt into her arms, holding her until she could collect herself while Lord Elyot waited a little way off, aware of the crisis, but keeping the farm manager and bailiff in conversation. There was nothing Amelie could do to conceal the effects of her distress from him, in spite of Caterina's mopping, the kindly matron's understanding and her soothing cordial. She could see at a glance where the problem lay.

Lord Rayne had been visiting the stables, coming to meet them as they emerged from the large stone porch on to the cobbled courtyard where their horses were waiting. With unmistakable authority, he took charge of Caterina's attempts to arrange her long skirts over her legs, brusquely changed her riding crop from her left to her right hand and told her to face forward properly in the saddle, which she thought she was doing. From his own saddle, he saw her attempt to move away and, reaching for her horse's bridle, clipped a leading-rein to it. Then he sat back, grim-faced.

'I can *manage*,' said Caterina, crossly.

'You need to concentrate.'

'On you, or the horse?' she muttered.

'On your *riding*. Walk on.'

Not another word was spoken by either of them on the way home, but a glance that passed between Caterina and her red-nosed aunt assured her that silence was no bad thing.

For that matter, there was no actual conversation between Amelie and Lord Elyot either, and what did pass between them was mostly monosyllabic.

To an outsider, one tear-stained face and a lack of communication between four people might have appeared disastrous, but to Lord Nicholas Elyot it was far from that. For one thing, his brother seemed to have accepted his advice about what young Miss Chester *really* needed and, for another, he himself had discovered what her aunt needed, if that little scene was anything to go by. Through the pane of glass in the ward door, he had seen how reluctantly she'd handed back the warm bundle to its mother as if it broke her heart to do so, and he had wanted to take her in his arms there and then to give her the comfort she craved so desperately. But the episode had, for him, answered the question about her zeal for the plight of fallen women, a discovery that did not unsettle him as it once might have done. With previous mistresses, the problem of raising bastards had been enough to cool his initial ardour. This woman disturbed him in quite a different way.

Back in the stable courtyard at Paradise Road, he lifted her down from the saddle, knowing that she would attempt to escape him as quickly as Miss Chester had dismissed herself from his brother's uncongenial presence. 'No,' he said, gently hooking a hand beneath the velvet-covered arm. 'We need to speak, in private, if you please.'

Lord Rayne was remounting, preparing to leave.

'Seton,' Lord Elyot called to him, 'go on up to the Roebuck and I'll join you in a few moments.' The sound of a door being slammed in the house made him smile and throw a wink in his brother's direction.

On the ground floor, the saloon and the dining room were connected by a pair of large doors, leaving Lord Elyot in no doubt that both rooms would compliment each other in similar tones of soft blue, white and gold, warmed by the honeyed oak floor and a huge vase of red and gold foliage. This woman certainly had style and a liking for Mr Wedgwood.

In the saloon, she stood rather like a deer at bay, prepared to defend herself without knowing where the first attack would come from. 'Don't ask me,' she said, in a voice torn with emotion. She put out a hand as if to ward him off. 'I can't explain. You would not understand. It would be best if you were to leave me, my lord. I'm not company for anyone.' She turned away from him to hide her face.

Slowly, he peeled off his leather gloves and laid them upon a small side table, watching the graceful curve of her back and the irritable stacatto pulls at the finger-ends of her gloves which, in the next moment, went flying across the room like angry bats, followed by her veiled hat, narrowly missing a blue Wedgwood urn.

'I will leave you, my lady but, before I go, allow me to tell you that my only reason for taking you up there was to put your mind at rest about the welfare of the mothers and infants, not to upset you. I wanted you to see how seriously the Vestry treat the problem. I can see where your pain is.'

'You cannot possibly know,' she retorted, angrily, still with her back to him.

'I *do* know,' he said, harshly. 'I'd have to be blind not to know.'

'It's none of your business,' she whispered.

'It is, Amelie. It's very much my business, and so are you.' He waited, but she did not contradict him, nor did she remark on his familiar use of her name. 'Now,' he said, 'so far you have avoided asking me about the two invitations. Well, one is to my sister's birthday dinner party at Mortlake.'

'When?' She turned at that, suddenly apprehensive.

'Tomorrow evening.'

'I cannot go…no, I cannot! Your parents will be there.'

'They won't. They're attending a court function in London. Only my sister's family and friends will be there, and Miss Chester will be among people of her own age. My sister would particularly like to meet you after Miss Chester told her about you.'

For the first time since leaving the workhouse, Amelie's eyes met his, holding them steadily, and Nick knew she was saying what she could not bring herself to speak, that she would be on show as his newest conquest, paraded, compared, discussed and judged, that this was a role she had no idea how to fulfil, nor did she have the aptitude for it.

'We shall be among friends. They will congratulate us, that's all.'

'Your sister is not like the Marchioness, then?' She had mused, on the way home, about the sewing group run by the mother and daughter who made clothes for those unfortunates so heartily disapproved of by at least one of them. There was nothing so strange, she had told herself, as folk.

'Not at all. You will like each other, I know it. They all will.'

'And the other invitation?'

'Equally pleasant. A soirée at Ham House. Professional musicians. I think you'll enjoy it. Interesting people, artists, poets, writers too.'

'When?'

'The day after tomorrow,'

'And Caterina?'

'Of course, that's why I shall accept, so that she can meet the best people. She'll be a sensation.'

Again, there was a long silent exchange of messages behind the eyes that said it was more likely to be she who would be the sensation, that she was the one he wanted to flaunt like a trophy. He sensed the struggle in her, the excitement of being desired by a man, the conflict of needs, her reluctance to adapt to her new role and her fear of passing control of her life to a complete stranger. To him.

'I don't understand you,' she said at last. 'Why are

you doing this? There must be easier ways of getting a woman to partner you.'

'A woman like you, my lady? I think not. Perhaps I've had it all my own way till now. Perhaps I need to work harder at it. Perhaps my other relationships were so brief because there was no incentive to make them last. I've certainly never offered to take a seventeen-year-old in tow before.'

'Then I should be flattered, my lord, as well as grateful.'

'I don't know about that. But I do know one thing—that no man who sees you with me will be surprised by my haste and, although they may wonder how I managed it, I shall be the envy of them all. If that comes near to answering my question about why I'm keeping a hold on you, then so be it. Call it pride, if you will. A search for the best and pride in having found a way to hold it.'

She had stood with head bowed and cheeks flushed as his somehow left-handed tributes were delivered quietly across the elegant saloon, their sincerity all the more believable for their unexpectedness.

'Captured, or bought?' she whispered, testing him. 'It doesn't seem to me that you have had too exhausting a time of it in this search and capture. I seem to think it all fell into your lap rather easily, my lord.'

His stroll towards her was deceptively languid, but his hands caught her in a grip that bit through her sleeves. 'I was not referring to the pursuit, my lady, as you well know, but to the holding of the prize. And I intend to keep you by my side for the foreseeable future. Make no mistake about it.'

'Until all the skeletons in my cupboard are let loose upon the world. That's what you mean, of course.'

His eyes searched lazily over her features. 'You are telling me something, I believe. *More* skeletons? Hurst? *Was* he your lover?'

In a sudden blaze of anger barely hidden beneath the surface, she squirmed in his hold. 'I might have known you'd not believe me,' she said angrily. 'Let me spell it out for you. *I have never had a lover. There, now take it or leave it.'

'Very well. So since we're spelling things out, hear this. With or without skeletons, I want you in my bed and at my board, and the sooner we put that to the test the better it will be for both of us. And if you had it in mind to delay the pleasure, think again. I agreed to take it slowly, but I am not inclined to wait for the first frosts of winter.'

The words and the cynical use of the term 'pleasure' seemed to find no warm response in her eyes, for his expression was anything but lover-like. 'You're squeezing my arms,' she whispered.

'Forgive me.' Taking one of the hands that moved up to comfort the crushed velvet, he raised it to his lips, palm upwards, to place there the lightest of kisses and to close her fingers over it. 'I do not mean to shock you, Amelie. Are you shocked?'

'Today,' she said, 'you have dispelled a trouble from my mind that has been with me since I arrived here. That is a great relief to me, my lord. If only my other concerns could be dealt with so efficiently. What is the hearing of a few down-to-earth manly intentions compared to that? No, I am not shocked, but nor am I prepared to gallop up to your bed so that you can notch up the score on your side of the board. I never wanted to be in your debt, I did not choose the stakes, and I won't pay out what is still mine just because you are not inclined to wait. I'm sorry, my lord, but you may as well know how it is.'

'*Brava*, my beauty,' he said, smiling. 'I would have thought you in very queer stirrups if you'd not fought back on that one. Well done.'

'Tomorrow,' she said, moving away from his laughing eyes, 'it will be evening dress, I take it?' Unthinking, she placed a cool hand to her cheeks.

'Yes, but not too grand. We shall bring the coach round at five. My sister dines quite late these days.'

Amelie nodded, all replies used up.

Taking his gloves from the table, he came back to her and lifted her chin with one finger, touching her lips with his in a soft salute. 'Go up and take a rest, my lady,' he said. 'You've had a rough day.'

* * *

She did not, of course, take a rest and, even if she had, she would not have been able to prevent so many conflicting thoughts from tangling into the most complex of knots. Apart from that, those heartrending moments of melting bliss when she had held the infant in her arms had left such a deep and aching void inside her that she felt drained and quite unable to pull herself back into shape. Lord Elyot had said he understood, but no one could share that all-consuming blinding passion to bear a child except those women like her whose need had never been satisfied. Was it not ironic, she asked herself, that the circumstance in which that need might now be filled was the very problem she had striven so hard to rectify? She would never find herself in the workhouse, but nor had he put her mind to rest about his share in the responsibility, should there be one, of accepting a fatherless child.

Throughout the mantua-maker's visit, the enormity of what she had agreed continued to disturb her, and it was Caterina who conducted the dress fitting with confidence, despite the woman's grumbling apologies for the continued absence of her young assistant and the inevitable lateness of the new gowns. When questioned about Millie's illness, the mantua-maker had to admit that she had not had time to make enquires about her.

* * *

Later that afternoon, the appearance of the recovered but pale Millie disturbed Amelie's conscience less than it might have done, her newest act of charity far outweighing the furtive transfer from the girl's former employer to a bedroom of her own, warm clothes, good food and sensible hours of work. The grateful lass was speechless at the offer of six guineas a year, and the unfamiliar smiles she received from Mrs Braithwaite quite overcame her. In lieu of words, she kissed Amelie's hands.

Millie was familiar with the new gowns that had just arrived, and it was soon clear that her knowledge of how they should be worn as well as how they had been constructed would make her an ideal dresser for Caterina. After a bath, a change of clothing and some food, Millie was suggesting adjustments like a true professional, trying out combinations of ribbons, draping lace and fur while the names of hairstyles tripped off her tongue and wove through her nimble fingers.

Upstairs in her workroom, Amelie propped an array of calling cards across her writing table and gazed at them. Most were from the best-known families in Richmond who could, with a little less natural caution, have left cards weeks ago. One or two with the corners turned down had been left in person by gentlemen she had danced with at the

Castle Inn ball, and some were from strangers who apparently wanted to know her. It was most gratifying, she thought, pushing the Oglethorpes' card behind the rest.

Pulling out the lid of the writing-desk, she took paper and quill and began to write: *Dearest and Most Esteemed Brother, I fear that, since receiving your last letter, so much has happened that I hardly know where to begin with my reply. Nevertheless...*

Nevertheless, once started, she was able to form a tolerably coherent summary of the events that had suddenly overtaken her tidy life, leaving out little except Lord Elyot's indecent proposal, his intimacies, and her own confused reaction to it all. Stephen Chester, Caterina's widowed father, had been a true, though not impartial, tower of strength, and any hint that Amelie had agreed to a physical relationship with Lord Elyot in return for his support and discretion was not allowed to colour her account. Not even between the lines.

For Caterina's sake, I have accepted the brothers' offers of escort...Caterina and he get on so well together...to their sister's dinner party...a concert at Ham House where she will meet...so many calling-cards already...quite spoilt for choice... and so on.

Amelie had never been good at deception; on the few occasions she had tried it, she had come woefully unstuck. Consequently, she found it easier to tell her brother-in-law of Hurst's passing visit while painting Lord Elyot as the knight in shining white armour whose support she had accepted just as she had accepted his in Buxton. She hoped that this would not offend his feelings, for she knew how he had hoped for an affection of a deeper kind after his brother's death. For him, it would have been the ideal solution. But not for Amelie, who had two genuine objections to the connection, one of which was that she did not love him. Nor did she believe she ever would.

The village of Mortlake lay on the other side of the royal park on a loop of the River Thames to the north-east of Richmond, making a triangle with Kew. Amelie had driven through it once or twice and thought that, had she known of its existence earlier, its prettiness and clean lines might have suited her well.

'We'll come by boat one day,' said Lord Elyot as the coach turned through the gates of Elwick Lodge. 'It'll take longer, but the approach is spectacular from the river steps.'

But Caterina's description of the house as 'white and enormous' had not done justice to the groups of limes and elms, the green sloping lawns, rose-covered walls and the sparkling boat-studded river beyond. And it *was* enormous, three-tiered and grand with wide steps leading up to a porticoed entrance even now swarming with liveried men and a bouncing rash of black labrador puppies followed by two small children dragging their nurse behind them.

It was as if the house had suddenly had its cork drawn, spilling its contents around the coach and fizzing with welcomes. If Amelie had had any reservations about her acceptance, they were dispelled at once by the extended Elwick family who absorbed her like a sponge into their continuous embrace as if she had always been one of them. Caterina was greeted like a long-lost cousin, narrowly rescued from four eager hands by nurse and paternal grandmother. With hardly a coherent introduction to penetrate the general hub-bub, the frothy company then reversed its flow through the double doors into a cavernous hall, marble-floored, columned, and spiralling upwards in a coil of delicate ironwork from which coloured paper streamers fluttered in the breeze.

'Mama's birfday,' the fair-haired little angel lisped, pointing upwards. 'Look…steamers…look, Unca Nick!'

Having conserved a kind of distance until now, Amelie was obliged to revise her assumptions about Lord Elyot's judgemental relatives, for this scene certainly did not fit her previous images of them. Whether Adorna Elwick was used to receiving her brothers' current partners or whether Amelie was an exception, there was no way of knowing, but her smiles seemed as genuine as the children's. 'You must call me Dorna as everyone else does,' she said. 'Our names go back for generations. We can't escape them.'

'Dorna, may I wish you a happy birthday?' said Amelie.

'Certainly you may. Thank you.' She eyed the large box that one of the footmen had carried in. 'If that's from you two,' she said to her brothers, 'it will be the first ever to have arrived on the right day.' There was laughter and warmth in her cultured voice, and a sisterly tenderness in her blue-grey eyes that made her sparkling smile even more remarkable. Unlike her siblings, she was fair-haired and fair-skinned, still girl-ishly slender and so modish that she could wear with self-confidence an unlined white-spotted muslin of such fineness that no detail of her dainty breasts inside the minuscule bodice was left to the imagination. Tied beneath with a wide pale-blue satin ribbon, the long ends were left to trail over her train, which the black puppies were convinced was one of the latest games and which concerned the wearer not at all.

For her part, Amelie saw an appealing insouciance in her hostess's manner that would be able to take an ugly tea urn in its stride, even to flaunt it before her friends as good for a laugh. All the same, Amelie wished now that she had not taken her anger out on Dorna, of all people, for she was sure she was going to like her.

There was nothing *not* to like about the Elwick family or their spacious lived-in house by the river, or easy-going Sir Chad and his gentle parents, or Dorna's aged godparents and her various brothers and sisters-in-law.

However, Colonel Tate, an old family friend and neighbour, fell into rather a different category. He had an annoying habit of saying whatever came into his head, often causing laughter, but sometimes irritation. Nudging his old-fashioned powdered wig into position, he lifted his quizzing-glass to examine the single row of pearls around Amelie's neck and, convinced of their value, dropped it with a squeak of surprise. 'Well, m'boy,' he said, swivelling round to fix Lord Rayne with his bloodshot eyes, 'you've found yourself a flush mort here and no mistake. What's she worth, eh? This one'll put you back in funds, if you can keep her, eh, m'lad? What?'

'You've got it wrong, Colonel,' said Lord Rayne, wincing visibly. 'Unfortunately, Lady Chester is engaged to my brother, not to me.'

'To Elyot? Eh?' The quizzing-glass was picked up again to find the elder brother. 'What does Elyot want with *that* kind of money? He's not in queer streets too, is he? Looking for a golden dolly, m'boy? When I was your age—'

'Thank you, Colonel,' said Lord Elyot, taking Amelie's hand and threading it through his arm, 'for your advice on our financial affairs, but I can assure you it isn't in the least necessary. Lady Chester's financial affairs are of no one's concern but her own. Shall we go through? Lord, Dorna,' he whispered to his embarrassed sister, 'why the devil did you invite that garrulous old turnip? You know what he's like.'

'I had no choice,' she replied. 'He invited himself. Please...' she leaned towards Amelie '...take no notice of him, will you? He means no offence.'

Amelie smiled. She had met the Colonel's type before. 'I am not in the least offended,' she said. 'One could be called worse names than a golden dolly.' She felt the quick squeeze of the arm over her wrist, but what had concerned her more than the old man's indiscretion was Lord Rayne's use of the word 'unfortunately'. Could it mean that he did not approve?'

She looked to see if Caterina had heard, but her attention was being held by a tall good-looking dandy with shirt-points up to his ears and a curly mop of light brown hair worn in fashionable disarray.

'That's Tam,' said Lord Elyot. 'Short for Tamworth. Sir Chad's younger brother. He and his sister live with their parents next door. That's Hannah over there.' Looking across the room, he indicated a petite lady of about Amelie's own age, quietly attractive but not conventionally pretty. 'She's the sedate one,' he said. 'Not a bit like her brother.'

'I'd like to meet her.'

But there were other more pressing introductions, first to Lord and Lady Appleton, another of Sir Chad's sisters and her supercilious husband for whom the whole event was a tedium to be endured with a minimum of effort. Kitty, his chattery wife, was happy to hear that her brother-in-law had begun to think more seriously about his relationships, but her intrusive queries were too much for Amelie, who was glad to leave all explanations to the man himself. Listening to him, she realised that there was no incident or remark that he could not deal with politely while giving away very little real information. She need not have been concerned about anything, not then or during dinner.

The giving of gifts, to which Amelie had not been looking forward, passed off with the same noisy good humour as the greetings. The controversial tea urn was exclaimed over and, after various impertinent suggestions as to its role in laundry or cellar, a place was found for it in a mirrored alcove where its ugliness, to Dorna's delight, was doubled. 'Pride of place,' she exclaimed, 'to show that my brothers *do* remember!'

Lord Elyot's shapely brows lifted a notch as he caught Amelie's sheepish expression across the table, and she was reminded that he had understood. But her eyes had wandered towards the lady who sat on his left, to Hannah, his sister-in-law, who was looking at him with such poorly concealed adoration that Amelie could see how her heart was aching with the pain of love.

Like Amelie, Hannah was no longer a young girl. She was fair haired and possessed of a serene expression that bluff Colonel Tate mistook for an un-natural lack of animation, and the remarks he made from the opposite side of the table brought flames to her pale cheeks. Amelie's heart went out to her, but she held back the invitation that was on the tip of her tongue until she'd had a chance to talk with her. If she was as in love with Lord Elyot as Amelie believed, an invitation to stay at Richmond might make matters more complicated than they were already.

To Amelie's relief, Caterina had accepted the new situation with remarkably little surprise, as if she had foreseen the event and was pleased to have her own future placed on a surer footing. Her only disappointment was that, as yet, there was no ring to show for it, and no celebrations planned.

More gifts were unwrapped between courses and passed round the table to be admired, amongst them Amelie's painting of purple irises, which even she believed to be one of her most successful.

'Good gracious me,' said Kitty's patronising husband, 'you can paint! I believe this is quite beyond the usual for an amateur, my dear.'

'I didn't know you were an authority on water-colours, Appleton,' said Lord Elyot drily from across the table. 'You're viewing it upside-down, by the way.'

Hurriedly, Lord Appleton turned the painting round, frowning at it as if it should have known better. 'Er…well, no old man. I suppose fishing's more my line.'

'That's what I thought. I should stick to it, if I were you. That piece was exhibited at the Royal Academy last year.'

'Eh? Oh…really! Good lord!' said Lord Appleton, sinking a little into his cravat. He passed the painting on, taking another longer look at Amelie.

Every other remark was complimentary, but the one whose look held all the approval Amelie needed had again shielded her from the merest hint of disdain, even that provoked by ignorance. As at the ball, she felt the warmth of his protection and, while talking to her table-partners, watched how his dark handsome head bent towards Hannah, giving her all his attention while caressing the neck of a dessert-spoon with long fingers and nodding at some serious point she was making. No wonder, Amelie thought, that Hannah was in love with him and how changed he was from the hard-bitten cynic she had first met in the London goldsmith's shop. How could the two counterparts ever be reconciled?

By coincidence, the answer to that vexed question came after the sumptuous dinner when she seized the chance to speak to Lord Rayne, who had left Caterina to the dedicated attentions of Tam, Hannah's brother. As if their meeting had been booked in advance, he offered her his arm and together they strolled out on to the rustic verandah that overlooked the river and the meadows beyond. They were not alone, but no one approached them as they perched on a low windowsill with the evening sun in their eyes.

'We've had little chance to talk, my lord,' said Amelie, adjusting the Chantilly lace shawl over her shoulder. 'Could we be friends now, or did my earlier resistance quite put you off? It was meant to, of course, at the time.' She could see why Caterina had lost her heart to this young man, and why she would fall some way short of his more cosmopolitan tastes.

His smile, though, was boyish as he looked out across the river at the gliding of late wherries and their passengers. 'Our family has a reputation for not being easily put off,' he said, turning to her. 'I've been waiting for the right moment to talk with you.'

'About your brother's offer? You disapprove of it, I fear.'

'Why should I disapprove, my lady? It's extremely sudden, I have to admit, but I approve of Nick's choice. No, I *envy* him and congratulate you.'

'But…but you used the word "unfortunately" to Colonel Tate. I thought that—'

'Heavens above, no, my lady. It's only unfortunate that you're not engaged to *me* instead of Nick. But I'm not in a position to offer for anyone yet, you see. Otherwise…' He sighed, and looked away again.

For Caterina's sake, Amelie thought it best to let the subject rest. 'Well, then, I'm glad we have your blessing. It would have made me very unhappy otherwise. I would like us to be friends, my lord, and your sister too, though I'm afraid I cannot say the same…' she looked over to the group where a loud voice shouted down the rest '…for everyone.' Seeing the amusement on her companion's face, she relented. 'Oh dear, I hope he's not a particular friend of yours, is he?'

But his smile told her otherwise. 'Old Colonel Dandyprat? No, he still thinks he's in the army. We've known him since we were children so we can take his silly prattle with a pinch o' snuff. We used to mimic him a lot. Still do, sometimes. You should hear him on do-gooders…philanthropists, you know. His favourite aversion.' His comely features adopted Colonel Tate's florid puffiness and petulantly wobbling mouth as if he had practised for years. '"Them young bits o'skirt ought to be *locked up!*"' he yelped, for her ears only. '"Vagabonds! Nobthatchers! And anybody who thinks 'em worth helping must be *addle-brained*! A load o' loose screws, that's what they are! The workhouse is too

good for tarts like that."' His features relaxed as
laughter overtook him again, and he did not notice
how Amelie's expression of astonishment changed
to sheer relief as the uncompromising sentiments
were spoken once more, this time in their original
context. 'We'd never take *him* up to the workhouse,'
he said, still chuckling. 'He and my mother have
fearsome arguments about it, but nobody ever gets
the better of her. "If only you knew what *trouble* you
people cause!"' he mimicked again. 'She tells him
to go to the devil.'

'She's very fierce, your mother?'

'Oh, she's a character,' he told her.

Amelie hoped he might have gone on to elaborate,
but his place was taken by his sister. 'Seton,' said
Dorna, 'be a darling and rescue Hannah from Mr
and Mrs Horner. The poor girl looks desperate.' She
took his hands and pulled him up. 'Besides, it's my
turn to talk to Amelie.'

But by now, Amelie's curiosity had been aroused
by several anomalies, one of which concerned the
fearsome Marchioness, another was to do with the
names handed down from the ancestors.

'Our names?' said Dorna, in answer to her query.
'Elyot and Rayne are both family names dating
back to Tudor times. The first Lord Elyot had a son
named Sir Nicholas Rayne who was assistant
Master of Horse to Queen Elizabeth. He married

the first Adorna whose father, Sir Matthew Pickering, was Master of Revels when the palace at Richmond was still used by the royals. Apparently, there were as many fireworks over that match as there were over the Queen's *affaire* with the Earl of Leicester. A huge scandal, there was. Since then, the position of Assistant Master of Horse and Keeper of the Royal Stud has been passed down through Sir Nicholas's family, which is how my father comes to hold the office. That's why he can't be with us.'

'But he's now the Marquess of Sheen.'

'Yes, he was created earl by King George III, then he became a marquess and, as you know, one usually has to be the earl or marquess *of* somewhere, so he took the name of Sheen, since that's where we've always lived.'

'The old name for Richmond.'

'That's right. So Nick took the handed-down title of Lord Elyot, and Seton became Lord Rayne. It must be so confusing to strangers, with all these names from the past.'

'But then, *you* are a lady by birth as well as by marriage.'

'Which is why I'm Lady Adorna Elwick, rather than just Lady Elwick. As if it matters,' she laughed, nudging Amelie, who knew that it did. 'The first Adorna had a brother named Seton who wrote stage-plays for the Earl of Leicester's company, and their brother Adrian acted with William Shakespeare.'

'Really? So Adorna's scandalous affair with the first Sir Nicholas…is that something the present Marchioness prefers to keep secret?'

'Mother?' Dorna's laugh rang out as she threw back her fair head, curving her long throat. 'Heavens, not a bit of it. Mama is no stranger to scandal. I sometimes think she thrives on it. Ah…Nick! There you are. Have you come to interrupt our cosy chat?'

'Yes. Have you told Lady Chester that *her* house is on the same Paradise Road where our ancestors once lived?'

'Oh,' said Amelie. 'I thought it was just a lovely name. Tell me more, if you please.'

He did. 'The original Sheen House overlooked the paradise garden at the end of the old friary that stood next to Richmond Palace. The road that ran alongside it was known as Paradise Road, but that house was demolished and rebuilt as Sheen Court on the edge of the royal park about eighty years ago.'

Dorna blinked at her brother, prettily. 'Hasn't Amelie been to see Sheen Court yet, Nick?'

'Er…no, not yet. We met in London, you know, and I've only been home for a few days.'

Sensing that it was her turn to help him out, Amelie intervened. 'It's not that he hasn't invited me,' she said, 'but things happened rather quickly and I've been quite busy attending to Caterina's new wardrobe, her visits and lessons. I had no idea a niece could be so time consuming.'

'Well, then,' said Dorna, 'you must go and be introduced to the ancestors as soon as Nick can take you there. They're all up on the walls. And we shall be having some country dances soon. You'll come and join in, won't you?' She rose, smiling as Nick took her hand and kissed her fingers.

'Lovely meal,' he said, as she tripped away. Placing his hands under Amelie's elbows, he drew her to her feet and led her down the steps as far as the water's edge.

His hand moved lightly over her waist, spreading the fingers wide over the pale aquamarine silk, and she read his thoughts as clearly as if he'd spoken them. Peeping up at him in the last light of the departing sun, she was caught unawares by the sudden thump of lust against her lungs. His lips were still, chiselled and well made, manly and firm, and she knew they were hers for the asking. Drawing her mind along a different route, she asked, 'Your sister-in-law is in love with you, did you know that?'

'Yes, I knew.'

'Does she know?'

'That I know it? Oh, yes.' He pulled her closer and, before she could protest, held her against the stone balustrade. 'You need not be concerned by it.

Nothing has ever been said by either of us. It's something we both recognise, and accept. She'll find someone eventually, as I have done.'

'You didn't find me, sir. We collided.'

'So we did,' he grinned. 'And I'm very proud of you, my girl. You look magnificent. Thank you for making such an effort. I know it was not easy for you, but you've carried it off with flying colours.'

'As a matter of fact,' she replied, glancing aside to see if they were being observed, 'it's been very worthwhile. I have discovered all kinds of things. However, my lord, I shall never be able to condone your methods. Are *you* in love with *her*?' Instantly, she regretted showing the persistent direction of her mind, and when he gathered her up into his arms in the shadow of a large stone pedestal, she knew what he was about to do, yet she did nothing to prevent it.

'I have never been in love with Hannah,' he said, softly, 'nor shall I ever be. There is nothing to be concerned about. She is not a rival in any sense.'

'I'm not concerned by it,' she lied.

She had not wanted her body to respond to him, but it had begun a course of its own and was already halfway towards him as his lips sought hers, at first tenderly, then with a passion that detected her need of him. Then, with all those comforting revelations that had come her way, something began to melt around the protective shell of her heart, softening her lissom figure in the clinging silk dress, bending it shockingly close to his, letting it welcome those hands again and allowing them the same access as before.

Held by his questing lips and the brush of his skin over hers, by the deepening sky, by the seductive swoosh and lap of the river near their feet, she trembled at the touch of his hand upon her shoulder, easing away the tiny sleeve, gently, carefully. His fingertips slipped into the front of her shallow bodice, and she felt a coolness upon her skin before her breast was covered by the warm caress, bringing it to life with a melting that reached her knees, flooding her with desire.

Her 'Ah…ah!' was a cry from the womb that he caught in his lips and spread downwards over her throat, while she breathed in the cold male scent of his hair in passing, touched the soft spring of his ear and tracked the sensuous progress of his mouth towards his waiting hand. She clutched at his wrist, closing her useless fingers over the edge of his sleeve somehow to prevent his lips from tasting her, and then it was too late, for the exquisite touch stifled the cry in her throat and held it there, waiting spellbound as the warmth of his tongue reached the peak of her breast and suckled, firming the nipple within his mouth.

Burying her face in his hair, she clung to him, gasping at the sweetness that overcame her as nothing had ever done before. 'Oh, no,' she breathed into the lush silkiness. 'No, you must not do this.' But she knew that he must. It was what she had agreed. It was what she wanted and feared above everything. 'Not here, my lord,' she begged, hearing the contradiction in her muffled voice.

His lips withdrew, pulling at the sensitive bud with a teasing last kiss. 'Where, then? Shall I take you home?'

The words came out like a sob. 'Not yet…please… not yet.'

Expertly, he eased her bodice and sleeve back into position and adjusted them while she stood there like a confused child being dressed for school. He was breathing hard, his voice a mere growl. 'I'll wait,' he said. 'You're right, there will be better places than this to light your fires, my lady.'

Chapter Six

Except for the distant clack of a carpenter's hammer and the soft thud of apples into the grass, the September morning on Paradise Road was quiet enough to support every thought, however fragile. Lise's footsteps on the verandah made scarcely a sound as she placed the tray on the table and began to pour out the dark steaming chocolate then, adjusting the Paisley shawl around her mistress's shoulders, she placed Caterina's cup where she could reach it, curtsied, and left.

'Thank you, Lise,' Amelie murmured, stirring her drink. To her niece, she said, 'Tell me, why was Lord Rayne so silent? Have you quarrelled?'

Caterina did not resent the assumption, since Aunt Amelie understood men much better than she did. But such things were not easy to express in words. 'Not quarrelled, exactly. He spent more time with Hannah than he did with me, that's all.'

'But you were with her brother Tam most of the time.'

'Yes, because he's far better company and he likes to please people. If Lord Rayne prefers Hannah's company to mine, why should I care?'

'So if he comes to call, you'll be unavailable, will you?'

'He won't.'

'But if he does?'

'No,' Caterina said, dipping one finger into the froth on her chocolate. 'I suppose I shall have to see him.' With a sigh, she licked it.

'Use your spoon. From what I could see, he was being quite masterful at the end. Was he angry, do you think?'

'Oh, I can't make him out. He ignored me all evening, then quite literally *hauled* me away from Tam to say my farewells to Dorna and *hustled* me into the carriage, and I had no chance to say goodbye to Tam. He was *so* high-handed. And when I grumbled, he said, "You can say it next time you meet then, can't you?" Did you ever hear anything so disagreeable?'

'You think he might be jealous?'

There was nothing Caterina would have liked better than to think so. Lord Rayne had stayed in his own corner of the carriage until a sudden lurch had swayed her in his direction and, when he caught her, his arms had lingered for a few moments longer than they need have done, making her believe that he would keep her there for the rest of the journey. But he had not, and now she was convinced that he was playing some kind of advanced game, the rules of which were unknown to her. His good night had been alarmingly abrupt, though his emphatic kiss upon her knuckles had sent a warm thrill through her that she was sure he must have seen with that one dark forbidding glance.

That, with its warning message, had followed her into her dreams, confusing her at every wakeful interlude. 'No,' she whispered. 'I fear not.'

'Would you like to invite Hannah to stay for a day or two?'

Caterina nodded and sat up straight. 'That would be nice.'

'She played well on the harp last night, I thought.'

'She seems to do most things well.'

'Her singing is not as good as yours. You surprised us all last night, you know. I don't know why, but I had not realised what a beautiful voice you have when you perform. We must cultivate it, my dear.'

'Praise the new singing teacher. He's teaching me to breathe properly. I have breathing exercises to do now.'

'And you've been doing them?'

'Certainly I have. Did Lord Rayne…?'

Amelie smiled. 'He watched and listened very carefully,' she said, kindly. 'Drink up. Time to get dressed.'

An hour later, thoughts of the birthday dinner at Mortlake were still dancing through Amelie's mind, not least about her own reaction to Hannah which she had not been able to conceal. Nor could she say why she cared, only that she did, in which respect she was not as different from her niece as she hoped to appear. In one week, she mused, the two brothers had begun to wreak havoc with their sensibilities, causing each day's plans to revolve around them. *For Caterina's sake,* she told herself. *Only for Caterina's sake. Then it will have to cease.*

Yet there was a secret part of her that quivered with anticipation at thoughts of the future, and Lord Elyot's words to her by the water's edge brought a flush to her cheeks even now. *There will be better places than this to light your fires, my lady.* No, it would not be long before he would find both time and place, and she would no longer be able to hold him off with excuses or wiles.

Laying down her sable pencil, she gazed unseeing at the vase of late roses on her work table while with one hand she cupped the breast he had fondled and teased, reliving in her mind the sensation of his lips and hand upon her skin. Recalling what his brother had told her, she breathed a sigh of thanks that he was not, after all, the hard-bitten cynic she had taken him for, and that what she had overheard in London had been a ridiculous but understandable mistake. Nevertheless, his deplorable methods of placing her in his debt for as long as it suited him demonstrated a kind of ruthlessness she could never approve of, even though a secret part of her craved to experience more of it.

In the event, it was not Lord Rayne who called to take Miss Chester out driving, but the two eager young captains, Flavell and Bessington, in a phaeton built for two but which, at a pleasant squeeze, accommodated three. Amelie had not the heart to protest at the wrong two instead of the right one. Consequently, Caterina's mood was distinctly lightened in time to prepare for the evening event at Ham House and to take in her stride whatever fault Lord Rayne would no doubt find with her. It was, however, her aunt's opinion that there was no fault to find, for she and Millie between them had made sure of it.

The pretty gold edgings along neckline, sleeves and hem of the new evening dress, sewn on by Millie, had transformed plain white lawn into something quite remarkable with the addition of a gold and diamond buckle beneath her bodice. White satin shoes with smaller gold buckles, long white kid gloves, a white and gold fan and a beaded reticule had been chosen for an exact match, while Millie's expertise with Caterina's hair was to crown it with a gold cord threaded through the chestnut curls like a badly tied parcel from which coils escaped prettily over ears and neck. Both Millie and Aunt Amelie had forbidden any other adornment. 'Time enough to pile on the jewels when you're as old as the rest of them,' said Amelie. 'At seventeen you have the advantage.'

At seventeen, Caterina would rather have been twenty-two.

By contrast, Amelie had chosen to wear a clinging gown of forest-green crepe deeply cut away at front and back, the tiny bodice of which was spangled with emerald beads that trailed across the train to complement the emerald and diamond necklace and pendant earrings. A matching green ribbon bound up her dark curls, but she refused the plume, the hair ornament and the turban. 'No, Lise,' she said, pushing them away. 'I'll not go looking like a harvest festival. Pass my fan and reticule, if you please.'

She was assured that the choices had been well made when she saw the expression of admiration change Lord Elyot's usual aloofness into something altogether more heart-warming and, when he assured them that they would take Ham House by storm, they politely protested, thinking that this must be an unusual show of exaggeration on his part. They might have known that Lord Elyot never exaggerated. From the moment they passed into the great hall at Ham House, a dozen or so conversations suffered minor fractures, sips of wine paused in midair, eyes widened and blinked and elbows nudged as the whisper went round, 'Who's that with Elyot and his brother?'

Amelie was no stranger to large gatherings, having entertained and attended functions with her late husband several times a week in Buxton and Manchester. Here at Ham House, just round a bend of the river from Richmond, she had not expected to know a single soul, though Lord Elyot had briefed them on the way there about their host, the cultured sixth Earl of Dysart who had been a widower for less than a year. His hostess, Lord Elyot guessed, would be the Earl's sister Mrs Manners, a widow who stood to inherit her brother's title unless he produced an heir.

Amelie saw how unlikely this might be when they were greeted at the door of the reception room by a distinguished-looking gentleman in a white wig and wearing the long embroidered frock-coat of twenty years ago. But nothing could have prepared Amelie for the look of recognition that beamed from the Earl's alert eyes beneath drooping lids and black bushy brows.

'Lady Chester, what an evening of surprises this is, my dear. Sir Josiah and I met often in Manchester, I recall. We must talk, you and I. We *must* talk. Will you promise me?'

'Indeed, my lord, I will,' she responded while not taking his enthusiasm too seriously with so many other guests to attend.

'Good,' he said. 'Elyot, good to see you here. Saw the Marquess in town only two days ago. And who's this charming young lady? Welcome, my dear.'

They moved on into a waving sea of plumes, frothy lace creations and turbans trimmed with yards of goffered frills, feathers and jewels, an abundance of scarves, veils and fichus, bits of gauze half covering bare backs and fronts, the wicked evening glitter of diamonds, and everywhere eyes that turned to look at the two ravishing creatures on Elyot's and Rayne's arms, some with envy, some with admiration, and all of them with interest.

Lord Elyot's deeply mocking voice in Amelie's ear was loud enough to be heard above the general hum. 'Well, well. So you *are* known, it seems.'

'He must be mistaken,' said Amelie. 'How could he have known Sir Josiah, except by name?'

'Could it have been in his capacity as High Sheriff of Cheshire, d'ye think? If Sir Josiah was active in Chester, Dysart might have banked with him.'

'High Sheriff? Is he really?'

'Was,' he said, nodding to someone across the room. 'He's a man of many parts. He'll not be mistaken.'

It was not the first time Caterina had met an earl, but it was her first experience of being surrounded by so many titles and, as she and her aunt were presented to viscounts and dowager countesses, marquesses and minor lords, knights and honourables, neither of them could doubt that the grand launch had begun in earnest and that the creak of opening doors could already be heard.

Through one polished door the splendid tide of guests flowed into the crimson plush seats of the grand hall and settled themselves over the black-and-white chequered floor with occasional glances at the gallery above where more plumes nodded and diamonds flashed. Briefly, Amelie caught sight of a lovely face that withdrew rather too quickly to suggest mere appraisal of the scene, and as Lord Elyot's eyes also withdrew from the same direction, it was only natural for her to assume some former attachment.

'You know her?' she said, competing with the tuning of strings.

His head inclined towards her and she felt the warmth of his skin just before she was caught looking at it. The smile in his eyes recognised her concern and soothed her with their caress. 'I know many of them,' he said, softly, 'but not in the way you think.'

'What way do I think, my lord?'

The smile deepened, just reaching his lips. 'Later,' he whispered as a tall black-clad gentleman walked onto the shallow dais at the far end of the hall. 'Here's Mr Saloman, the concert master.'

To her other side where Caterina sat contentedly
with Lord Rayne, she whispered, 'Mr Saloman,' but
the word *later* had found a niche in Amelie's mind
and so, missing most of the impresario's introduction, she did not know what to expect until she recognised Handel's familiar *Water Music*. Then, when
she ought to have entered into the trotting rhythms
and weaving patterns of sound, her thoughts lingered
on the touch of his arm against hers, on the hand
spread over his thigh, on the long fingers, and on her
desire to smooth the dark hair that dusted the back
of his wrist.

She knew he had noticed her inattention when he
caught her eye with the remnant of his smile and a
lazy blink, sharing those thoughts that were not to
do with Herr Handel's artistry. With deliberation, he
gave his frilled shirt-cuff the slightest tug, then
watched with a deepening grin as her long neck took
on a deeper hue. Glancing at Caterina, she was satisfied to see her fingers tapping, and not for the first
time did Amelie wonder at the cost to her own heart
of this very dangerous and unorthodox liaison.

As the evening progressed, however, she began to
make the discovery that high society in this part of
the country was not quite what she had been used to
in more introvert northern circles where the strait-
laced elite would have enjoyed a bonanza of malicious speculation concerning her sudden appearance

as the notorious Lord Elyot's 'intended'. During the intervals, Lord Rayne kept up a running commentary for Caterina's enjoyment, pointing out to her as many irregular liaisons as conventional marriages. Indicating yet another mistress, another *ménage à trois*, an ex-mistress of the Prince of Wales, a lover of several earls and viscounts, all beautiful, intelligent and popular women, Lord Rayne smiled and nodded to them while keeping Caterina close beside him to hear his outrageously pithy comments, not quite shocking enough to make her blush, but frank enough to make her feel womanly. In a perverse way, it was worth any number of compliments about her appearance.

While he amused Caterina, Amelie realised that what would have degraded these women forever in the eyes of this exalted society was not so much their selective promiscuity but the wrong background, a far greater sin. Lord Nelson's mistress, Lady Hamilton, was sometimes denied the salons of certain hostesses whose invitations stipulated 'Lord Nelson only', for she was of common birth, ill-mannered, and an embarrassment to them. Even that might have been tolerated if, like Lady Caroline Lamb, for instance, she had been a somebody instead of a nobody.

In the company of Lord Elyot and his brother, Amelie and Caterina were accepted as respectable ladies of impeccable breeding, and no questions asked that could not easily be answered. But this did not remove the nagging worry that the man to avoid was Lord Dysart, their host, who had known Sir Josiah Chester and who would presumably feel free to tell his guests about him being a northern industrialist, a banker, and the victim of a duel. Not a perfect pedigree by any standards. As for herself, her family's wealth was well-established and her education of the finest, but here where everyone blithely owed vast sums of money to everyone else and whose general level of education was not high, it was still the trade connections and the degree of scandal that Amelie believed would earn the loudest condemnation in these exalted circles. Once he had heard her story, Lord Elyot himself had endorsed that view, despite the hint from his sister that scandal was written into their family's history. Especially their mother's.

The shaking of this belief came when Lord Dysart and his elderly sister eventually caught up with her during an interval. The handsomely coiffured black-laced Mrs Manners bore down upon her like a tidal wave. 'Here she is!' she announced. 'At last! Now, my dear Lady Chester, I shall take you away from all these admirers because my brother and I want to know what has brought you to these foreign parts.'

The Earl was a good listener, a sociable and intel-

ligent man whose contact with Amelie's late husband
had been of a business nature in Manchester. He had
heard about his sad death, and although he and his
sister could sympathise with Amelie's reasons for
moving away, they were adamant that her concerns
were ill-founded and that duels were not as
uncommon hereabouts as she had thought them to
be. 'In fact, my dear,' said the Earl, looking around
the crowded supper room, 'I would not be surprised
if almost half the men here had not been on the end
of a duelling sword at some time in their lives. Even
Elyot has.'

'Pistols, Wilbraham,' said his sister. 'I believe they
use pistols nowadays. Not nearly as interesting to
watch. You can fire into the air with a pistol whereas
you can't quite do that with a—'

'Yes, my dear Louisa,' said Lord Dysart, patting
her arm. 'Thing is, it takes much less to scandalise
'em up north than it does down here. I'm not saying
that duels happen every day, nor is the gossip any
kinder, but here they're far more likely to kick up a
stink over bloodlines than they are over a whiff of
scandal. It's all about honour, you see. Duels are
soon forgotten, my dear. Soon forgotten. Bloodlines
ain't. I seem to recall that your future mother-in-
law, the Marchioness, got up to some party tricks in
her youth, though perhaps I should not let the cat out
of the bag too soon, eh?'

Beyond Mrs Manners's powdered and feathered hairdo, Lord Elyot stood within earshot, talking to a gentleman and, as they turned, Amelie found herself face to face with another acquaintance from the past who had painted portraits of her and Sir Josiah in the year of their marriage.

'Mr Lawrence,' she said, smiling. 'You're here too. What a delight.'

With his usual theatrical flourish, Thomas Lawrence bowed and, taking her hand, kissed it and held on to it to extend the contact. Once a child prodigy, he was now a witty and popular portraitist for whom Amelie remembered sitting with great pleasure. 'My lady,' he said, gravely, so that she knew he was about to say something teasingly complimentary, 'is it possible that you could have grown even lovelier? Now, I have an idea. You shall put aside the first portrait and allow me to paint an up-to-date version to put in its place. My lord,' he said to Lord Elyot, 'you must back me up on this. You *must* have seen how her beauty has changed?'

A denial would have appeared strange, but he knew at once what was needed. 'Of course she has,' he said, 'but we cannot dispense with the first one. We'll have two. Shall we make a date for it?' And without showing the least surprise that Amelie and the Royal Portrait Painter should know each other, he swung the conversation smoothly away from Amelie's past towards the painter's recent commissions, to the music, to young Miss Chester's interest in the singers, to anything except Lawrence's sojourn in Buxton.

'Thank you,' Amelie whispered as they strolled back into the hall for the next part of the concert. 'Does anything *ever* put you in a quake, my lord?'

Once more, the slow blink revealed laughing eyes that held a reply well away from the subject of conversations. 'Oh, yes,' he said, softly. His gaze slid downwards past the emeralds. 'But no need to be surprised, my lady. I promised you my protection and now, as a reward, I shall insist on seeing the portrait. Where do you keep it?'

'Er…' She studied a displaced bead on her reticule.

'Well?'

'Somewhere private.'

Now there was a bubble of laughter in his voice too. 'Then you will have to admit me to this private place, or how shall I ever know how much you've changed?'

'How did you know my gift to your sister had been accepted by the Royal Academy?' she said, still poking at the bead.

'The label was still on the back. I saw it first in your folio stand. You were not going to tell me of that either, were you?'

'I have to keep some secrets from you.'

'Not for much longer you don't.'

'My lord…' she said, looking to see who might overhear them.

'What?'

'Hush...please!'

Taking her hand, he clasped it in his and held it upon his thigh until the four vocalists walked onto the dais and were applauded. Solos, duets and quartets by Purcell were followed by a *furioso* performance on the pianoforte of Steibelt's celebrated 'Storm Rondo' which, if anything could, drowned out all the inconsistent information about the importance, or not, of scandal to this society. Lord Elyot had implied that his parents would not tolerate any whiff of scandal, yet Lord Dysart had said that few people hereabouts would care one way or the other, citing the Marchioness's own indiscretions, though vaguely. In fact, the only difficult moment had been as a result of this so-called betrothal to Lord Elyot himself who was expected to know more about her than he did. How ironic was that?

But there was also a disturbing conclusion to be drawn from her conversation with Lord Dysart, which went some way to confirming what Amelie feared that, despite the *illusion* of good breeding, if it was not borne out by fact, she would be unacceptable in the eyes of a potential husband and his family. Bloodlines, the Earl had termed it. And now, his pronouncement lay like a dead weight upon Amelie's heart, for it was her *own* bloodlines that concerned her most, a pedigree so insubstantial that it faded into nothing. Even if no one discovered her secret, she could never go through with such an appalling deception, and the shaky contract she had entered into with Lord Elyot would be broken with some with relief on his part.

It would have mattered less, no doubt, if she had not allowed her feelings for him to get out of hand. But she had. She had thought that her love for Josiah was 'being in love'. Now she knew the ache, the yearning, the churning inside like a sickness, and there in the great hall, in the midst of a sublime quartet that told of love, betrayal and anguish from four different viewpoints, her heart swelled, her eyes filled with tears and her breathing staggered and trembled as the overlapping voices soared upwards towards the dark gallery, tearing her composure apart, pulling at her heartstrings.

A large warm hand moved across to cover hers, but the thumb that smoothed her skin added yet another layer of sensation to those already brought alive by the music, and it took every ounce of her self-control to close the doors of her mind while clinging to his hand as if to a life raft.

The applause was appreciative and prolonged, and when Amelie leaned towards Caterina to comment, she saw tears in her eyes too. 'Like it?' she said, above the noise of applause.

Gulping, clapping and craning her neck to see

more, Caterina nodded. '*Loved* it!' she replied.
'That's what *I*'m going to do. Wonderful! *Bravo!*'

'What, sing in public?'

'Yes. I can do that.' Her voice dropped with the volume. 'I *could*, you know.'

'What can she do?' said Lord Elyot.

'Caterina wants to be a vocal artiste.'

'Then we must introduce her to Signor Rauzzini. He's the tenor. He composed the last song. The best singing coach. Lives in Bath.'

'You know him?'

'Not personally, but Salomon will introduce us.' He looked closely at her. 'You all right now?'

'Yes, my lord. It's the music, that's all.' She knew he was not convinced, though he appeared to accept her explanation.

Whatever it was that had gone askew in the relationship between Caterina and Lord Rayne, it seemed to have been straightened out by the heady events of the evening and, by the time they were packed into the dark intimate space of the town coach for the short journey home, the atmosphere could be described as companionable. Very little was said except the occasional, "Did you speak to…? Did you see…? Did you like the Telemann?" after which all four of them found their own thoughts enough to keep them occupied.

Dwelling on her most recent discoveries, Amelie would like to have tackled Lord Elyot head-on about the glaring discrepancies in his reading of her difficult situation, which he had used to his advantage, but this was hardly the time, and the hour was late, and it would have been churlish to thank him with an argument. Better to save it for another time when she'd had a chance to weigh up the implications.

It appeared that the brothers had made plans of their own when, on arriving at Paradise Road, the ladies were handed down, escorted into the hall, and were then left rather hastily by Lord Rayne who wished the remaining three a very good evening before striding back to the carriage.

'Where's he going?' said Amelie, staring after him.

'Home,' said Lord Elyot, quietly, handing his cloak to Henry.

'You mean...*home*? To Sheen Court?'

'Shall we go in? You're going to show me a portrait, I believe.'

Amelie waited for Caterina to reach the first landing. 'No...look...this is late. What am I going to tell—?'

'You're not going to tell them anything,' he said, taking her elbow. 'And I think it's time you had a butler as well as a housekeeper.'

'I don't *need* a butler.'

'I think you do. This way, is it?'

This was not what she had wanted, not while her

emotions were pulled taut like harp strings, not when there was so much that was unclear in her mind, not when she wanted to talk to Caterina about their evening or when she could feel the deception swirling about her like a mist. And not at *his* bidding, either, damn him. With an unusual lack of graciousness, she led the way into the Wedgwood-blue saloon, which Lord Elyot had admired and which now lay open to the matching dining room through two white-and-gold doors. Pale blue velvet curtains fell to the floor at both ends, and an oval table reflected in its brown satin surface a large bowl of cream roses and the soft flutter of candlelight. The scent wafted towards them as the door closed.

'That was not very subtle, was it?' Amelie complained, tossing her gloves and reticule on to a silk-covered settee by the wall. 'Will you help yourself to brandy while I go and say good night to Caterina? I shall not keep you waiting.' Suddenly, the magic of the evening was giving way to the fulfilment of a certain business contract.

Ten minutes later, she returned to find her guest reclining in the corner of the settee with a brandy glass on the table beside him, his long legs crossed in complete repose. He stood as she entered. 'May I pour you a cordial?' he said. 'Blackcurrant juice. That's it. Where do you keep it?'

'No, perhaps I'd better have some brandy too.'

He was laughing softly as he came towards her, drawing her to the settee and seating her by his side. 'Come, lass,' he said. 'Is this such an ordeal?' From the curved back, he reached out a hand to touch one dark curl that spiralled in front of her ear. 'Well?' he said. 'Do I get to see Lawrence's portrait?'

Though small, the gesture vibrated through her body to her knees, reminding her yet again how inept she was in the finer points of dalliance and that, while she had poise to spare for an evening in company, she had no experience to help her through this kind of intimacy. She sat, rigid as a poker and almost as aggressive. 'It's all very well for you,' she whispered, 'but I have not done this kind of thing before. I'm not sure that I can. Is there not some alternative?'

Uncurling himself, he stood and took her hand to pull her up beside him. 'We'll continue this conversation upstairs, I think,' he said. 'Is your maid waiting for you?'

'No, I've dismissed her.'

'Good.' Taking her shoulders, he held her chin up with one finger. 'Perhaps you should stop thinking that I'm expecting you to do something, my lady. You need do nothing, unless you wish, and I shall not do anything you don't want me to. That's not my way. Our arrangement will make no difference to that. Do you understand what I'm saying?'

She nodded, unable to speak for the dryness of her mouth and shaking with the realisation that, though she had tried to prepare herself mentally for this moment, she was in fact as unprepared as one could be. She swayed, suddenly overcome with tiredness, with her attempts to make some sense of what she had heard that evening, and with the extraordinary effort at Ham House of holding her emotions in check. She felt that she ought to warn him of her inadequacies, but she did not, for it was in her own interests to make an effort. In Caterina's interests.

Placing an arm about her waist, he supported her up the wide staircase as she supported her train, while from the quiet landing a door opened to let a shaft of soft light fall across their feet. Lise emerged from Amelie's room, curtsied, and whispered, 'Good night, my lady.'

'Good night, Lise.'

Struck by the uniqueness of being ushered into her own bedroom by a man, Amelie leaned against the Chinese wallpaper and watched Lord Elyot's ghostly shadow slide across the polished floor and over the bedposts until his white-fronted reflection halted in the gilt-framed chimney mirror. A low fire had just begun to burn in the grate. She would have liked to saunter into her room as if his presence meant nothing to her, to kick off her shoes and to drop her shawl, to fall back upon her beautiful curtained bed for some moments of contemplation. Now, she dared not go near it. She spread her hands, helplessly. 'My lord, can we talk about this?'

In the soft light, he appeared larger and darker than ever, yet by now she knew every detail of his immaculate dress and how he had outshone every other man that evening with his grace, elegance and devastating good looks, how the envious glances of women had scanned him from head to toe to approve the muscled calves beneath tight white stockings, the bulge of thighs and the deep chest that swelled the black coat. She saw how their eyes had lingered, hoping for a hint of recognition from him, a word, a bow, following his progress with thoughts as readable as a book. And how many of them, she wondered, would have given much to be in her place now?

He reached her, making a buttress with his hands on the wall on each side of her, hunching his head into the great span of his shoulders to look into her eyes, wide and black with apprehension. 'Yes, my lady, we can talk about it, if that's what you want.' His deep voice caressed her, and she recalled how he had said he would seduce her, how he would light her fires, which, had he but known it, were already beginning to scorch her by his closeness.

'You may have to remind me…a little…about how…to…er…'

'Yes, I understand. You are not unwilling?'

'No…I, er…' The touch of his knuckles moved softly over her throat above the glowing emeralds and, unconsciously, she stretched and lifted her face to his like a cat with half-closed eyes.

'Yes?' he said. 'Go on.' Bending his head to her throat, his lips followed the trail of his hand until they reached hers, hovering, drawing her mouth towards his, nudging and lapping while he cradled her head in both hands, spreading his fingers over her skin and warming her to his purpose.

'The music was so…' she breathed.

'Purcell, or Mozart?' His mouth teased a response.

'Let me think.'

'No, don't think.'

Half sentences, phrases and odd assorted sounds served as some kind of link between past, present and future, which, he realised, was only to be expected in these most unusual circumstances. Rarely had he needed to be so attentive or inventive, for this remarkable and sensitive woman was not dropping herself like a ripe plum at his feet, nor did she know how to make it easy for him to reach her. And because he wanted her more than he'd ever wanted any woman in his life, he was prepared to take the time, to make the effort, to play whatever musical game she wanted. Her inexperience, though bewildering, was delightful, he thought.

When he felt her hands slide beneath his coat he

knew it was time to do what she had allowed before when she was tired and unresisting, this time sliding over the green silk of her buttocks and hips, sweeping up to her waist with a boldness that bent her in to him like a bow, perfectly curved. And when she fretted at the stiff collar beside his cheeks, he said, 'I am without my valet, my lady, as you are without your maid. Could we help each other, do you think?' But he could tell it was not familiar territory when, between kisses and caresses, she searched for non-existent buttons and had no idea where the ends of his cravat could possibly be. Her fingers trembled and fumbled. So, he thought, she had never done *this* before.

Drawing her towards the chair by the fireside, he sat her down in her blaze of emeralds while he proceeded slowly to undo each item of his own clothing and then assisted her to remove it as if she was not sure what she might find underneath. Each shoe, each stocking was placed neatly aside so as not to litter her perfectly appointed room, and when at last he knelt before her clad only in his linen drawers with the firelight casting a warm sheen over his very large male torso, he took her silent wonder for a comparison with the much older man she had last seen in this state.

He could not have known that she had never seen any half-naked man at close quarters, that she had never encountered a man with soft downy hair that funnelled downwards from collarbone to navel as dark as that on arms and head. He could not have known how the sight enthralled her and sent waves of excitement deep into her hidden places, as did the glimpses of his long strong legs with the same masculine accessory. Amelie had never initiated intimacy of this kind before, and now curiosity overcame her shyness, as he had intended it to do, as she reached out first one hand and then the other to touch the wide column of his neck. Exploring with the palms of her hands, she found that the smooth skin belied a hardness beneath, that he had hills and valleys where she had none. Her hands slid over his shoulders as he moved closer and, without thinking, she leaned forward to meet his mouth, feeding on the sensuous taste of him, on his scent and the cool pressure of his bare arms on her skin.

The fire blazed and crackled as they drew apart, casting a halo around his faultless head. 'Turn around for me,' he said, huskily.

It sounded more like a command than a request, and although she could not have undone the hooks of her gown by herself, the idea of a man undertaking such a task made her hesitate at the inevitable consequence.

'Amelie,' he said more gently, suspecting that this also was a new experience for her.

Slowly, she presented her back to him while holding on to the arms of the chair, feeling by the quick snap and click of each hook that he knew exactly how to manage the business of undoing a lady's bodice with its built-in straps and supports. He could not, however, slip the bodice off her arms without her cooperation and, though he waited, the thought of showing herself naked to him was not easy for her to accept.

Again, he said, 'Amelie,' but now his hands spanned her slender waist while he placed his lips to her long backbone. The silken skin felt like the cool bloom of rose petals. 'Turn to me,' he said. 'Come on, turn round, sweetheart.'

She turned like an exotic bloom rising through forest-green leaves and sparkling with the dew of diamonds dripping into the cleft between her full perfect breasts, and neither of them spoke, not then, or for quite some time until the moments of Amelie's unsureness had passed and until he was almost drunk with a surfeit of her beauty. Then she fell slowly forward into his arms and was swung down on to the warm soft pile of the rug where he covered her with his body, raining kisses upon every surface in a release of passion that dizzied her and made her cling to him, half-tangled in the green silk train and alive with the warm pressure of his skin on hers.

With a deft pull on the cord around her hair, he

brought the dark curling mass falling about them, and then they were rolling over and over, pressing every part of themselves to every other part and now, in the growing heat of their ardour, there seemed to be no time left for the long slow seduction he had intended. Nor did Amelie protest at his urgency, for the fires he had lit were raging without direction, and she knew only vaguely how to channel them after her years of waiting.

Masterfully, he led her on, luring her to let go, to lose herself. He had said that he would not expect her to do anything, yet her hands were already searching the slender hips and firm buttocks under the linen of his drawers, roaming along the muscular valley of his spine and up to the powerful shoulders that rippled with strength. With his mouth on hers, on her throat and breasts, he held her quiet and still, throbbing with want of him and moaning gently through the veil of her hair as his suckling brought her to the peak of desire.

Caressing her thighs with firm sweeps of his hand, he moved towards the soft tenderness between them and was instantly trapped by her legs, his wrist caught by her hand and held without explanation. Patiently, he waited until she relaxed again before continuing with the skilful touches that opened her to him with a gasp and a cry of ecstasy. 'My lord,' she whispered, 'tell me…now…what…'

Pulling at his last remaining buttons, he nudged her legs wider, pushing himself against her with an eagerness that made her catch again at his hand, warning him, 'Please…be careful…my lord….please…'

He hesitated. 'Let go, Amelie. I know. It's all right, I'll be careful. It's been some time, sweetheart.' With her release, his hand slid over her again, teasing, melting her.

'What…how shall I…?' she whispered.

'Shh, it's going to be all right.'

In the soft firelight, she saw him hunch over her and felt the exciting weight of his supported body, demanding, controlling her, and the deep kiss that followed filled her senses so that when he pushed himself against her, then paused, then pushed harder, the cry that escaped her lips was like a tremble of sound, not meant to be heard.

But he *did* hear it. He waited. 'Amelie?' he said, looking for the corresponding pain in her eyes. They were closed tightly against him, and suddenly he understood.

'No…go on…please…do it,' she whispered, trembling. 'Don't stop now. *Please.*'

'Are you sure?'

'Yes, I'm sure. It's nothing. Go on. I want you.'

His lips were gentle over her face as he waited inside her for the tension to abate, for her panting to slow, and for her hand to signal with a caress that she meant what she said. Then he began to move, filling her with each slow thrust, further and further, until she knew that he was part of her, joined with a sweet pain that brought tears to her eyes, though she was not weeping.

This was something he had certainly not expected. Breathing his sighs over her face, he watched her eyes gradually open. 'Beautiful woman,' he said. 'Adorable, desirable, perfect woman. Now I have you…at last.' Later, when she began to moan, he said, 'Am I hurting you?'

'Not hurting…no…something else…I don't know what…'

'Do you want me to stop?'

'No, don't stop. It's amazing…I didn't know…'

Still later, as their excitement reached unbelievable heights within all those newly explored caverns of her body, she was unable to control the surge of emotion that came, in a flash of lucidity, from knowing that here was the only man ever to have captured her heart as well as her body, the only man she could ever want to possess her like this.

Timed perfectly to her mounting fervour that tossed her from side to side beneath him, his pace quickened and took her even further towards an ecstasy she could never have imagined. And although she was rocked by the sheer force of his rhythm that nothing could have stopped, the growing exhilaration stretched her breathing to its limits before sounds and sights collided into an earth-shattering void, shimmering like stardust through her eyelids. Floating in space and gasping for breath, she clutched at him for support.

Above her, his magnificent body convulsed with what sounded to her untutored ears like a deep groan of despair into her shoulder, though when she turned to look, she could find only his ear, which she took between her lips while breathing in the scent of male vigour from his thick glossy hair. Now for the first time in her life, she knew the completeness of belonging and of being possessed by a man, though she was sure that, to him, she was simply keeping her side of the bargain after he had kept his. He would never know of her heart's involvement, for by the time she had paid her dues in full, he would have tired of her, despite his impassioned words. She would have to find a way of dealing with that, as she had dealt with the tragedy of Josiah.

For a few startling moments, his withdrawal left her feeling diminished and incomplete, but not for long. With one hand under her back, he lifted her, pulling his linen drawers beneath her and between her legs in a caring gesture the significance of which she did not fully appreciate, at the time. 'Thank you,' she whispered.

'Keep it there,' he said, gathering her into his

arms, 'while I carry you to your bed. Tell me where to find a towel.'

Between the cool sheets he enclosed her with his arms, tucking her head into the angle of his shoulder, with the emerald necklace and earrings peeping through a dark cloud of hair like distant planets. His fingers carefully adjusted the lowest and largest gem precisely between her breasts before continuing their own meandering journey over the lovely moist contours of her stomach, now quite sure that they travelled over virgin territory which she had ceded to him without a word of explanation. Even now, she believed she had deceived him, that he would not know the difference, indeed that there was no difference for him to know about. What an innocent this woman was. What an amazing contradiction of a woman. What more skeletons did she have hidden away to explain the phenomenon of being a virgin wife?

'Amelie?' he said.

'Mmm?' It was the satisfied sound of a woman sated by loving.

'Do you have something to tell me?'

She yawned and covered her hand with his own. 'No, but I do have something to ask you.'

'Oh?'

'Is this what you do with all your lovers?'

She did not see his smile in the distant candle-light, but it was there in his voice for her to hear. 'No, my lady,' he said, struggling against outright laughter. 'Not by any means. You are singular in every way.'

'Oh, I see. Then could we do it again, please?'

The laughter won. 'What…*now*?' he gasped.

'Yes, now. Are you too tired?'

Still chuckling, he lifted himself up on to an elbow to watch how her heavy almond-shaped eyelids opened for him like the gates of heaven, bathing him in their depths and showing him a side of her he had never thought to glimpse so soon. It was a side he guessed would be hidden again by daylight when she was more in control. 'Too tired to make love to you, sweetheart? Never. But are you sure…?'

She smiled. 'Just do it again,' she said, 'but slower.' The deep pools closed with a sweep of lashes against her cheeks, and this time she offered him her lips in a manner that was some way from being virginal.

'So slowly that you'll beg me to take you,' he whispered.

'Very probably,' she replied, wrapping herself around him.

Inch by slow inch, he explored the seductive curves and surfaces that lay under his hands, about which Amelie herself knew so little and which made him wonder why her late husband had never discovered them. His skills were such, however, that her responses were at the same time wondering and rapturous, shy and permissive, hesitant and then eager, and gradually he began to see more clearly how all the previous signs had pointed towards her ignorance of a man's body as much as to the precious and erotic parts of her own. Yes, every encounter with this amazing woman brought out yet another facet of her complex character and, just as he had solved one mystery, another one came to overshadow it.

Nervertheless, there was one problem very dear to the lady's heart that, like it or not, he was actively involved in solving and which, for the first time in his adult life, gave him pleasure instead of concern. The problem of conception. Her childless state was now explained, and what he had earlier dismissed as unlikely could easily be made fact.

In her languorous state where inhibitions still lay dormant, Amelie allowed herself to be swept along by his passion that seethed like deep currents below the surface, ever under control but possessed of a power that disturbed her, making her respond to him. Lacking nothing in purpose, his hands searched more uncharted places, reminding her of their first daring journey over stomach and thigh and, when she squirmed into position, drowsily inviting him while teasing him with her lips, his entry this time was more leisurely than the first assertive attempt, lingering over the theme that would develop gradually, sensuously.

For her, he brought their loving as close to a concerto for two as he could and, since she was so new to the varied rhythms, cadences and tempos of lovemaking, nothing he did was lost on her, or ignored, rejected or wasted. And when the beat of his loins heightened her rapture, the music of her sighs and cries of delight carried them both into a suspended gasp at the summit of paradise, which, for Amelie, was the beginning of yet another kind of need she had been unaware of until then. This could not, she was convinced, have happened with any other man. That was the only minor key in the score.

Lying once more in his embrace, floating again upon warm sighs of wonder at the raw beauty of male nakedness, especially his, Amelie recalled the strange circumstances of this event and that this was not designed to have been her reward, but his, that she'd had little choice in the matter, in theory, and that she must not allow him to believe that it was the major event it actually was. Quite sure he could not have discovered her secret, she kept her elation to herself.

His hand moved gently along her arm, smoothing her. 'Incredible,' he murmured. 'Out of practice or not, my lady, that was exceptional by anybody's standards. So if that's the way you fulfil your side of our agreement, I shall lose no time in putting you back into my debt as often as I can devise it. Miss

Chester's feet will hardly touch the ground. Nor will yours, for that matter,' he added as an after-thought.

Something in her heart leapt a little at his words, but she would not betray herself, not even by a hug of agreement. 'I shall keep my side of the bargain, my lord. If I must have a man in my life for a while, then it might as well be one with a reputation like yours that will not suffer unduly from another failed relationship.'

'Thank you,' he said, yawning, 'but there isn't going to *be* another failed relationship. And I think it's time you called me Nick.'

She could, of course, have put it another way. She could have told him that it was not so much *his* suffering that concerned her, but her own and that, if she could have chosen any man to share her life, however briefly, it would have been a man like him, reputation or not. She could have said that the past few hours spent in his arms had been for her a glimpse of heaven and that, here on Paradise Road, he had made a complete woman of her at last. She could also have said that, when they finally parted, as they must one day, he would take her heart with him and she would be left more incomplete and alone than ever. But the bargain they had made was not about sentiment, and he would not want to know of such mawkishness.

Her last thought before she slept was that she must show him her portrait, if only to avoid more difficult moments.

The revelation was not, however, left entirely in Amelie's hands for, as Lise came in to draw the curtains and to place a tray of tea on the table, the light washed across the pretty chinoiserie room and on to the opposite wall, where the portrait of Lady Chester looked with interest at the two rumpled lovers in her bed as if she was about to congratulate them on their night's work. It needed no explaining to Lord Elyot, staring back at her, that the size of the canvas had made it impossible to hang it next to her husband when so many bookcases lined the walls of her workroom.

She was very beautiful in the year of her marriage, he thought, taking in the swan-like neck and the smooth flesh tones of her upper body in the clinging empire-line gown, white and innocent. Her hair was braided up in a soft pile as it had been last night, her lustrous eyes full of vitality, her lips parted as if caught in conversation with Lawrence, the artist. A fan lay half-open upon her lap, and a sunny garden could be seen just beyond her left shoulder, no doubt as a reference to her interest in botany.

He recalled the portrait of Sir Josiah, his greater age and almost repressive stolidness in comparison to this young untamed creature's restless energy, and he wondered why she could not have done better for herself than a middle-aged tycoon, for all his wealth. It would have been the mother, he told himself. The mother's ambition for title *and* wealth. It was always the mother's all-consuming quest for the best catch for her only daughter. He should know.

But yet there was some unidentifiable familiarity that kept his eyes riveted first on the portrait and then on the beauty in the bed beside him whose face was half-shrouded in glorious brown tresses with a heap of green gems around her neck, reminding him of his childhood and a significant moment in his life when he had met a truly astonishing woman and rec-ognised beauty for the first time. After which he had grown up rather quickly and been able to see the effect she'd had on others, old and young alike, just as Amelie had done last evening. It was, he thought, what they called 'a rite of passage,' like taking a woman to bed for the first time.

But why should the portrait have reminded him of that? What had triggered that hazy memory? And who was it that she reminded him of? No, they were a Manchester family; it was most unlikely that there could be any connection. Would Lord Dysart know? He would be about the same age as Chester, had he lived. There would be no harm in asking the Earl what he knew of the man's family.

He smiled and lay back upon the pillow, removed

his creased linen drawers from the untidy sheets and studied them, suddenly intent upon a small blood-red smear down one side. That, he thought, would have to be dealt with by someone other than the laundry maid.

Chapter Seven

Amelie's mother, the late lamented Mrs Anne Carr, while carrying out a mother's duties in most other respects, had never managed to pluck up enough courage to explain to her daughter in any precise terms what to expect from her husband once they were married. Strangely, she had expounded on such matters as orders of precedence, forms of address, the correct attire to wear when visiting a bishop's wife and the depth of a curtsy to a duchess, but about the mysteries of a marriage bed she had remained silent except to say that Amelie must try to please her husband in all things. Which was one of the few things Amelie already knew.

As was to be expected, throughout her adolescent years Amelie had deduced that a male and female of any species could produce an infant, and she had seen enough pregnant women to dispel any doubts about that side of things. But the technicalities had remained well beyond her reach and, when dear Mrs Carr had assumed that Sir Josiah would do the rest, she had been quite mistaken. He had not. Not even when Amelie's marriage failed to produce a Chester heir did Mrs Carr enquire if all was as it should be, nor did she offer any advice except to take a trip to Switzerland, where she herself had first thought of adoption.

Consequently, Amelie's first experience of love-making had passed off, she believed, remarkably well in view of her appalling ignorance. So well, in fact, that her former misgivings about the act itself were in danger of being replaced by an eagerness that bordered on a greed she found difficult to hide. Though she *did* try to hide it from Lord Elyot, it was often more than she could manage when he appeared to know that her protests were merely a matter of form, a ladylike attempt to maintain a seemly reticence in view of his uncomfortable hold over her. It was far from an ideal situation to be in when she had thought, for a time at least, to hold the upper hand. Now, she was not so sure, for there was more at stake here than her debt to him; there were feelings, too. Having sampled the intimacies of Lord Elyot's debt-collecting, she threw herself wholeheartedly into the system of martyrdom. For Caterina's sake, she told herself repeatedly, wondering who she was deceiving most.

Nor was it easy for her to know what Lord Elyot's

views were on their deepening relationship, him not being one to quiz her about how she felt or express his own sentiments except indirectly through satisfaction with her progress in bed. This was unstinting and, she believed, quite genuine, but just as she could hardly expect a man like him to speak of love, nor could she tell him of the way *she* felt when it would be sure to embarrass him and reveal even more of her vulnerability. What was more, in a matter of months, it would all be irrelevant anyway.

It had been at third-hand via Tam and Caterina that she had learned how he had been a captain in the Prince of Wales's own regiment, the 10th Light Dragoons, and Amelie supposed that it might have been this experience that had shaped his attitude of inconstancy towards women, for he had lost several of his married friends fighting against Napoleon's armies. Tam had told Caterina how his brother-in-law's former mistresses had all been society hostesses, experienced women on the lookout for exciting, handsome and wealthy lovers, and how he had apparently grown weary of them within a few weeks. Of course, Caterina had hastened to assure her aunt, he had never *offered* for one until now.

No, Amelie thought, I don't suppose he blackmailed them, either.

This was still a sore point with her for, since that evening at Ham House where she had seen things in a different light, it had become clear that her predicament was not as serious as he had made her believe. Though she had not broached the subject as she had intended to do, she could hardly help feeling that it was *she* who was sparing *his* reputation by not making a public denial of their engagement. It was partly the fact that she had been responsible for it in the first place that prevented her from reopening negotiations. That, and the secondary fact that she might win.

Her next big test as his partner was to hostess a dinner party at Sheen Court the following week, primarily as a platform for Caterina to sing before an invited and friendly audience to include Signor Rauzzini while he was still in the area. Among the guests were Sir Chad and Lady Adorna Elwick, Tam and Hannah and their parents, Sir Joseph Banks and his wife from Kew, Lord Dysart and Mrs Manners, Thomas Lawrence and several noble couples, neighbours who had kindly made themselves pleasant to Amelie and Caterina since the ball at the castle.

A dinner party on this scale was well within her capabilities, even in the very large and unfamiliar Sheen Court, which was many times larger than her own home. From the start, she struck up an instant rapport with the Marquess's chef and butler for whom, after the initial interview, she could do no wrong. It was an occasion for which she spared no effort or expense to create a visual and epicurean feast of the most harmonious kind, warm and friendly, dazzling and tasteful, and unusual in its predominance of white, intended to set off the varied colours worn by the guests. Most of all, it was meant to complement Caterina's performance after the meal.

For one so young, Caterina's singing voice was truly remarkable, strong and secure over an astonishing range, luscious with the fruity mellow tones of a mezzo-soprano. Signor Cantoni's careful tuition of only a few weeks had already made a difference to his pupil's confidence, bringing out her natural grace of expression and her understanding of the music. As he accompanied her on the pianoforte, the dinner guests sat entranced by the ravishing sounds and by the sight of the chestnut-haired white-clad young woman against a bank of white lilies and roses, pouring out her heart as if she were singing to each listener personally.

Signor Rauzzini was ecstatic. The discovery of the decade, he insisted, pumping her tutor's hand. It would be a tragedy if she did not continue with her training. He wished Miss Chester was his pupil. Could she be persuaded to sing for him again, privately, before his return to Bath?

Not only could she be persuaded—it would be beyond anything she could have hoped for. The evening was an unqualified success, for now Caterina was making a splash not only as a well-connected young woman with a very wealthy guardian-aunt, but with the added attractions of a lovely face and an amazing voice too. That was something quite beyond the usual.

Amelie's grand sacrifice was bearing fruit, but she did not mean Lord Elyot to think that it was *all* his doing or that he should be the one to claim all the rewards when it was she, Amelie, who had shouldered most of the preparation for the event. Certainly it had nudged Caterina further into orbit, but he had gained too. Everyone was remarking on the breaking of new ground: Elyot playing host, at last, in his own home with his future wife. What a step forward, to be sure.

So when he escorted Amelie and Caterina back to Paradise Road in the early hours of the morning and discreetly suggested that he would like to stay, Amelie's excuse of tiredness was not too far-fetched to believe. Taking the rejection with a good grace, he returned to Sheen Court.

The next few days were spent by Amelie and Caterina in preparing, vocally and sartorially, for the visit of Signor Rauzzini, in attending church, in receiving guests and returning calls, in writing letters, interviewing several butlers chosen from Mrs Braithwaite's shortlist, and in rescuing a sad young mite from a Richmond gutter, which he appeared to believe was his home. Like a runt piglet, he was revived in the kitchen, scrubbed, fed, reclothed and set to work with Riley in the warm stables where a lad was needed, according to the groom. And to add to her benevolent disposition, Amelie paid a solo visit to the workhouse to see the babes and mothers and to unload a bundle of cast-offs from Caterina's wardrobe and money for the matron's use. At the same time, she told the matron that if Emily's mother ever wanted a job as laundress at Paradise Road, there was a vacant place and a room to live in for her and the babe, and plenty of hands to help with it. That, she told herself on the way home, was going through the proper channels.

A visit to Kew Gardens took up most of the day after that and, when Lord Elyot and Lord Rayne came to call, they were told by the new butler that the Director of Kew had invited her ladyship to visit the glasshouse and that she would not be home until dinner time. Miss Chester was out driving with Mr Tam Elwick.

'Your name?' said Lord Elyot.

'Killigrew, my lord,' said the butler with a dip of his shining bald head. He was as tall as the two brothers with shoulders as wide as a wrestler's, his bearing every inch that of the no-nonsense protector who would know which callers to admit and which to keep out. The face was kindly, middle-aged and polished, but not one to be argued with.

'Settling in, are you?'

'Most comfortable, my lord, I thank you.'

'Good.' Lord Elyot regarded the silver knob of his cane. 'You might inform her ladyship that I shall call again after dinner.'

'Very good, my lord. This evening?'

'This evening.'

'Very good, my lord,' Killigrew repeated, without a blink.

'Looks as if they've both got the bit between their teeth,' Lord Rayne remarked laconically as he took his seat in the perch-phaeton beside his brother. 'That's the third time they've been out when we called.'

Lord Elyot flicked his whip above the horses' ears and caught the lash smartly, settling the matched bays into a high-stepping trot up Paradise Road with an expression hard to read.

But Seton recognised the hint of annoyance in the tight line of the lips, and did not envy anyone on the receiving end of his brother's cool unamused gaze. 'Lady Chester's not avoiding you, is she?' he asked, bracing his feet as the phaeton bounced. It would be most unusual if that were the case, for it had always been the other way round.

'Very probably,' said Nick in the bored tone that did not deceive his passenger for a moment. 'I intend to find out. Unfortunately, I shall have to go to town again, sooner or later.'

'Oh? Father, is it?'

'And Mother. They want to see me personally about my plans. I almost wish I hadn't written.'

'So when do you go?'

'I shall try to delay it for as long as possible. It really isn't convenient to leave Richmond now, of all times. Highly *in*convenient, I have to say.'

'D'ye want me to go and speak to them?'

'Lord, no, Sete. I need you here more than ever.' He cast a sideways glance at Seton's profile. 'You'd lose that lass to Tam if you were to leave now, you know.' When his brother made no reply, he persisted. 'Don't you care?'

'Yes, as a matter of fact, I think I do,' said Seton. 'I care because young Tam is a fly-by-night and a coxcomb, and she's still a country miss who thinks she can flirt with him the way she does at home. And he's taking advantage of that, Nick. If she's not more careful, she'll be up to her neck in trouble, and all your efforts gone for nothing. They're out driving together now, alone, and heaven only knows where the idiot will have taken her. Lady Chester ought to be warned, you know. I'm surprised she's allowed it.'

'Lady Chester thinks Tam is a highly amusing dandy who tries harder to be pleasant to her niece than you do.'

'And what do *you* think? You know him as well as I do. He may well try harder to please her, but that's because he's got his sights on a different goal. He's an unprincipled little bounder, Nick. Somebody ought to plant him a facer, but I doubt it will be that showy little filly.'

'You don't think she's encouraging him just to annoy you, then?'

'Oh, more than likely. She doesn't care to be taken in hand, and Tam's appeared at just the right time to convince her that she's fine as she is. Granted, she pulled out all the stops when she had an audience at her feet last week, and to her credit she took us all by storm. But it's not going to do her ambitions much good if she gets tangled up with Tam Elwick, is it?'

'No, it isn't. Perhaps we could persuade Hannah to chaperon Miss Chester when she goes out with her brother, but if I were Hannah I'd not see the need. She believes the sun shines out of Tam.'

'That's the problem. They all do. They ought to have sent him to Winchester instead of Eton. His father ought to find him something to do.'

'Better still, he should have bought him into a regiment by now, or sent him to sea. Should I suggest it to Chad?'

'His brother? No! By the time Chad gets round to thinking about it, the wars will be over. You might suggest a grand tour, though. That would give the lout a chance to sow his wild oats and get him out of the way for a year or two. Argh! Just listen to me, Nick. What the hell do I care what they get up to?'

The grim but expressive mouth stretched a little at that. 'I cannot possibly imagine, brother. Unless you'd like me to breathe a word into his father's ear. He's the only one of the tribe who'd be glad to see the back of him, I think.'

'Would you?'

'Yes, and I'll have a word with Aunt Amelie about him too, though I'm not so sure I shall be received with quite the same accord.'

'Oh? Why not?'

'Because, my innocent, we've reached an interesting stage when anything I suggest appears to take on the aspect of a challenge that usually ends up as a set-to before we get an agreement. Entertaining, but quite time consuming.'

'Which is why you stay the night, I take it?'

'Of course. How else would I keep hold of the ribbons?'

Seton, who thought he might be in danger of losing *his*, had no answer to that, but watched in admiration as Nick swung the phaeton round in a tight horseshoe to bring them, within an inch, to the steps of Sheen Court.

Mrs Braithwaite and Mr Killigrew were in deep discussion about what best to do with the almost cold rack of lamb and an unhappy lemon soufflé when Lady Chester arrived alone, on foot, very weary, smeared with mud, hatless, and coming apart along one shoulder-seam. She had no time to hide any of this from the one whose beaver hat, gloves and riding whip lay on the hall table before he came down the staircase faster than she had ever seen him move before.

Too tired to smile and in no mood for detailed explanations, Amelie wished Lord Elyot had not been there to see the effects of her misadventure, for these things always looked worse than they were, and now he would demand to know why she had not taken Riley, or her maid, or the curricle, or indeed the whole retinue of servants with her to Kew.

'What happened?' he said. 'Are you much hurt?'

The housekeeper and butler hovered, obviously concerned.

'Not much,' said Amelie. 'My horse is outside. Lame. Will somebody take him round to…to the… stables…oh! I need to sit.' Before the last words were out, her legs were scooped from under her and she was swung up against her guest's charcoal-grey lapels so firmly that her protest was squashed at source.

'See to the horse,' said Lord Elyot from halfway up the stairs. 'Send Lady Chester's maid up, and you'd better come too, Mrs B.'

'Put me down,' said Amelie in a muffled voice. 'It was only a fall. No harm done.'

'Did no one escort you home?'

'No, they offered, but I didn't…. Anyway, the light was still good.'

'And I suppose you took a short cut?'

It took the best part of an hour to put Amelie to rights, to assess the bruises and to clothe her in a warmed pelisse swathed in a large Norwich shawl that made her look like an invalid, she grumbled.

Lord Elyot led her to the sofa in the parlour next to her bedroom and, lowering her on to it by both elbows, lifted her feet up and arranged a rug over them. 'You will be an invalid for sure if you go careering off on your own across unknown countryside without an escort. You jumped a fence, did you?'

'A ditch. Well,' she retorted, stung by his rolling glance at the beautiful Joseph Rose ceiling, 'it looked perfectly harmless, and indeed it would have been so, had it been just a little narrower than it looked. How was I to know?'

'Exactly,' he said, without emotion. 'How *were* you to know without looking? Did the horse close its eyes too, or just you?'

'He changed his mind at the last moment, the coward.'

'I would say he had enough sense for both of you, then.'

'And I fell off down the muddy bank, so I had to walk him all the way round because he'd hurt a leg. I couldn't ride him.'

'Who allowed you to come home alone? Wasn't there anyone who could accompany you? If you'd asked me, I would have gone with you. Who *were* you with, anyway?'

'I didn't need anyone with me. I was with Sir Joseph Banks and his wife. I was perfectly safe. What good would it have done to request your company when you have little interest in horticulture? I could not even subject Caterina to an account of Sir Joseph's voyage with Captain Cook in the *Endeavour*. She'd have been bored to tears. And as for looking at hothouses and orangeries and pagodas…well!'

'And what makes you believe that my mental capacities have anything in common with Miss Chester's, I wonder? She may believe that the banksia is so-called because it grows on banks, but I know different.'

Amelie treated him to a stare of utter amazement. 'What do *you* know about the banksia?' she said.

'I know, my dear Lady Chester, that it grows in Australia, that it was named after Sir Joseph who discovered it, that it is related to the protea of South Africa, and that it also grows in my father's heated glasshouse. Admittedly not a prime specimen, but it's there.'

At this revelation, Amelie's voice lost its sharp edge. 'But you have never shown me your father's glasshouse. And I didn't know you knew that.'

'There's a lot you don't know about me. You had only to ask.'

'But I thought…well…that…'

'That because our arrangement is unorthodox, there is little point in making any more discoveries than necessary? Well, I cannot compete with the more exciting revelations that *you* disclose from time to time, but I may have a few modest contributions to make. Of course, in order to be shown them, you would have to strive to be more available, my lady. Have you been trying to avoid me, by any chance?'

'Not intentionally.'

'Unintentionally trying, then.'

'No, indeed. You are wilfully misunderstanding me, my lord.'

'Correct, my adorable invalid. I cannot resist teasing you. Now, before we find ourselves agreeing on anything else, which would shock my system beyond repair, I have to mention another matter.' He glanced at the door. 'Is Miss Chester likely to interrupt us?'

A knock on the door was followed by a supper tray bearing a silver-covered plate, cutlery, a glass of wine and a dish of lemon soufflé disguised as a syllabub. Placing the tray across her ladyship's knees, Mr Killigrew revealed a succulent de-boned woodcock surrounded by a sprinkling of tiny vegetables and a triangle of fried bread. 'Cook's compliments, m'lady,' he said. 'She thought the game would be more appropriate.'

'Tell her thank you.'

'A horse with some sense and a cook with a sense of humour,' said Lord Elyot. 'Whatever next? Eat your dinner.'

'Pass this to Lord Elyot,' said Amelie to Mr Killigrew, indicating the glass of wine, 'and bring me some water, please. And pray enquire of his lordship if he would like to have a tray of food sent up.'

As if her instruction was the most natural thing in the world, he passed on the message. 'My lord says that, since he forfeited his dinner to be here, m'lady, and since you were not…'

'Oh…yes, or *no*?' Amelie groaned.

'Er…yes, please, m'lady. I believe so.' The butler glanced briefly at his lordship's long crossed legs and then at the handsome face now studying a fine horse painting by George Stubbs with an air of detachment. Already he was beginning to get the gist of this ambivalent relationship.

'Then go and request one, if you please.'

Within moments, a duplicate tray was being placed on a small table and a chair drawn up for

Lord Elyot. 'Cook says she thought you might,' said the butler.

'A mind-reading cook,' the guest was heard to murmur. 'Does she juggle too, or would that be expecting too much?'

'Eat your dinner,' said Amelie, picking up her napkin. 'Thank you, Mr Killigrew. I'll send for you when we've finished.'

'Very good, m'lady.'

There was a preoccupied domestic silence for some time until Lord Elyot leaned back and repeated his former query regarding Caterina.

'Miss Chester is staying overnight with the Elwicks,' Amelie said, licking her fingers. 'Tam is hosting a small dinner party and a rout for some young friends. It's his birthday on Sunday.'

Knife and fork were laid down and the napkin dabbed at each corner of the mouth. 'And you approve of that, do you?' said Lord Elyot.

'I should hardly have allowed her to go, if I did not.'

'Without you?'

'Yes, without me.' She looked across at him. 'She's being chaperoned by Mr and Mrs Elwick and Hannah, and there are other females known to the family. I was invited, but I declined, so Mrs Elwick asked if Caterina could stay, rather than have me send the carriage for her. What could be more proper than that?'

'Tam Elwick could, for a start.'

Amelie laid down her fork, regarding his serious face with concern. 'Are you saying that Tam Elwick is improper? In what way?'

'I am not about to slander him to you, Amelie. Tam is my brother-in-law and therefore family. He is also Miss Chester's friend. Could you simply accept that it might be best if she was not encouraged to develop her friendship with him? Suffice it to say that he's not the kind of acquaintance who will add any prestige to her good name if you really want her to move in the best circles. There, I've said too much already.'

'You haven't said enough, my lord. In what way is the young man deficient?'

'In propriety, Amelie. Take my word for it.'

'Well, I *will* take your word for it, but without any details it seems I am to tell Caterina that, after being allowed to spend the night with the Elwicks, she may not spend any more time with young Tam. That might pose rather a problem.'

'She *can* spend some time with him as long as you are there with them. You don't have to give reasons. Just devise it.'

'In a two-seater curricle, that would *certainly* pose a problem,' she said, removing a stray pea from her shawl. 'I don't suppose your warning has anything to do with Lord Rayne, has it?'

'None at all.'

'Oh. I just wondered.'

'Amelie, Seton doesn't need any help from me along those lines, I can assure you. But both of us *are* concerned about Miss Chester's moral safety, as I'm sure you are also. She is a delightful, spirited young woman, and my lively young brother-in-law has not yet realised that overstepping the mark by a whisker can have the same serious consequences as ignoring it altogether. It's a very fine line, as you yourself know. To Miss Chester, Tam may look every inch the sophisticated beau, but unfortunately he appears to have left his moral conscience behind at Eton. If, indeed, he ever took it there. And now I've said *far* too much.'

'No, you haven't. Thank you for telling me.' She put her head back against the cushions. 'But I wonder how Tam Elwick's moral fibre differs from that of his two older brothers-in-law, both of them reputed rakes. You don't suppose he's following anyone's example, do you?' She smiled up at the pretty ceiling. 'Or could your warning have something to do with titles? Aristocrats get away with it, but not commoners.'

'That remark is quite unworthy of you, Amelie,' he said, taking the dish of syllabub and looking hard at its creamy froth. He took up his spoon. 'It's Miss Chester's future we're talking about, not Tam's. He can go any way he chooses, but she may not. If you prefer to ignore my warning, then go ahead and do so. I am neither Miss Chester's father nor her guardian.'

'Yes, I'm sorry. It was a cheap remark. You've done so much for her, and I'm grateful. We both are.'

He dug the spoon into the soft dessert. 'No, I've done it for *you*,' he said, 'but the choice is entirely yours.' Between dish and mouth, his hand hesitated. He looked across at her. 'Does your head hurt?'

'Not my head. No.'

'What, then?'

With an uninhibited motion of her hand, she slid it beneath the tray. 'Here,' she said, 'the pommel… bruised me…here…when I fell.'

His spoon clattered on the tray and, in one stride, he was across the room, removing her tray so that he could sit against her legs, facing her, taking her hands in his. 'Tch! You should be in bed instead of talking about this nonsense. Come on, sweetheart, I'll see you tucked up, then I shall leave you in peace.'

'I don't want you to leave me in peace,' she whispered, eyes closed. 'I want you to stay with me. Is that why you came?'

'That *is* why I came. Because I have not seen you for days.'

'Then stay. Will you?' She did not see the way his eyes softened, nor the flicker of sheer delight that darkened the grey to almost black. It was the first time she had asked him to linger.

'I'll send for Lise,' he said as he carried her through to her room. 'Then I'll join you, just to keep on eye on the invalid. Eh?'

'Mm…m,' she said, smiling into his shoulder.

He thought of asking her whether it took a fall from her horse to obtain an invitation, but the time for scoring points was passing with each new day, so he read to her from the newspaper instead, then spent the night holding her carefully in his arms. Making no demands upon her, he scolded her gently for being such a rash little fool, to which she smiled and snuggled closer.

After an early breakfast, Amelie and her guest took the coffee-coloured barouche first to Sheen Court to collect Lord Rayne, then up to Mortlake to the Elwicks' house to collect Caterina. But Mr Tam Elwick was not pleased with their plan to visit Hampton Court on some business of the Marquess of Sheen's, nor was he about to relinquish Miss Chester to her elders without a fuss, as a result of which the invitation was extended to him and to Hannah. So there they were, three ladies in the barouche with straw hats sparkling and scarves flying in the September sunshine, and three men riding beside them against a background of blue sky and leaves tinted with the first colours of autumn. Everything indicated a perfect day.

The drive across Richmond Park and Ham Common passed off pleasantly, with enough repartee between them to keep smiles on faces for the most part. Crossing the river at Kingston-upon-Thames, they took the road towards a dense plantation of trees in the centre of Home Park in the grounds of Hampton Court Palace, past fenced paddocks where grazing mares came trotting to see them.

'Is this it?' called Amelie. 'The King's Stud Farm?'

'Yonder, in the trees,' Lord Elyot replied. 'The Marquess asked me to take a look, just to check on a few things.'

'The Marquess values Lord Elyot's opinion,' said Hannah, sweetly. 'And I can quite see why, can't you? He knows as much as anyone about horse breeding.'

'Don't be such a goose, Hannah,' said Tam, scornfully, hauling his horse round. 'Anyone with half a brain could pick it up in no time. Isn't that so, Seton?'

Lord Rayne refused to be needled. 'Oh, certainly, if you say so,' he drawled. 'It so happens that my brother picked it up, as you put it, with *both* halves of his brain. It's a habit of his.'

Amelie said nothing, but thought that Tam's attempt to belittle her lover exposed a basic insecurity in his own character, but she wished he would not try so hard to impress them all as he had done most of the way there with exaggerated and unnecessary feats of horsemanship.

Used to being called a goose by her younger brother, whether it was deserved or not, Hannah was not in the least put out, for such was her good nature that she was ill-equipped to recognise antagonism. She wore a close-fitting yellow straw hat tied under the chin with a yellow ribbon, and a pale yellow day dress with ruffles round the neck that shortened the distance between chin and shoulders. But the tones were a sickly mismatch, and her yellowish hair that strayed from beneath the straw hat made Caterina long to tidy her up, and again she wondered why dear kind Hannah had made so little effort to find a mate.

Their hour spent at the Royal Stud Farm gave the three women a glimpse of the responsibility that Lord Elyot himself would one day take over from his father, the palatial stables with name plates and gleaming brass, polished wood and leather, the liveried grooms, the glossy manes and tails and polished rumps. Stallions and yearlings were paraded by their proud keepers, papers checked, plans discussed, and all the time they were obliged to endure the advice of Tam Elwick, who had no hesitation in contradicting his brother-in-law on any point, however small. When Lord Elyot found Tam lecturing one of the senior grooms about the treatment of an injured hock, he thought it was time to intervene.

'Tam,' he said, interrupting the homily, 'we shall

be taking a light lunch at the Chequers on the green next to the Royal Mews. I would be obliged if you would escort the ladies there. Seton and I will catch you up in a few moments.'

'Oh...er, well...yes. But can't Seton go with them?' He caught Lord Elyot's frosty eye. 'Well, if you insist.'

'I need Seton here, and I *do* insist. *Now*, if you please.'

There was no possibility of Tam mistaking the command, for the captaincy still lingered in the deep strong voice, and Tam's perception was not deficient in every respect. Nodding his carefully tousled head the colour of hazelnuts, he strode away towards Amelie, Caterina and Hannah who were admiring a herd of frisky colts in a paddock. 'We've been dismissed,' he called to them, laughing. 'Apparently we're getting under the exalted feet of the son of the assistant Master of the King's Horse. Come, ladies, we must retire gracefully to the Chequers to sit and drink cordial until his supreme lordship is ready to receive us once more.'

Amelie was not amused. 'Mr Elwick,' she said, quietly, 'will you try to remember that I am engaged to Lord Elyot, please? If he wants us to go on to the Chequers I'm sure his reasons need not be questioned. I am quite happy to wait there with a glass of cordial, to rest my legs a while.'

'Lord, m'lady,' said Tam, helping her up into the barouche, 'I mean no offence, believe me. I dare say my brother-in-law can talk about his mares till the cows come home, eh?' He kept the schoolboy grin across his face until all three occupants of the carriage were seated, but, although Caterina and Hannah saw nothing untoward in the remark, Amelie's frown lasted until they had reached their destination.

The green at Hampton was a long field that ran alongside the river between the palace and the village. Converted from one of the royal stables, the Chequers stood on the south side of the green adjoining the Queen's Coach House while further on, the King's Coach House was now the barracks for a troop of cavalry. Within a railed compound, conical tents and splendid marquees crowded across the parched grass and, at one end, soldiers drilled to the bark of commands. Others in red-and-white uniforms stood in groups or lounged upon the grass, openly staring at the barouche, its cargo of females and its dandified escort.

No sooner had they alighted outside the inn than Caterina took Hannah's hand, intending to stand near a group of red-coated officers whose eyes they had caught. Tam, however, who saw himself as being outnumbered by at least five to one, redirected the two very firmly and properly towards a table and bench outside, ordering ale and cordial from the landlord, earning Amelie's approval. But this did not prevent the determined officers from occupying the next table to theirs, introducing themselves, smiling and flirting, while Tam looked helplessly on, unable to apply any brakes to the silly but harmless chatter, the toasts to bright eyes and the request for names, which were withheld. It was only when the two brothers arrived and, dismounting, signalled with the merest tip of the head for the men to clear off, that the intrusion suddenly stopped and the soldiers dispersed silently towards the barracks in a matter of seconds.

Sitting down beside Amelie, Lord Elyot took her hand in his. 'You all right, sweetheart?' he whispered, adding a droll wink for good measure.

The laughter in her eyes belied the otherwise solemn expression that swept past Tam's vexed face and Hannah's blushes. 'Don't be too hard on him,' she whispered.

'He'll survive. I'm more concerned about you.'

'I'll survive too,' she said, returning the squeeze of his hand.

The alfresco refreshment at the Chequers, augmented by pasties, pickles, cold ham, salads and plum cake, became a lunch enlivened by a pageant of uniforms and strolling sightseers, the coming and going of carriages and the grooming of the cavalry officers' horses. But the tensions that had been steadily growing between Tam and Lord Rayne did not relax as Amelie had hoped, for now the thwarted young man was keener than ever to restore his credibility as the ladies' entertaining escort. And because he was using every device he knew to keep them in a state of constant amusement, Caterina at least felt that he deserved some recognition for his efforts while wishing that Lord Rayne would bestir himself half as much for her sake.

Tam's insistence on taking Caterina and Hannah into the palace maze was ostensibly to show them how good he was at finding the centre and back again in record time, though it had not escaped the notice of three others that their tiresome chaperonage of Caterina was irksome to him. Despite all their efforts and with so many differing opinions about which turn to take, with them all in single file, with the meeting and sidling past of bewildered strangers, with the confusing blind alleys and the worn hedge that looked the same everywhere, they managed somehow to become separated except by calls of, 'Where are you? *Here…* Where?'

Amelie waited beside Hannah, thinking that Seton was near them too, but he was striding back the way they had come, disappearing round a corner. There were shrieks and shouts, and so many people calling and squealing with frustration that Caterina's voice could not be identified.

'I don't care much for labyrinths,' said Hannah. 'Where has Lord Elyot gone?'

'He'll find us. I think we should wait,' Amelie replied, having doubts about both statements. 'Caterina! Where are you?'

It was not Caterina who replied, but a man's deep bark of anger, unmistakably that of Lord Elyot, followed by a shout, a scream, and the sound of crashing branches. A well-dressed young man in brown fell heavily backwards through the ragged hornbeam hedge further up the path, thrashing and struggling, held fast in the tangle and shouting with fury.

Recognising her brother's wild brown hair and his voice, Hannah ran, dodging round surprised onlookers whose helplessness had not so far led them into violence. 'Tam…Tam, my dear…ah, no! Are you hurt?' She could not reach him, and his threats were not directed at her.

'Damn you, sir! I shall call you out for this…this *insult*! How dare you…get away from me…name your seconds. My man will—'

'Get up, you stupid fool!' came Lord Rayne's voice. 'You'll do nothing of the sort. Here, take my hand or you'll be there for hours.'

'I don't need your help. I shall thrash you both for this.'

'And I shall see that your father hears of *your* behaviour,' said Lord Elyot. 'Time somebody knocked some sense into you, lad. Get up or stay there, but you'll apologise to Miss Chester for your insolence immediately.'

'Tam…Tam dearest,' Hannah whimpered, trying to reach him from her side through the untidy hole in the hedge. 'What have they done to you?'

Amelie held her back, keeping her out of the way of the astonished passers-by who lingered and walked on with pitying looks and giggles. Hushing her, comforting her, Amelie felt her sobs of distress, then a warm patch of dampness seep into the fabric on her shoulder. 'It's nothing,' she whispered. 'Only men. Only a bump. Nothing broken.' And while she comforted Hannah for Tam's indignity, she would prefer to have known what Tam must apologise to Caterina for, and which of the brothers had taken him in hand.

Neither she nor Hannah were kept waiting long, for through the press of curious men and shocked women came Caterina, close to tears and with one hand to her face, hiding her blushes. Though she was blameless, it was the first time men had come to blows over her, and the first time she had ever seen a man knocked down. She was not the kind to fall into hysterics, but neither was she insensitive to Tam's humiliation.

Mortification, not pride, was deeply etched on Caterina's very pink face. 'It was nothing,' she whispered to Amelie, with downcast eyes. 'I'll tell you later. I'm sure he meant nothing by it. Oh, I was never so embarrassed in my life.'

The incident put a damper on what had begun as a pleasant day's outing, and now no attempt was successful in lightening the mood that hung over their cheerless journey home. There were, in fact, few attempts except by Hannah whose third observation of the deer herds ended in a muffled squeak as the sight of her bedraggled brother hove into view. No one in the carriage dared to speculate on whether his distress was mostly for his swollen face, his ruined neckcloth and torn coat, or for the curious stares of strangers who would be drawing their own conclusions from his distance some way behind the others.

Without any explanation from either Lord Elyot or his brother, Amelie could draw no such conclusions about their handling of Tam apart from no one deriving any satisfaction from the disgraceful public fracas except, perhaps, those spectators who were glad of a diversion. Hannah was very upset by her brother's treatment at the hands of her hero. Caterina was deeply confused by the vehemence of Lord Rayne's reaction, and sorry for it. And Amelie blamed herself for not keeping Caterina more firmly by her side. She was, after all, the one person most responsible for her, and she had been warned. What the two brothers thought of the matter she could hazard a guess from their inscrutable expressions and their unremitting cold-shouldering of their brother-in-law.

Nor was the earlier mood of goodwill restored on Amelie and Caterina's return to Paradise Road, Lord Elyot and his brother being so keen to make an immediate call on Tam's father before his son's version of the incident became the only one. There was just time for Amelie to hear a brief statement of regret that the outing should have been marred, though no apportioning of blame was suggested before the two escorts left them with thanks for their company and a hope that Miss Chester would not be too distressed by her experience.

Miss Chester *was* distressed, though apparently not for the reasons Lord Elyot might have expected. She sat on the piano stool, twisting a damp handkerchief into a rope while trying to stem her tears of anger with the back of one hand. 'I *thought*,' she sobbed, 'that he was holding me away from a group of elderly people who were...well, very *wide*, and he...kind of...swung me away from them against the hedge.'

'With his arms around you,' said Amelie.

'Yes, there was so little space for them to pass, and I suppose he held me for just a mite longer. Oh, this is so *silly*, Aunt Amelie. He meant no harm.'

'But you should not have been alone with him, my dear. He should not have—'

'I've been alone with him many times, Aunt. You know I have. His conduct has never been such as to give me cause for alarm. I would not continue to call him my friend, had it ever been otherwise.'

'So he's never attempted to kiss you? Is that what…?'

'What Lord Rayne thought he was doing? Yes, I expect he did, but then, Lord Rayne has been looking daggers at him all day as if he was waiting for a chance to…well, *hit* him.'

'And *did* Tam try to kiss you?'

'If he did, I didn't realise it. I really don't know. His face *was* very close to mine and I suppose it may have looked a bit like that. He flirts, you know. Nobody takes it seriously. I certainly don't. Oh, I wish it had been anybody but those two who interfered. I'm sure there was no need for it.'

'They know Tam better than you do, my dear. We have little choice but to trust their judgement. I take it that Lord Rayne does not flirt with you?' She knew she need hardly ask, but one must be sure.

'No.' Caterina's voice dropped an octave. 'He's shown his annoyance with Tam before, remember, but now he'll be more than ever annoyed with me, for I'm sure he'll think I was encouraging him, which I most certainly was not. But I couldn't snub Tam after all he was doing to please us, and I *so* wanted to reach the middle of the labyrinth before the rest of you. Tam told me that if you place your left hand on the hedge wall and keep it there all the way through, you're sure to get to the centre no matter where it leads you. Then, when you leave the centre, you do the same with your right hand, and you'll come to the entrance again. He's tried it before and it's foolproof.'

At that point, the full weight of Tam's disgrace fell upon her once more. Instead of winning the race to the centre of the maze, she was now lost in a maze of recriminations for which she herself, somehow, was responsible. And for the second time that afternoon, the shoulder of Aunt Amelie's pretty blue pelisse-gown was dampened by tears.

Disappointed, angry, and plagued by conscience, Amelie found it impossible not to sympathise with her niece, her version sounding plausible enough, her truthfulness never in question. Though Caterina was an innocent, she was not so whey-faced that she would not have given Tam a very clear indication of his impertinence, had any been intended. Bearing Lord Elyot's warnings in mind, Amelie could not help thinking yet again that the two brothers had perhaps been waiting for a chance to discipline Tam, overreacting when they thought they had found one.

There was no singing practice for Caterina that day.

* * *

The next morning, reminded by a note from Lord Elyot about the ball Lady Sergeant was to give for her daughter that evening, Amelie and Caterina agreed that it would serve no good purpose to cry off without a better reason than disinclination.

Theodosia Sergeant had been a latecomer to her parents' marriage, and despite her widowed mother's best efforts to find her a husband, she had remained on the shelf, looking more and more unlikely to be rescued. The balls, routs, parties and picnics meant to entice the local talent had not had the desired effect, her prime target—and his brother too—having escaped her net once and for all. Lady Sergeant had met Lord Elyot's final choice of wife at the Castle Inn asssembly and had been satisfyingly rude to her. Lord Rayne was, by all accounts, about to receive his papers any day now, so he was also out of the running.

The desperate hostess, however, had a trick or two up her lace sleeve which, if it did not exactly help her daughter, might at least steer things off course for the lovers. She had invited two particular guests to the ball who would be sure, one way or another, to tweak the pretty nose of Lady Chester, the newcomer who had been so instantly successful where her daughter had failed miserably after years of trying. Besides, banking, cotton or lead mines, the woman was *trade*, however one looked at it.

Keeping to his policy of accepting all invitations likely to give Caterina an advantage, Lord Elyot felt that he, his brother and Lady Chester could steer the young lady safely through any undercurrents that might threaten to spoil her enjoyment. Had he known that it was Amelie's 'enjoyment' Lady Sergeant had in mind, not her niece's, he would certainly have advised giving it a miss.

As usual, Amelie and Caterina made every effort to dress to perfection without intending to outdo the habitually drab Theodosia Sergeant. Not a word had been said about the fracas of the previous day, both parties tacitly agreeing to leave that discussion for a more appropriate time. Even so, there was a noticeable reserve during the journey to the top of Richmond Hill, and Caterina hardly dared to look at either of the men for fear of seeing censure in their eyes, deserved or not.

On reflection, Amelie was still inclined to think that Tam's misdemeanour was the result of misunderstanding and, although she would like to have heard what his father had to say, a certain coolness towards the two brothers was as far as she could go without more information.

Fortunately, there were several people known to Amelie and Caterina at the Meldish House ball, making them both less dependent upon their escorts. Before being claimed by admirers, of whom there were many, Amelie stood up with Lord Elyot to dance with hardly a word between them. She was extremely gracious to the frosty hostess and her twenty-two-year-old Theodosia, who looked as if she would rather have been anywhere but by her mother's side, and was pleased later on to notice how Caterina was making an effort to engage her in conversation, which could not have been easy for either of them. She caught sight of Lord Elyot doing the same and, ever mindful of his duties as a guest, leading Theodosia into the dance.

But she also saw how well he knew two of the guests, both of them beautiful and well dressed, young and confident, how gallantly he danced with them, and how he failed to introduce them to her when he might have done. When she had chance to ask why, he said, 'Do you wish it? I suspect our hostess has invited them solely to embarrass me, and you, too, and she will even now be watching like a hawk to see whether she's managed it. So far, I think I've convinced her that she has failed.'

'Oh, I see,' said Amelie, quietly. She darted a quick look towards Lady Sergeant, but it came to rest instead upon the two elegant, slender creatures draped in fabric so sheer that one could see the outline of every limb, every curve, as if the stuff was still damp from the wash. Diamonds flashed from deeply plunging necklines, diaphanous scarves floated like mists, graceful arms waved and embraced, and gold-painted toenails peeped out from hems just a hand shorter than anyone else's. 'Well, then,' she said, 'yes, I *do* wish it. Why should I not meet your ex-mistresses when I shall be one of their company by and by? Better to join them now while I have the opportunity.'

'Very well, if you insist on it,' Lord Elyot said, casually lifting a finger to summon Lord Rayne to his side. 'But allow me to remind you, my lady, in case you are in danger of losing sight of the fact, that we are here for Miss Chester's benefit rather than to provide a diversion for Lady Sergeant's guests. Which is exactly what she has in mind. I would suggest that you and I put on an act of total disregard, as if the two women you are watching so closely are of no consequence whatever. As indeed they are not.'

Until then, she had not been aware that she *was* watching them, but now she saw the wisdom of his advice. There would be other times and less public places, and what would be the use of creating an incident and stealing the attention from Caterina? Who would be satisfied by it except Lady Sergeant, and her own perverse curiosity?

He whispered something in his brother's ear, but Amelie placed a hand on his arm. 'No,' she said, smiling. 'Another time, perhaps? Lord Rayne, will you ask me to dance with you?'

Offering her his arm, he bowed. 'That is exactly what I was about to do, my lady,' he said. 'May I have the pleasure?'

Amelie's heart ached at the sight of Lord Elyot walking away with the grace of a cat, erect, tall and commanding, watched by those two who had known him once, intimately. It meant little to her at that moment how he had exchanged them for others, unsatisfied, or how he had wanted *her* badly enough to use dubious means to win her. Now, the only rhythm pounding through her body was the beat of time, like a distant drum. How long would *she* last? Would she ever seek an introduction to his next lover, and would she then appear as carefree as they did?

The dance with Lord Rayne was a lengthy one, and when at last she was free to return to his brother, neither he nor the two women were there. She wanted to run screaming through the high ornate corridors of the house in search of him, to stop him doing whatever he was doing, to make a scene to end all scenes and be damned to Lady Sergeant's malicious game.

'I'd like to sit a while,' she said, 'and take a glass of water.'

But by the time Lord Rayne had returned with a glass of sparkling pink punch, others had come to talk to her and Lord Elyot was weaving his way towards them, giving her not the slightest hint of his business while she had been dancing. She would not ask, fearing to have her assumptions verified, and he was not about to tell her unless she did, paving the way for all her demons of doubt and anger, jealousy and rivalry to run riot through her imaginings. Already, she thought, he was turning his attention to others. Once a rake, always a rake. What had she expected?

The two ex-mistresses had vanished and Caterina was being returned to her aunt by a partner who showed all the symptoms of being smitten. But the young lady's eyes, peeping up at Lord Rayne, were to Amelie as transparent as crystal, showing how she longed for his approval, how she yearned for him to take her on to the floor for a second dance, to show her the same warmth as at the beginning of their friendship. But he did not, and the brave resignation on Caterina's face and the quick sag of her shoulders was pitiful to see.

Catching sight of Amelie's gentle caress upon her niece's arm, Lord Elyot spoke quietly to her alone. 'Have you had enough of this?'

'Quite enough,' she said, coldly.

'Shall we go, then? Home?'

'If you please.' She had no need to look at his eyes to know exactly what he meant by home, for it had the same intimate sound as 'bed'. Her painful anger advocated a rejection of his company to punish him for having led her into this wretched situation, and the plan that etched itself on her mind like a creeping frost was to take him as far as the bedroom door and then to close it, sending him off with a flea in his handsome ear. It was at the same time both attractive and unattractive, for it would certainly hurt her more than him. Which, she recalled, had ever been the way of things.

The return to Paradise Road was not long enough for Amelie's anger to simmer down, or for her plan of retribution to develop beyond an idea, and Lord Elyot was not so impervious to her mood that he could not tell what was coming. Bidding a curt farewell to his brother, he followed Amelie and Caterina into the house with an authority that took them both off guard. Caterina immediately went up to her room and, ascending the stairs ahead of Amelie as courtesy dictated, he was inside the main bedroom before she could think of a way of keeping him out.

Once she was inside the room, he stood with his back to the door as if she might bolt. 'Now,' he said, with an infuriating calmness, 'tell me what this is all about, if you please.' Leaning back, he folded his arms and waited, expressionless.

More than ever incensed by her failure to evade him, Amelie pulled off her velvet cape and, with a flourish worthy of a matador, flung it aside, whirling to face him from halfway across the room. Then, because his intrusion into her private space made her wild with resentment after his close physical contact with two of his former mistresses, she tightened her grip on her spangled reticule and hurled it at his head with all the strength she possessed. 'That!' she shrieked. 'That's what it's about, damn you! Don't pretend not to know.'

He caught it in midair with one hand and tossed it across to the cloak. 'Know what?' he said. 'Just tell me.'

She could not tell him. Words had not been invented to describe the paradoxical loving and hating of a man, her insecurity and his command over her, her wanting and not wanting, her agonising confusion. Lacking words, she leapt at him, intending to beat him with her fists before he could catch them. 'You *do* know,' she yelled. 'You do…you *do*! Those women…how *dared* you speak to them… *dance* with them…*smile* at them…let them *touch* you and ask you about *me*? You are not *theirs*… you're *mine*!' Tears rolled down her face, the mere mention of her rivals making her distraught while his capture of her hands prevented the assault to his chest punctuating the accusations with pain. 'You went with them,' she sobbed, 'and I needed you…with *me*…'

'You were dancing with Seton,' he said in surprise.

'I needed *you*, you oaf! Why did you walk off…to see those…'

'Hush, lass. I did not walk off to see—'

'You *did*…I saw you…and them…gone. Don't lie to me.'

'I have never lied to you.'

'You *have*! You lied to me about scandal. You lied about how severe your mother is….and about…oh, helping me…everything!' she croaked.

'I think,' he said, grimly, lifting her into his arms, 'that this argument… can best be settled….over here.' Placing her without ceremony on the turned-down bed, he purposely sat on the long skirt of her evening gown and began to remove his shoes.

After the first few furious tugs and pushes at his unyielding back, she knew it was useless. But, more than that, she wanted him as would any woman who had seen how those two, far from holding a grudge against him, had basked in his admiration as they had done in the past. As she had done. Had she been certain of him, she would have been less concerned, but he was by far the most attractive creature there, exuding an animal magnetism that affected every woman upon whom he bestowed the slightest attention, young and old alike. With one look, he could make her think of nothing but him, of what he was saying, of how he was saying it, of what he really meant by it, and of what it would be like to be taken to bed by him. Amelie knew, and those women knew too, and they wanted him again as if it was written across their foreheads. After witnessing that, how could she now believe that it was only *her* he was thinking of when he made love? Was she really destined to be only one of many, waiting in line to be remembered with pleasure, as they were?

The thought of it lent a passionate fury to her struggles and a determination not to cooperate in the slightest degree while her fear and rage were at their peak. But his far greater strength wore her down at last, making her ineffective against his control, and her body was soon to feel the dangerously exciting touch of his skin covering her like a softly sensuous blanket. Her aching arms could no longer hold back his great shoulders as they lowered, keeping her still at last.

She could not tell him of her longings or of her greatest fear, nor did she realise how she had already betrayed herself by word and action. But nor did he attempt to explain to her that it was none of his doing, that he was innocent of any impropriety, or that he had every reason to behave the way he had. There was still more that he must discover about her and, while she clung so firmly to unreason, she was in no mood to accept his explanations.

Consequently, to anyone permitted a glimpse, their dynamic loving might have looked more like a conquest in which Amelie fought for her honour, which was the impression she intended. At that moment, it was her pretence, her justification which, fortunately, Nick understood and went along with, using just enough force to hold her, but not hurt her, speaking no lover-like endearments but converting her wild, willing objections into moans of desire with sublime caresses. Teasing, taking, and luring her towards forgetting, he drew from her cries of, 'Ah…ah, brute!' as he tormented first one nipple and then the other with lips, tongue and teeth, making her wait upon his slow erotic entry instead of the fierceness she had expected.

Even then, there were no loving words to spoil the illusion of dominance, no sighs or tender compliments to soothe her resentment, for she believed herself to be the injured party and tonight had provided one grievance too many. He would not spoil that for her. She needed to fight someone, to win and to lose, to pretend that it was none of her doing, to add to her injuries while indulging herself, body and soul, in his gloriously expert lovemaking.

She lay quiet under him, panting softly and reeling with the potent rippling plunges of his body that seemed to know intuitively how best to pleasure her until the world slowed to a standstill, waiting, keeping her balanced on the tip of a giant wave that would not break and fall. On and on he went, hearing her pleas and cries that sounded to her like distant sirens calling her to let go, to dive and drown in rapture. And she did, wailing and mewing softly into his ear as he bent low into her, taking her over the crest with a renewed surge of energy, buffetting them both on to a long steep shore where they clung, half-hoping to be dragged back into the maelstrom.

Thinking of jumbled and delicious things that could not be explained, she slept, rocked comfortably in his enclosing arms. Then sleep overcame them both, but not exhaustion, for she had only to turn her supple body against him for their hands to begin another journey of exploration and discovery as if for the first time. So twice more during that tempestuous night, she demanded from him the full price of her doubts and dreads while his intention, apart from taking his fill of what he desired, was to provide her with every possible reason to stay with him permanently.

Chapter Eight

So few words had been spoken during those intense hours of loving that when Lord Elyot's absence was discovered next morning, with only Mr Killigrew to see him leave, and no message left to explain it, Amelie was understandably puzzled, then vexed, then deeply fearful. She could have asked Mr Killigrew about the manner of his leaving, but that would have looked odd. If there *had* been a message, she would have received it by now.

A casual enquiry at the stables revealed that her guest had borrowed her grey hunter and would return it that same morning, but the offhand manner in which the groom from Sheen Court, later on, let slip the information that his master had set out for London ''ell for leather' caused Amelie the greatest concern. A sudden nausea made her sit down on the mounting-block until it had passed, then with shaking legs she returned to the house to rejoin

Caterina, whose puffy eyelids and red nose were not much better than they had been at breakfast.

'London,' said Amelie. 'He's gone to London.'

'Without telling you?' said Caterina, accusingly.

Amelie shrugged, studying the silver top on the inkpot. 'I suppose he must have mentioned it,' she said, searching for a convincing line to take, 'but I really can't remember. He has duties to perform for his father, you know, like yesterday. London's not as far as all that. He could be back in no time at all.'

'Did Lord Rayne go with him?' Caterina asked in a small voice. She was writing a letter to her father, and the quill she held was about to break under the extreme misuse she was subjecting it to.

'Er…I don't know, my dear.' Blankly, she looked into Caterina's deeply unhappy topaz eyes, saying more eloquently than words that she knew absolutely nothing about what either of them were doing, that she and Caterina were not likely to find out for certain, that communications appeared to have broken down even after a night spent in the deepest and most personal intercourse of all.

'What about Tam? No word of him either?'

'Nothing was said. I didn't ask.'

'I would like to know,' whispered Caterina.

'Yes, dear. So would I. If I'd realised…' The sentence was left open. If she had realised how abrupt the end would be, or that the amazing night they had spent together was to be a kind of farewell, she would have been more prepared for his sudden departure. Even now she could scarcely believe that he had gone without waking her, no doubt to avoid any more angry scenes. Yes, that had been a mistake. A spontaneous, but costly, mistake. Perhaps the other women had brought things to an end in the same way. Heaven knows what she had screamed at him.

More disturbing news arrived that morning in a letter from Signor Rauzzini addressed to Lady Chester. The maestro was full of regrets that he had been summoned urgently to Bath, post-haste, and that his visit planned for the day after tomorrow would unfortunately have to be postponed until his return. He did not know when that would be. He had been so looking forward to hearing Miss Chester sing for him, but meanwhile she must take care not to overtax her voice, to take plenty of fresh air, exercise and sleep. 'Your very obedient servant, Venanzio Rauzzini,' said Amelie, passing the letter to Caterina. 'Oh, my dear, this is a *bitter* disappointment. After all your preparations.'

Caterina's letter to her father suffered a temporary hiatus until her tears had dried, after which she tried again, telling her father of the great set-back to her singing career with an exaggeration typical of young people in love. She told him that things did not always flow smoothly since Aunt Amelie's engagement, and although the dinner at Sheen Court had been a great success, the outing to Hampton Court had not, the dance last night had been a great crush and they had come home early. Significantly, Lord Rayne was not mentioned.

It was to be a day of letters, for among the day's post was one from Caterina's father and sister, always first to be read and devoured for gossip, congratulations for Amelie and a hint of envy from sister Sara. But hidden in the pile lay one which, in her thirst for news from Buxton, Amelie had not noticed. Her heartbeat raced, and she stifled a gasp of annoyance as she recognised Ruben Hurst's handwriting. From London, the postmark said. So, he was still there, and still not out of her life, and the one who had assured her of his protection was not here, after all that, to deal with the problem, nor would he even know that Hurst was still pestering her. She would have to deal with it in her own way, as she had done before.

An hour later, she took the letter to her workroom where, over by the window, she broke the wafer with shaking hands and stared at the page of neat writing, hating it already. Skipping over the salutation, she read:

At last I am able to give you an address where you may contact me and, if our last sweet meeting had not been so unkindly interrupted, I would have found a place sooner, with your generous assistance. I could see your distress at the dilemma, but I have never given up hope that we shall soon come together for all time, and I pray that meanwhile you will not be so ill-used by that man as you were with the other. You will know who I mean. I need say no more on that painful subject.

As for myself, I am making contacts here of which I am convinced you will approve. Last night, for instance, I met a Manchester couple who, when I mentioned the Carrs of that city, told me that they had known Mr and Mrs Robert Carr very well in the old days, which I found strange—that memories can stay so fresh for so long. What they had to say about your parents made me feel ever closer to you. However, I did lose a substantial pocket to them and would be obliged if you could forward a contribution to my growing expenses. I already owe 200 guineas and am like to need more soon. Keep up your spirits, my dear love, and trust that I am working towards our future together. Your most obedient servant...

For a long time, Amelie stood with the letter in her hand, listening to the thud of her heart, her mind every bit as convoluted as the maze at Hampton Court, but without any simple key to the solution. Two things were clear from Hurst's letter: one was that his menacing overtones of devotion were meant to distress her while giving Lord Elyot a clear message that, in spite of her denials, there *was* something between them. This she was able to disregard, since Lord Elyot was not there to see the letter. Indeed, it was a huge relief that he never would.

The second point was even more serious: he had met someone who had known her parents, presumably before she was born. What exactly had he discovered? And what did he propose to do with the information if he did not receive her 'contribution to his expenses'? One thing was certain; he must be paid before he made another effort to discredit her in Lord Elyot's eyes and before she could do it herself at her own convenience.

Staring out into the garden, the minutes came and went before she laid the letter to one side. Should she destroy it immediately? No, it had the address of his lodging on it, somewhere. Was she reading too much into it all? No, she did not think so. Should she ask Lord Rayne's advice? No, she had handled Ruben Hurst on her own before, and Lord Rayne knew nothing of the man, anyway. And why had Lord Elyot gone off to London without explanation? 'Hah!' she whispered. 'I think I can guess the answer to that.'

One hand pressed tenderly upon a certain place just below the gathers of her bodice where, as if by magic, a memory rose and wound itself around her, melting her limbs, closing her eyes, parting her lips in a deep moaning sigh. That had been a night of nights. Even he must have thought so, with his years of experience and ardent mistresses.

With a last casual glance at the letter, she took it up to put it in a safe place until later, but a tap at her door took her by surprise and, just as Henry opened it to announce her visitor, she turned quickly and slid the letter beneath a pile of paint sketches on the corner of her work table, her mind already on words of greeting to the elegant Lord Rayne.

The distant sound of Caterina's sweet singing reached them from the morning room across the white landing, then Signor Cantoni's instruction, followed by another line of melody. Lord Rayne paused as if to catch every note before the door closed. 'My lady,' he said, bowing. 'I hoped I might find you at home.'

Amelie smiled. 'Yes, my lord. You were away last night before we had chance to thank you for our evening. Have you come to see my niece?'

He glanced towards the door. 'I came to see you, to explain.'

She waved a hand, inviting him to sit, then took a seat near the window, arranging her skirt of sprigged muslin smoothly over her knees. 'Explain what, my lord? You mean—about Mr Elwick?'

If he was taken aback, he was careful not to show it. 'About my brother. His sudden departure for London,' he said, sitting down.

'Of course. Yes, he does move with astonishing precipitation at times, doesn't he? Did he have time for breakfast?'

He caught the caustic overtones, but continued with his errand while his eyes lazily followed the arc of her slender throat and the dark curling wisps of hair that clung to it. 'No, he was away after only a change of clothes. Well—' he smiled '—he could hardly travel to London in evening dress, could he? Though by all accounts he turned a few heads in his way through Richmond on your grey. Nick didn't think you'd mind him borrowing it.'

'I don't mind at all, but why the sudden departure? Has there been some kind of crisis? Your parents?'

'No, not that. But there *is* an urgent matter that's cropped up quite suddenly. He asks me to say that he hopes you will not be too inconvenienced by it, though of course I shall be at your disposal to escort you where you will. He doesn't know how long he'll be gone. Meanwhile, if there's any way in which I can be of service to you and Miss Chester, I shall be more than happy to oblige.'

Far from being mollified by this insipid and vague excuse, Amelie was not inclined to salve his conscience by accepting Lord Rayne's offer, though she had no doubt it was kindly made. *Doesn't know how long he'll be gone, indeed. Urgent matter he has to attend to. Poppycock!*

'You are too kind,' she said with a marked chill that Lord Rayne had heard before. 'You have both done *far* more for two complete strangers than either of us had ever expected or deserved, and we are *extremely* grateful to you. Caterina has already begun to make a good impression, for which she has you and Lord Elyot to thank, and we must therefore not trespass on your time any longer. You have been the kindest and most *tolerant* of escorts. It must have put your own plans sadly out, at times.'

There was some smoothing of feathers to be done here, for the frosty inflections of her voice had all been noted. Leaning towards her, he saw the pain amongst the icicles in her eyes and thought that, although his brother's handling of women was usually faultless, this time he might have made an error of timing for such a sensitive creature as this. And he, Seton, would not like to predict the days ahead. 'It was not done out of *kindness*, my lady,' he said, softly. 'My brother and I have never spent a more enjoyable month in anyone's company, believe me. But Nick cannot always explain what his business involves since he is bound by royal command not to say more than is absolutely necessary. Even I don't know what my father wants of him. All I can say is that both my parents will return with him and that he is looking forward to introducing you to them.'

Naturally, he had expected this pronouncement to interest her, so the frown that passed like a shadow across her forehead caused him to ask, 'The prospect does not please you, m'lady?'

'Oh, yes…er, yes, indeed. That will be…er… something to which we shall look forward with, er… I've heard so much about them.'

'As they will be hearing about you at this very moment, I dare say. And Miss Chester, too. I believe she's having her singing lesson.'

'Yes. Did you hope to take her driving?'

'Not exactly. I came to deliver my brother's message and to offer my services.' Again, he admired the graceful curve of her neck as her head bent forward to watch her fidgeting fingers. 'An errand, perhaps?' he teased. Then, looking across her work table at his side, he espied a pile of paintings resting on a large piece of brown paper. 'Who frames your paintings?' he said. 'Someone in Richmond? Mr Pallisy is very good, I hear. A Huguenot family. Been here forever.'

'Yes, he's done very well for me. Those are waiting to go to him.' She indicated the paintings with a nod of her head, wishing above all things that it was Lord Elyot who sat there instead of his charming brother and that she had not been told of their parents' imminent return to Richmond.

'Then, if you will allow it, I shall take them to him on my way home. I shall be passing his shop. He knows what you require, does he?'

'Oh, yes, he knows what to do with them, thank you.'

He folded the brown paper neatly around them

and tucked the package beneath his arm. 'I am glad to be of some use, my lady. I came in the phaeton, so they'll be quite safe.'

'Thank you again. It was kind of you to come. Give us a few days' grace, if you will. Caterina is still…'

'A little upset? Yes, that's quite understandable.' He moved towards the door, clearly debating whether to say more on the topic. 'I think you should know,' he said, 'that Mr Elwick has sent young Tam away for a while. Oh, don't be alarmed. It's not banishment. Hannah has gone with him for a few weeks until things settle down. It's for the best, I'm sure you'll agree.'

'A few weeks? And then what?'

'Well, then his father may have long-term plans for him. We shall have to wait and see.' He smiled, looking very unlike the angry man who had knocked his brother-in-law down two days ago.

'Yes,' said Amelie, thinking not so much of Tam and Hannah speeding away in a coach to some unknown destination, but of Lord Rayne's smile, which was so like his brother's that her breath was caught on a sob. Now she did not know how long it would be before she saw it again or to whom it would have been given by then. 'As you say, we shall have to wait and see. Good day to you, my lord. Mr Killigrew will show you out.' She dipped a curtsy and watched the way he seemed to flow like liquid down the stairs, disappearing round the corner.

She waited, hoping to catch another sound of Caterina's voice, but all was quiet. Before she could turn away, the door of the morning room was held open by the singing teacher for his pupil, who had been standing by the window, her face clouded by melancholy.

'Ees all right,' said Signor Cantoni to Amelie. 'Ees all right, we all 'ave *emozione...*' he pressed a hand to his heart with an indulgent smile at Caterina '...but we cannot make good sound when we 'ave weeping. Then we do—' and here he squeaked a note so flat that even Caterina broke into a pained laugh. 'They will not mix. Another day, when the weeping has gone. Yes? Then we will be *brillante.*' His expressive hand opened like a mouth, while his counter-tenor top note hit the high plasterwork ceiling.

'Yes,' Caterina whispered. 'Thank you, Signor Cantoni.'

'Ees good,' he said, nodding. His affable expression and swarthy skin fell back into deep folds as if it was a size too large for him, and dark oiled hair swept off his forehead in a thick cap that poured over the back of his collar. Thirtyish and hardly taller than Caterina, his deep dark eyes were alight with vitality, his attractive mouth mobile like his hands, moulding and shaping each word as if he could feel it between his fingers. 'But,' he said, dropping his voice, 'Meez Chester says that we are not to 'ave the pleasure of Signor Rauzzini's visit on Sunday. Now that is *so* tragic, my dear lady. *So* unfortunate.' He hugged a pile of music sheets to his waistcoat and fixed sorrowful eyes upon Amelie, hoping for an instant solution.

'I'm afraid it's true, *signor*,' Amelie said. 'I don't know what else we can do except to wait for his return. Bath is such a long way away.' As soon as the words were out, a small door opened at the back of her mind, showing her a way through the labyrinth of her problems. She hardly heard Signor Cantoni's gentlemanly argument.

'From Richmond?' He swung his head like a metronome, ticking off the mileage. 'Not the end of the world, surely? The maestro organises the concerts there, you know, so I expect his musicians are missing him. Ah, well, you and I, Meez Chester, will 'ave to wait upon his return and keep on improving. *Bon giorno*, my lady. Meez Chester.'

'Thank you, *signor. Bon giorno.*'

With a bow, he, too, disappeared down the staircase, leaving Amelie and Caterina standing where he had left them, waiting to hear the click of the front door while their eyes linked, holding an idea between them.

Amelie could not ignore her niece's anguish. 'You saw him leaving?' she said.

Caterina nodded, knowing to whom she referred. 'Didn't he want to wait?' she said.

'He had some business to attend to. It wasn't exactly a social call. He'll be back. Don't look like that, dearest. He heard your singing, and he *did* ask about you.'

'It doesn't matter. Really. Anyone could see by last night at Lady Sergeant's that he didn't seek my company, and I'm not going to ruin my singing voice by weeping about it. Did he mention Tam?'

'Tam and Hannah have gone away for a time.'

'Hannah too? How ridiculous. Everybody is leaving.'

Amelie took Caterina's hand and gave it a gentle tug. 'Come with me in here,' she said. 'Perhaps it's time we thought about leaving too, then. And Bath isn't the end of the world, is it?'

Only three days later Lady Chester, her niece and their two maids descended upon the spa of Bath in the county of Somerset, their housekeeper, butler and cook having preceded them with most of their luggage the day before. Taking the journey in easy stages, they had rested overnight at the Castle Inn, Marlborough, coming into Bath in the early afternoon with the sun still washing the honey-coloured stone of Lansdown Crescent with warm light. Amelie had almost forgotten what a beautiful place it was.

Situated high above the town on the green northern slopes where white dumpling sheep dotted the fields, Amelie's elegant four-storied house had been given to her by Sir Josiah as a wedding present where she could entertain during the season. She had not visited it for several years, but had rented it out to friends who vacated it only two weeks ago, and now it offered a retreat from ever-worsening problems.

Indeed, the problems had grown so alarmingly that what had at first seemed like a satisfactory solution to Caterina's disappointments became a full-scale escape for Amelie herself once it was known that Ruben Hurst's insinuating letter had fallen into the wrong hands. After an hour or so of frantic searching and an abortive visit to the picture framer, the letter had at last been returned to Paradise Road by a servant from Sheen Court, sealed within a paper cover, but with no note to reassure Amelie that it had not been read, no regret for her inconvenience, and no intentions of calling on her, either.

The only conclusion to be drawn was that Lord Rayne *had* read it, and that it would only be a matter of time before his brother was made aware of Hurst's insistence. The question was then whether Lord Elyot would believe, after all, that Hurst *was* her lover. Would he bring their engagement to an abrupt end, too soon? Or had it already begun to falter after the appearance of *his* old paramours and Amelie's furious reaction?

She did not, as she had at first intended, send Hurst any money, for though he could not be prevented

from making mischief, he would find it more difficult to communicate with her for a time. As would
Lord Elyot and his parents. Especially the parents.

For the rest of that first day at Lansdown Crescent
it looked as if Caterina's despondency might be
lifting at last as she flitted from room to room,
admiring the pretty flocked wallpaper, the tasteful
colours, the matching curtains and pale carpets, the
camlet and calimanco bed hangings. Her own room
was on the third floor next to her aunt's, a delight-
fully pretty place with a canopied bed, gilded mirrors
and a dressing room with a fitted washstand and
water-closet. From her window, she could view the
long garden that led away to the stables and coach-
house, then the road at the back bordered by trees
and the green of Lansdown Hill.

The views from the south-facing front windows
across the whole of Bath quite took her breath away,
however. 'Down there,' said Amelie, pointing
through the smoke haze, 'is the abbey tower with the
Roman bath and the Pump Room beside it. See?'

'And the Assembly Rooms?' said Caterina.

'About ten minutes' walk down the hill. We'll call in
tomorrow to find out what's on, and we'll find out
where Signor Rauzzini lives and leave a card. Shall we
go and inspect the piano? It's sure to need tuning again.'

'What does one do all day in Bath?'

Amelie smiled, recalling how she had asked the

same question, once. 'One dresses up in one's finest gowns,' she said, slipping an arm through Caterina's, 'and then one goes out to see who's better dressed, and why. We go down to the Pump Room in the mornings straight after breakfast to see who's there and where they're staying, and tomorrow we must write ourselves into the book of intelligence so that others know we're here. Things are not nearly so formal here as they are at home, my dear.'

That same night, as Amelie looked out over the darkened town with a crescent of lamps burning below her on each of the wrought-iron arches, her worries were brought out for an airing after being closeted in her mind all day long. She had not shared with Caterina the other more formidable reasons for being here in Bath, nor why she longed for her lover to come and find her and demand her return, nor why she believed her flight could be the beginning of the end. So soon. After only a matter of weeks.

These last few days ought to have produced her courses, yet so far there had been no sign of the one thing she had always been able to depend on. Not even the closest examination, or wishing, or recalculating of dates had made any difference to the disturbing verdict.

Behind her had been years of yearning, envy and unfulfilment when symptoms such as this would have been both miraculous and welcome. Now, she did not know what to feel except, perhaps, a sense of wonder that she might bear a child to the man she wanted more than any other, the man of whom she was unsure, and who was unsure of her. She could stay here in Bath and bear a summer babe, pretending to her Richmond neighbours that it was a fosterling rescued from a poor woman in need. No one would be too surprised by that. But how could she continue to live in Richmond when her child's father lived there too? She would have to move. Caterina would not, after all, find her aunt a good example to follow, and Stephen, her father, would wonder which of them needed a chaperon most. He would take his daughter back to Buxton and she, Amelie, would lose his friendship. The repercussions rippled ever wider into the darkness, unanswered and unanswerable.

Yesterday, the coaching inns on the road to Bath had been brisk with travellers, for the town season was just beginning and soon lodgings would be hard to find for those hoping to drink the medicinal spa waters, or to bathe in them, or to contact old friends. Caterina was convinced there would be no one of her age in Bath, only dowagers, invalids, and middle-aged hopefuls on the marriage-mart.

The walk down the hill into the bustling noisy crowds did not at first reassure her as they swerved to avoid horses and sedan chairs, Bath chairs and walking sticks. But the shop windows along Milsom Street delayed and delighted them, acquaintances hailed them with waving hats, and by the time they had reached the colonnade leading to the abbey churchyard, several young blades had eyed them boldly, to Caterina's great satisfaction.

Standing solidly next to the great medieval abbey was the Pump Room, even at that early hour alive with visitors as eager as Amelie to contact friends both old and new. A wave of sound enveloped them as they entered the large sunny room through which the musicians strove to be heard, and a sea of white muslin and pink faces surged gently upon a tide of feathered and beribboned bonnets and the darker flotsam of men's coats.

Amelie need not have been too concerned about her long absence, for within minutes it was as if she had never been away, greeting and being greeted by the Ellisons, the Cranleighs, Sir Monty and Lady Mountford, Mr Grace and the usually elusive Lady Nelson, whose admiral husband had deserted her years ago.

Dutifully, Caterina curtsied and smiled, taking pleasure from the interest generated by her aunt and herself, by the admiration of her pale blue velvet spencer over the white spotted day dress. The veil of her matching jockey bonnet fell almost to the floor, thanks to Millie's suggestion. Her wardrobe had matured by several years in a matter of weeks, promoting a more graceful posture and a lessening of the embarrassed giggles to which she had once been prone. And though she lowered her eyes demurely, this did not prevent her from taking stock of any contemporaries who might be doing the same.

As if wishing might make it happen, she searched also for the impeccably handsome form and broad shoulders of Lord Rayne, who might by some miracle have flown along the Bath road in his curricle to be with her. But there was no one in the stuffy Pump Room who came even close to his perfection, and Aunt Amelie was taking her hand, urged by friends to enter their names in the book over by the window.

Just as important was to scan the most recent pages to see who had arrived. Amelie's gloved finger followed the names down, sliding sideways to see where people were staying this year. Then came, 'Good heavens! It cannot be!'

'Who is it, Aunt?'

'It's Dorna. Look...here!' Decisively, her finger flattened the page.

Caterina bent to look, reading out loud. 'Lady Adorna Elwick and family, Mr Tam Elwick, Miss Hannah Elwick. Four Sydney Place. Oh, my goodness. When did they arrive?'

'Yesterday, as we did,' said Amelie. Lowering her voice, she tried to prevent the overtones of crossness. 'No matter. You don't have to meet him if you'd rather not, dear. Though I must say—' She entered their names and place of abode in the book, checking her tongue. *Now he's going to think I brought Caterina here just to defy him. Why could Dorna not have taken him to Worthing or...or Hastings, even? Does it matter what he thinks?*

'But I do want to see Tam, Aunt Amelie. Heavens, with *three* chaperons I can hardly run into much danger, can I? Anyway, Tam's all right. He'll be as glad to find a friend in this place as I am, I expect.'

In that assumption, however, she was only partly correct, for when she saw Tam, he appeared to be not in the least forlorn or friendless.

It was only an hour later when they took out a month's subscription to Meyler's Library adjoining the Pump Room that a wander along the bookshelves brought them face to face with Hannah, whose unfeigned delight convinced them of a welcome at Sydney Place.

'Dorna will be *so* pleased you're here,' she said, wistfully. 'She had to come without Chad, you see. Business, I believe. And she's missing him so terribly, poor dear.'

Without questioning Hannah's well-intentioned

opinion about the gregarious Dorna missing her listless husband, Amelie felt bound to wonder how much persuasion had been needed to prise her away from him to join the Bath *ton* at the beginning of the season. 'Then we must join forces for a stroll, now and again,' she said, not wishing to take Dorna's pleasure for granted. 'Where is Lady Dorna? And is your brother here too?'

'Tam is over there,' said Hannah, looking. She laid a gentle hand on Caterina's arm. 'Don't think you were in *any* way responsible for Tam and me being sent here, will you? My father knew Dorna was planning to come, and she offered to take us with her. It was more coincidence than anything else. Quite sudden, but convenient.' Not the most tactful of remarks.

'Yes,' said Caterina, blinking. 'I can see that it would be.' Her attention had now been drawn to a group of young people with Tam in their midst, two young gentlemen of about her own age and three young women, rather older.

As usual, Tam was holding all the attention while reading from a book with far more melodrama than was necessary, his audience dutifully responsive to every intonation. Glancing up, he saw Caterina, passed the book to his neighbour and came over to her with a purpose that corrected in an instant all the negative thoughts she had had about the future of their friendship. He *was* pleased to see her and, by his smile, appeared to harbour no resentment about what had happened, although the magenta bruising around one eye was less forgiving.

'Dear Miss Chester,' he drawled, imitating the world-weary accents of the nonpareil but negating it with his laughing eyes, 'my prayers have been answered. I knew it...I *knew* it! You *flew* down to Bath because you could not *bear* to be without my company for a *moment* longer. Admit it, now. Make her admit it, dear Lady Chester.'

'I did no such thing, Mr Elwick. Release my hands, if you please,' said Caterina, blushing. 'It's far less romantic than that, and we're both meant to be avoiding each other.'

'Really?' said Tam, looking affronted. 'Lady Chester, is that so?'

'I think,' said Amelie, 'that some consultation would have been useful. In fact, Mr Elwick, we have come to meet up with Signor Rauzzini. It's as simple as that.'

Tam pulled a face while the rest of the group looked on, clearly amused and fascinated by this unexpected drama. 'But I may borrow her, may I not, Lady Chester? For a drive...a walk...a *dance*? Heavily chaperoned, of course? No labyrinths? With my hands tied behind my back?' The young flirt was irresistible, and he knew it.

'If Caterina wishes it,' Amelie said, 'but first I

must speak with Lady Dorna and see what she has to say about it.'

They had not long to wait; as they trooped out of Meyler's, the lady in question, as modish as ever in apricot and white, came fluttering through the great west door of the abbey held open for her by a very good-looking gentleman who, as soon as he perceived Amelie and the others, bowed and strode off smartly in the opposite direction. Unabashed by this obvious retreat, Dorna stretched out her arms towards them and, in the next moment, put an end to any of Amelie's reservations about a welcome. Soon, they were walking arm in arm along the South Parade as if their meeting had been planned from the first and no hitch had ever existed to spoil their enjoyment. There was so much to do here, Dorna agreed, that not an evening would pass without a party, an assembly ball, a theatre visit or a fête at Sydney Gardens opposite their house.

With this lift to their modest expectations, it was hardly surprising that Amelie's original plan to contact the maestro as soon as possible was delayed in favour of Caterina's more immediate diversions with Tam and the new friends he had attracted. Reviewing her niece's soaring spirits as she strolled through the crowds between Tam and Hannah, smiling at his teasing, free of Lord Rayne's disapproval, Amelie decided on a few days' respite before the attention to more serious matters. Meanwhile, closely chaperoned, Caterina would come to no harm, and not a word of protest or disappointment was heard.

Exactly why and when Caterina began her strange behaviour was not clear, for she had not been her usual self since Lord Rayne's coolness towards her. That she had been hurt and bewildered by it was obvious to Amelie, who suffered for her, but was unable to advise her on how to deal with it. Such advice, had there been any, would have been as useful to Amelie herself in her dealings with the elder brother. Caterina had tried hard not to let her pain show while taking pleasure in Tam's company which, in many ways a blessing, had come at a time when she needed an alternative admirer, even one as superficial as he.

In the following few days, neither Amelie nor Dorna laid on the chaperonage with a heavy hand, there being a group of six or seven young people on each of their excursions to the hills surrounding Bath, Dorna's children with their nurses, Hannah and Amelie, sometimes horses, waggons, drivers and grooms too. At intervals, Caterina would return to her aunt as if to reassure her that all was well, seemingly carefree, sometimes poetically dreamy, at other times bursting with energy. If Amelie was surprised by these remarkable swings from disconsolate to highly charged, then to the dreamy young lady, then to some astonishingly moving singing practices, after which Caterina would fall asleep, there was nothing to which she could attribute it except, perhaps, the invigorating Somerset air.

Four days after their arrival, they took a box for the grand opening night of the new Theatre Royal in Beaufort Square on October 12th, during which Caterina's perception of what was happening on the stage so overwhelmed her that she wept uncontrollably and, halfway through, Amelie and Dorna had to take her into the foyer to comfort her. The performance of Shakespeare's *Richard III* was not thought to be so very painful to one so young, they both agreed, until it was revealed that Caterina's tears were not for sadness but for the event itself. The splendid crimson-and-gold décor, the ambience, the stunning scenery and costumes, the clever lighting, the superb acting and the dazzling magic of the occasion were all too much for her. Poetically, she described to them the colours, shapes and patterns she had seen, the sound of music and voices heard as if through resonating mirrors, a kaleidoscope of senses and illusions, which they were unable to recognise in that exaggerated form.

'Has she been taking anything?' Dorna whispered.

Amelie frowned. 'No,' she said, 'she's as healthy

as a young ox. You saw how she almost *danced* her way here this evening.'

Coming from the opposite end of town, Dorna had not. She shook her head. 'Odd,' she said. 'Has she been like this before?'

'Not that I know of. She's very artistic, you know. Very sensitive. Music affects her, as it does me.'

'Mm…m,' said Dorna. 'That's probably what it is, then.' The hour was late when the two sedan chairs deposited them on the doorstep, but Caterina was still of a mind to write to her family to tell them of the amazing sights she had witnessed that evening, writing well into the night until the candle gave out. Before sealing it, she remembered to add a post-script asking her father to send an extra allowance of money, as things in Bath were so very costly.

Across the breakfast table next morning, Amelie waved a letter. 'From Signor Rauzzini,' she said, happily. 'He's responded very quickly, my dear. I think he must be eager to hear you again. He invites us to visit him tomorrow afternoon. Would you like that?'

'Yes, that would be nice. Where does he live?'

'A little village called Widcombe on the outskirts of town. Only a walk away. Are you all right?'

'I have a slight headache.'

'I'm not surprised, with all that weeping. Did you sleep?'

'I think…a little.'

'Thinking about things?'

Caterina nodded, once. 'I thought he might have come by now.' Placing a hand on her breast, she stared down at the bright white reflections on her plate. 'It hurts,' she whispered, wincing. 'Why doesn't he come?'

'Yes, dearest. I know it does.'

'Do you hurt, too?'

'Yes.'

'Did you quarrel?'

'Not seriously. I don't really know.'

'Not to know is worse, isn't it?'

'No, my dear. As long as you don't know, there are grounds for hope. It's knowing that's unbearable.'

'I suppose we should go to church, but I'm not sure that I can.'

'We could try the abbey. There's a good organist, and a choir, and there's plenty to see. We need not stay for the sermon, unless you wish it. Then we can walk on to Sydney Place, then to the gardens. There's a pleasant ride all the way round. We can take the phaeton.'

'Would you rather walk, Aunt Amelie?'

'No, dear. I'd rather drive today. Wear something pretty. There's nothing like dressing up to dispel headaches and heartaches.' Not for one moment did she believe it, but had Caterina not needed a boost of some kind, she herself would have gone back to bed with a book and a cup of hot chocolate in port wine instead of meeting Dorna's party in Sydney Gardens. Last night, Caterina had been intoxicated by her experience at the theatre. Today, she was back to despair again. 'Have something to eat,' she whispered, placing the honey pot from Rundell's in front of her. 'Do you remember that *dreadful* tea urn we chose that day?'

A new day and still no sign that would have put an end to at least one of her concerns, the one that preyed on her mind night and day. She had told Caterina that knowing was unbearable, but it also forced one to drag out of hiding every possible ploy to deal with the problem. She had lately considered begging him to marry her, but had quickly put that idea back where it belonged. That would be too shabby, even for a womaniser like him. The answer was to wait. Anything might happen while one waited.

The house that Dorna had leased for the season was in many respects like Amelie's, stone-terraced and stylish, but without the lofty position of Lansdown, or its exclusivity. As they had done at Mortlake, the occupants tumbled out of the front door on to the pavement where Dorna exchanged places with Caterina in the phaeton, intending to keep pace with the walkers. There was more to this strategy than Amelie's courtesy, however, for she intended to use the opportunity to ask Dorna about the formidable Marchioness who, according to her eldest son, was highly intolerant of adult misbehaviour. More than once, Amelie had received mixed messages about this, and now she felt she knew Dorna well enough to ask her outright.

So, while gentle Hannah walked with the nurses and children in whom she delighted, Caterina walked with Tam in sight of the phaeton, leaving the path now and then to push the swings, to examine the grottoes or to linger on the Chinese bridges over the canal. The children threw bread to the ducks under a waterfall, and here Amelie rested the two beautiful dapple-greys for Dorna to watch the fun. 'You promised to tell me about your Tudor ancestor, Adorna Pickering,' she said. 'The scandal. Remember?'

Wrapped in layers of frothy pink and tinkling like a bell, Dorna laughed. 'If you have the heart to take on my brother for a husband, then you'll not mind hearing about Adorna, who apparently appeared half-naked in a masque before Queen Elizabeth and was netted by Sir Nicholas Rayne and dragged half-across the floor in front of the whole assembly, before he carried her off.'

'Really? Now that's what I call scandalous behaviour.'

'And at Kenilworth, on a royal progress, she acted before the queen in place of her brother Seton, and then fled with Sir Nicholas chasing after her. And by the time they reached Richmond, she was pregnant. Her father was livid, but they married just the same. It caused quite a stir at the time.' There was no element of censure or shame in Dorna's account. Quite the opposite; she sounded rather envious, if anything, of the excitement her namesake had generated. 'I think,' she said, 'that most of our ancestors have had stories attached to them, one way or another. What about yours, Amelie? Are they all squeaky-clean?'

'Oh, I doubt it,' Amelie smiled, treading carefully. 'But you said that your mother was no stranger to scandal. Did you mean the ancestors, or personally?'

Plucking at the double layer of frills around her neckline, Dorna gave a gleeful chuckle at the prospect of talking about it. 'She's a larger-than-life character, if ever there was one,' she said. 'We all adore her. My father adored her when she was the Duke of Asenthorpe's mistress, and so did plenty of others, I believe. You may think it's bad enough that Nick and Seton have taken mistresses, but Mother was almost as bad before Father snared her. We tease her that it's the Royal Stud connection she fancied more than my father, but then she settled down and had us, and pretends to be as respectable as anyone else. She'll be as pleased as Punch that Nick has found someone like you to marry. She and my father have been telling him for ages that it was time he started a family. Oh, I'm not saying,' she said, placing gloved fingertips on Amelie's arm, 'that Nick would *ever* take anyone to wife just to please them. He wouldn't. But we've all seen how he looks at you, Amelie. He's in love, this time.'

Amelie had her own cynical views on that subject. 'He must have been in love before, surely?'

'I don't think so…no…I'm sure he hasn't.' She turned to Amelie as she recalled something else she had to say. 'By the way, you know Hannah fancies herself to be in love with Nick, don't you…? Yes…well, don't let it concern you. She's in love with the idea of getting married and having a large family as much as anything. Look at her. She'll make a wonderful mother and wife to somebody, but she's not Nick's type. You're his type, not Hannah.'

'What *is* his type, exactly?'

'I'd say class, beauty and intelligence, mostly. But particularly class, and you have oodles of that. Father would never allow him to marry beneath him. Family lines and all that. Having mistresses lower down the scale to practise on is one thing, but marriage is different, isn't it? Even our mother comes of a good family, or Father would not have made her his wife. That's how it goes.'

'What about Admiral Lord Nelson's poor wife,

deserted for a woman of low repute, though? The Viscountess is a near neighbour of yours.'

'That she is, poor dear. Put aside for a common little nobody. I feel so sorry for her, and she's *so* well bred and accomplished. Did you know that her husband fathered twins on that Hamilton woman, and that one of them was put into the Foundling Hospital in London because she felt she could not cope with both of them? Yes, it's true, Amelie.'

Amelie struggled to keep her expression within her control, neither too pitying nor yet too alarmed. This was a clear reminder, if she needed one, that those high up the social ladder were as dependent upon Foundling Hospitals and such places as those lower down. Even a man as besotted as Lord Nelson had not found a way to keep both his offspring with their mother during such a very public relationship. 'How do you know this?' she said, glad to be sitting down.

'Gossip filters down,' whispered Dorna, 'especially from Mother. She's in touch with the Foundling Hospital, but she's a shocking gossip.'

'So why do you suppose your brother painted such a forbidding picture of her to me? He made it sound as if she was easily offended.'

'I cannot imagine, dear thing,' Dorna said, waving to Tam and Caterina. 'Teasing, I expect. Even I don't know when Nick is teasing. Look at those two. Where have they been?'

'I don't know,' said Amelie, realising that it was true.

Caterina was laughing as if she had not a care in the world.

For Amelie, the remainder of the visit passed in a daze of puzzling thoughts that, far from unravelling as she had hoped, were now even more tangled. Dorna's informed opinion that her brother was sincere about marrying, that he was in love at last had, naturally, to be taken with a pinch of salt since Amelie knew the truth behind the arrangement better than Dorna did. His determination to get her into bed was the reason for that, especially in view of her resistance to the plan. Amelie was not such a goose as to fall for Dorna's conviction, for she had seen with her own eyes how he had been attracted to those two women. Well, she had seen him *dance* with them. The rest she could easily imagine.

But why, when the Marchioness's past was so improper, had he represented her as one who would hesitate to help Caterina if she knew of the skeletons in the Chester cupboard? She did not sound like a vindictive woman. The rest of Dorna's revelations were just as puzzling. Amelie knew, as did everybody, of Lord Nelson's baby Horatia, but how many people knew that her twin had been abandoned simply because the mother wanted only one, not two, by the man she claimed so stridently to worship? If *they* couldn't manage to rear two, who could?

At first, the disturbing news had frightened Amelie into supposing that Lord Elyot might insist on her using the same amenity, but by the time she and Caterina had returned to Lansdown, her resolve had hardened like tempered steel. *Nothing* would induce her to part with any child of hers. Not for any reason. Not even if it remained the best-kept secret in the world, or if the whole world should know of it.

The enigma of Caterina's unsettled behaviour plagued Amelie for the rest of the day, for now her mood was so bouyant that nothing would persuade her to practise for tomorrow's meeting with Signor Rauzzini. Instead, she picked armfuls of seed-headed foliage from the garden, insisting that it was the most colourful she had ever seen and then, to Amelie's utter despair, vanished for three hours while every possibility was investigated except the one actually employed. She had walked alone up to the top of Lansdown Hill to see the view.

'By *yourself?*' Amelie said, not bothering to hide her anger. 'Could you not have taken a maid with you? Or said where you were going? What on *earth* were you thinking of, Caterina?'

Dishevelled, wind-blown and quite unconcerned, Caterina smiled, her hair tumbling down her back like a fall of horse-chestnut leaves in autumn. 'Of views,' she sang with her eyes half-closed, 'of hills…like home…ah!' Tears of joy squeezed through her lashes as the jewel-words fell from her lips. 'Home, hills, sheep, the wind in my hair…and peace…and no pain. Oh, Aunt Amelie, you should have seen it, heard the birds…the harp-songing birds.' As Amelie opened her arms, Caterina fell into them, whispering through her tears about the beauty she had experienced, which Amelie knew was being compared to home in the Derbyshire hills.

'Shh…shh,' she crooned. 'I'm glad it gave you such pleasure, my dear one, but we were *so* worried about you. You must not wander off on your own again. Shh, it's all right. Come and eat. You must be starving.'

They had accepted an invitation to spend the evening with the Ellison family at Laura Place and, in spite of Amelie's reservations concerning Caterina's strangeness, she believed that to take her mind off things was preferable to having her dwell on them. So they went, the young son and daughter being among those they had first met in Meyler's Library, a lively pair but well bred and respectful. Caterina would be in good company. There was music and a cotillion or two, even on a Sunday, card games and mild flirtations, a very good supper and then, to the dismay of some of the elders, waltzing. The Ellisons, Caterina told her later, were an unconventional family who happily turned a blind eye to such harmless capers. Amelie would like to have tried it herself.

They were in bed by midnight, Amelie lying wakefully in the soft candlelight, comparing Caterina's breakfast mood with the rest of the eventful day and the almost feverish energy she had displayed later. To her relief, Tam had behaved more soberly, but she hoped he would stay away tomorrow, for Caterina must relax and prepare herself for the singing assignation.

Her failure to appear at breakfast next day, her disappearance from the house apparently dressed for riding, and the lack of any message, while causing alarm, was at first taken to be another visit to the top of the hill. But no one had seen or heard her go, and not even the groom who slept above the stable knew she had taken her mare until later. Riley was sent post-haste up the hill to find her, but returned with nothing to report. A man sent to Sydney Place came back with the same, but said that Mr Tam Elwick was still at home and knew nothing of Caterina's whereabouts. Amelie thought he might come to help in the search, but he did not.

Sick with worry, she sent servants to every part of Bath, to the Pump Room, the abbey, the libraries and the favourite shops in the abbey precincts and Milsom Street, to the milliner's and to the apothecary in Wade's Passage, thinking of her headache. The apothecary, Mr Carey, said he had not seen Miss Chester since Saturday.

'Mr Carey saw her?' said Amelie, incredulous. 'Did you ask him what she wanted?'

'Yes,' said Millie, who had no reservations about asking such a personal question, 'I did, my lady. He said she went in to purchase some laudanum drops. He suggested that pills would be safer, but she said she preferred the drops and that anyway they were for you. She even gave him her bottle to fill.'

Words and imaginings did a slow somersault in her mind before she could force them out. 'Laudanum? I sent her for no such thing. Did he sell some to her?'

'Yes, m'lady. The best. He said she had only just enough money to pay for it.'

'And she had a bottle…to be *refilled*? God in heaven, Millie. Did you know anything about this?'

'I swear to God I didn't, m'lady,' said Millie, stoutly. 'Miss Chester must've been very careful to keep it hidden, 'cos I didn't even smell it. And I know what it smells like 'cos my mother takes it for her pains.'

'But Caterina didn't have any need for it. Why would she want it? And who has introduced her to it? And where?'

'On her visits with the young ladies and gents, m'lady, I dare say. I know people like them take it for fun. Lots of them do. It makes them happy, though I must say I never thought Miss Chester would do it. Still, she's been a bit down lately, hasn't she?'

Clapping a hand to her forehead, Amelie uttered a long slow sigh of despair, sitting down suddenly to fight the wave of nausea that swept hotly over her. Laudanum. Easy to obtain as a painkiller, used in small doses on teething babies and feverish children, more widely used to relieve war wounds and the pains of the elderly and the incurable, but deadly dangerous for young people unless administered by a doctor. The liquid version was a mixture of opium and alcohol coloured yellow with saffron, the pills brown and easier to measure accurately. No wonder Caterina was sky-high between bouts of unhappiness. For the pain of rejection, laudanum would do wonders.

'Then young Tam Elwick must know something about this business,' Amelie said. 'That must be why he's keeping out of my way, though I thought he'd have shown *some* concern. Tell Riley to bring the phaeton round, Millie, and then go and look in Miss Chester's room to see if you can find anything that might help. Ask Mrs Braithwaite to come up.'

Millie disappeared, talking as she went about not worrying, while Lise lit the spirit stove beneath the little brass kettle.

Things did not improve, nor was it young Mr Elwick who called ten minutes later, but Caterina's travel-weary father.

'Mr Stephen Chester, m'lady,' said Mr Killigrew, sonorously.

Next to the appearance of Caterina herself, or Lord Elyot, this was the most comforting. 'Stephen! Oh, thank heavens you're here!'

The enthusiasm of her welcome was as much of a surprise to him as *his* timely appearance was to Amelie, though the new butler's serious face had warned him that something was amiss, and his first words were not an enquiry after her health but, 'What is it? What's happened, Amelie?'

'How on earth did you know?' she cried, taking both his hands in hers, but misreading his questions.

'I don't know anything. Tell me what's going on. Where are you off to?

'But how did you get here so soon?'

'In my carriage, of course. How else? Caterina's last letter sent from Richmond was so disturbing that I thought I'd better come and see for myself what the situation is. I'm glad I found you at last.'

'So you went to Richmond first?'

'Of course. They told me you were in Bath. Look, Amelie, sit down and tell me. We're talking at cross-purposes here.'

Only then did she actually look at him to see the dear friend and brother-in-law whose kindness had been her mainstay in Buxton. Like his late elder brother, he was tall but more physically active and slender, almost willowy. Dark red and thinning, his hair looked as if he'd been standing with his back to the wind, and his gingery eyebrows sloped downhill to give him an air of scepticism that was quite undeserved. His usually merry brown eyes were now almost green with concern as they searched affectionately over Amelie's face, absorbing her agitation.

Moment by moment, his expression darkened as he heard in some detail of his daughter's strained relationships with Lord Rayne and Tam Elwick, which were innocent but not without risk. It was a saga which, in the telling, made Amelie realise what emotional turmoil Caterina was suffering, together with the excitement of a new life among complete strangers without her family to talk to, the sudden discovery of a remarkable voice, and the emergence of the butterfly in all its first trembling beauty, only to find that none of this was enough to turn the head of the man she wanted. Amelie now saw for the first time that her own lightning-speed engagement to Lord Elyot must have seemed to Caterina like a normal wooing when, in fact, it was exceptional by any standards. She had not set her niece a perfect example.

'I'm sorry Stephen,' she whispered. 'I'm deeply ashamed to say that I've failed her. And I've failed you, too. Where on *earth* can she have gone?'

'You have not failed either of us,' Stephen said. 'You have your own life to lead, and I placed you under an obligation that I should not have done. But she needed a woman's hand so much. Sara too, now.'

'I know, dearest. I know. I was…still am…happy to have her with me. She's been good company and now she's made dozens of good connections too. She has an appointment with a world-famous singing teacher this afternoon and now I fear we shall miss it. Perhaps she didn't really want it, after all. Have I been pushing her too hard, I wonder? For my own benefit?'

'From what you tell me, my dear, I feel an urgent need to go and find this young Elwick and flog him,' said Stephen with a rare flash of anger. Striding to the window, he looked out across the town. 'Where does he live, the little bounder?'

Amelie caught at his arm. 'No, Stephen…no! I really cannot believe Tam would wish her any harm. He may well have introduced her to drug-taking, but he's just irresponsible, not…not like *that.*'

He pulled his arm away, turning to her with a fury she had not seen since his brother's death. 'Not like *what*, Amelie? He's a young scoundrel who was floored only days ago by the brother-in-law he sees as a rival. Do you think he'll have forgotten and forgiven? Already? No man would. He was humiliated in front of women. He's getting his own back, isn't he?'

'On Caterina?'

'On Lord Rayne *through* her. You've got your charity blinkers on again, Amelie. You were always too damn charitable. And as for getting yourself hooked up to this Richmond family to help launch Caterina into society…well…even a blind man could see what *that*'s all about. Elyot's name and exploits have reached Buxton, you know, since he sent his man up there, and now he's gone off to London already, and no word from him in a week. Hah!'

'Oh, *do* say what you think, Stephen. Don't be too nice for *my* sake,' Amelie snapped. 'You're saying it's a sham, I take it. Well, you're right. It is. I'm not *so* charitable, you see, that I don't know how I'm being used. But even *you* will have to admit that Caterina has made a *huge* impact locally, and will do so in London, too, if I can hold on long enough.'

Shocked into a new realisation, Stephen stared at her. 'You *know*? You're allowing yourself to be *used*, for Caterina's advancement? Amelie, tell me it's not true. That's not what I wanted to happen.'

'I know it isn't, but I can't tell you it's not true because it is. To all intents and purposes, I am Lord Elyot's betrothed until I have done what I agreed to do for Caterina and you, and if that means going to bed with him, well, that's the price of success down here as it is elsewhere. And now I think we have to get out there and find her before something terrible befalls her.'

Gripping her elbows, he held her still before him. 'Amelie, you had no need to do this. That was *not* part of the deal. Was it Hurst? Did Elyot find out about…you know…Josiah?'

'He knows about the duel, yes. Hurst is still in London.'

'Tch! I was right to come. I should have come sooner. You know I would have…well, you *do* know, don't you? I never wanted you to be tied to a man like Elyot who uses women and throws them away again. It must be so painful for you, after Josiah. He was so—'

'Yes, Stephen. He was. But I had to buy Lord Elyot's silence. I had no choice, but he was more than a match for Hurst. We'll not see *him* again. Now, we must go and look for Caterina. You saw nothing of lone female travellers on the London to Bath road, did you?'

'Nothing at all. Where does this singing teacher live?'

But Caterina was not there, either, and the rest of the day was spent in fruitless searches in and around Bath, especially on the many hills and lovely glades that had brought back memories of home. Stephen alerted the town constables who could do little now that the light was fading, but agreed to begin an investigation in the morning. One by one, the servants would arrive only to be sent off again on another wild goose chase while Amelie, sick with distress, was told to wait at home in case there was news of her. Unable to eat, to sit down, or even to think clearly, she watched the darkness fall and, with it, a steady rain that would chill anyone to the bone. Beguiled by her own reflection in the window panes, she threw a heavy shawl around her shoulders and waited inside the open front door, willing all the lights in the town below to yield up to her, alive and unharmed, the girl she had grown to love like a daughter. 'Bring her back to me, Stephen,' she prayed. 'Bring my lovely girl back to me, please. *Please.*'

When Stephen returned, it looked as if her prayers had been ignored, for his face was haggard with worry and the futility of empty searches. 'Nothing,' he said to her, passing a cold hand across his face. 'Nothing.' He staggered up the steps as his carriage moved away with white clouds rising from the horses into the lamplight, and Amelie caught him in her arms to stop herself from bursting into tears.

'Come inside,' she said. 'You're shivering.'

The sound of hooves and the rumble of wheels over cobbles made her glance over his shoulder. One of the neighbours, perhaps? The coachman hailed her from a distance. 'Lansdown, is it, lady? Looking for Lady Chester's residence.'

'Here!' Amelie shrieked. 'It's *here*! Who is it? Have you news?' Thrusting Stephen away, she ran along the pavement to the door of the carriage with her shawl flying behind her, grabbing at the handle as it opened from the inside to release the tall dark figure of Lord Rayne, who leapt onto the pavement even before the wheels were still.

'Go inside!' he barked at her. 'You'll get drenched. We'll bring her in. Nick's with me. Go on, we can manage.'

'Caterina?' she yelped.

'Yes. Go inside.' He turned to the carriage to receive Caterina into his arms, then strode with her past her stupefied and speechless father into the soft glow of the hall.

Mrs Braithwaite's face crumpled. 'Upstairs, my lord, if you please,' she said.

Chapter Nine

In their relief at Caterina's safe return, there was no time for more than an exchange of meaningful glances between Amelie and Lord Elyot before attending to the comfort of the two exhausted Chesters, though she could see from the grim countenance that there would soon be a demand for detailed explanations. Nevertheless, his presence in Bath, at last, gave her more pleasure than she was prepared to admit until she was sure that it was for her pleasure he had come. While Caterina was being settled into her bed, it was enough that he was here.

The drowsy young woman was in no fit state to provide her aunt with a coherent account of her adventures, though she did indicate that she had been riding to Richmond to find Lord Rayne since he had not come to find her. She had been quite sure it was the best thing to do and well within her capabilities. Which, Amelie thought, she would do, being high on laudanum. Amelie had asked no more questions about how she was found and brought home in a blanket by the one she had been seeking. If this was not mere coincidence, Amelie thought, then Someone had been watching over her rather well.

Alternating between sleepiness and shivering, Caterina was otherwise unharmed, had no idea what day it was, whether she was in Richmond or Bath, though the brief contact with her father brought an angelic smile to her face before she let go of his hand, probably believing that she might be in Buxton.

Leaving her to be tended by Lise and Millie, Amelie returned to the candlelit parlour to an atmosphere of concern and relief, but also to an icy civility hardly thawed by a roaring log fire, Madeira wine and fruit cake. 'She's going to be all right,' she said. 'She needs to sleep it off, then we'll see. Have you been introduced? Yes, of course, you will have guessed, I'm sure. My lords, Stephen and I cannot thank you enough for bringing Caterina home. We were frantic with worry. A most *dreadful* day. May I ask how...where *was* she, exactly?'

'On the road to Richmond,' Lord Elyot growled, 'which you might have guessed if you'd both used some imagination. We were heading for Bath when we took a stop at Chippenham. Seton recognised her horse in the stableyard. It had cast a shoe, and Miss Chester was out for the count on a bench in the taproom with an audience of travellers debating her identity.'

'I came along the Bath road myself this very morning,' said Stephen, tetchily, 'and there was no sign of her *then*.'

'The upper road, or the lower road?' said Lord Elyot, fixing his wine glass with a frosty stare.

'Er…well, the lower one, I think. Through Devizes.'

'That's why you missed her, then. She was on the upper road.'

Sensing that the conversation would veer in the usual masculine fashion towards routes, distances and timing, Amelie came to Stephen's rescue with a defence that was perhaps unnecessary. 'My brother-in-law arrived only today,' she said, 'quite by coincidence. He's not had time to familiarise himself with the routes.'

'Really,' said Lord Elyot, lifting an eyebrow. 'So you will not have had chance to introduce Mr Chester to the utterly harmless Mr Elwick, who is also here. Have *you* had time to change your mind about his morals, yet?'

'If you are implying, my lord,' Amelie said, 'that we came to Bath to follow that young man and his sister, then you must have a very low opinion of my intelligence, after what happened. We came here to meet Signor Rauzzini because our first appointment was cancelled and because we both needed a change of air. Your sister and I have chaperoned Caterina closely.'

'As we have seen,' said Lord Elyot. 'And did young Elwick help you to search for her?'

'No,' snapped Stephen. 'He did not. And when I catch up with him tomorrow, he'll be looking for the shortest way home.'

'Stephen!' said Amelie. 'First we must allow him to explain himself. What interests me at this moment is why Caterina was so very unhappy that she wanted to…oh, dear, I've made such a mess of this, haven't I? I thought…thought I was….doing…' She sat down, holding the back of her hand to her nose.

But Stephen seemed ripe for an argument. 'Surely there are better ways of dealing with un-happiness than dosing it with laudanum. When I'm unhappy, I take—'

'Well, you're not a woman, are you, Stephen?' croaked Amelie. 'At least young Tam was helping her to deal with it, which is more than I was able to do. And I don't think it helps at all to start looking for the blame until we know what caused the problem in the first place.'

Placing his glass upon the mantelshelf, Lord Rayne looked sadly at Amelie. 'The problem and the blame lie with me,' he said, quietly. 'As I think you know, my lady. She must have talked to you, surely?'

'She did, my lord. Some would call it the blind leading the blind.'

'Then you have no cause to feel guilt. On the

contrary, you have done more for your niece than some mothers do for their daughters.'

Promptly, before Amelie could reply, Stephen stood up, addressing himself pointedly to Lord Elyot. 'Indeed she has. *Much* more. Under duress too, I believe. And if Lady Chester had accepted *my* protection with the same promptness she was obliged to accept *yours*, my lord, then none of this would—'

'Stephen!' cried Amelie, jumping to her feet. 'Please say no more. You are overwrought, and I think we should talk about this again in the morning. This conversation is getting out of hand, and I am not to be discussed as if I were a commodity. We shall all regret saying things when we're so tired.'

'Then I shall have the last word,' said Lord Elyot, 'so that Mr Chester goes to his bed knowing exactly where he stands on the subject of protection. Lady Chester is engaged to *me*, sir. Let that be quite clear to you. The promptness of her acceptance has nothing to do with you or with anyone else, nor is there any possibility of you taking my place either now or in the future, just in case you had any ambitions in that direction.'

'My lord!' said Stephen.

'I am aware of the help you have given to Lady Chester in the past, and I understand the reasons for it, but she has agreed to be *my* wife, and that is what she will be. Your doubts, if you have them, do not concern me. Now, it's time we took our leave of my lady. Where are you putting up, sir?'

There was a noticeable pause as Stephen exhaled, noisily and tight-lipped. 'At the White Hart, my lord. My luggage is already there.'

'Then I believe one carriage may do for all three of us, for that is where my brother and I shall be staying. Will you share it with us?'

Stony-faced, Stephen nodded, curtly. 'Thank you.'

A few uncomfortable minutes later, as two of the men filed downstairs, Lord Elyot slipped a hand beneath Amelie's arm to hold her back, searching past the ravages of worry on her face to find a hint of warmth. 'I know you're angry,' he said, softly, 'but we can discuss all this in the days ahead. You heard what I said just now. Whatever he is to you, whatever he has been, it is me you will marry. So if you had any thoughts about taking flight again, alone or with him, forget it. I shall find you and bring you back, Amelie.'

'I have no such plans,' she replied. 'But you are wrong. I cannot marry you. This was a temporary arrangement, and that is how it will have to stay. Now, you can safely go to the White Hart, my lord. You are only right about having some talking to do. To be more exact, *you* do.'

'So do you, wench.'

'Why did you come, you and your brother? Was it Hurst's letter?'

'No!' A smile and a tip of the handsome head dismissed that idea in one second. 'I came to take the waters. Why else does one come to Bath?'

When her hopes had been at their lowest that day, a good night kiss from the one she hungered for would have been on her list of miracles. But now his lips sought hers just as hungrily, warm, like his arms hard around her shoulders, holding her upright as she sagged like a doll against him. Dizzy with emotional tiredness, she tasted the wine on his mouth and knew without asking that this was not the kind of kiss he shared with others.

'I seem to be having a problem making myself understood tonight,' he whispered, 'and you usually so sharp-witted. Let me say it again, my lady. Whatever clever scheme you have hatched between you for Chester's journey down to Bath, you will not be allowed to marry him. Have I made myself clear, or is there something I've missed out?'

The obvious and angry retort was suppressed, for now she heard the unexpected overtones of jealousy in his assumption that Stephen had come to Bath at her request rather than in response to Caterina's letter. That's how it would look. She fled from Richmond. Stephen joined her to provide an escape from a hopeless situation. How convenient. She could have reassured him, but chose not to.

'Good,' he said. 'You're the only woman I've ever

chased after, Amelie, and, by heaven, I'll chase you to the ends of the earth, if I have to. *Shall* I have to?'

'No,' she whispered, clasped within the hardness of his arms. 'You won't.'

'Then I shall come to you tomorrow, though I shall be delayed. I'm going to call on Dorna first. What number Sydney Place is she?'

'Four.'

He kissed her again, more gently, but she held his arm as he turned to go downstairs. 'My lord... please...don't hit Tam, will you?'

His laugh was more like a bark. 'Hah! I'd like to do more than hit him, but I won't. I shall take Chester to see him. He can hit him if he wants to.'

'Oh, dear.'

'Go to bed, sweetheart. You look all in.'

Waiting until the door had closed upon her visitors, she went upstairs, where the relief of seeing Caterina peacefully asleep settled upon her like an eiderdown. 'Go and take your supper,' she said to the two maids. 'I'll stay here.'

She sat by Caterina's bed and laid a hand upon hers, feeling the searing pity of a mother for her child's suffering, more so because she was herself caught up in the same kind of net. Lord Rayne, she thought, had obviously intended to assist his brother by partnering Caterina without realising the devastating effect he would have on an untouched seventeen-year-old heart. But she was not the kind of woman he wanted and inevitably it had showed, causing her more anguish than she had ever experienced before. Nor was he the kind of man to tell her sweet lies or to take pleasure from her adoration. She would have to be told the truth of the matter, and the pain would be terrible without laudanum to dull it. 'My poor brave little lass,' she whispered. 'Knowing will be unbearable. I should never have allowed it to happen.'

Taking it in turns with Lise, Millie and Mrs Braithwaite to stay with Caterina throughout the night, Amelie used the empty hours to view her own unsettled situation in which every negative thought was silenced by the fact that he had come to find her, angry, determined, possessive, and resentful of Stephen. If this latter element gave her no pleasure, it added at least a gram or two of weight to her dwindling confidence. It served him right. Perhaps she should not put his mind at rest too soon. Stephen would find her attention soothing after that very forthright and quite undeserved put-down just now.

Creeping back to her own bed in the early hours, she fell asleep to the memory of her lover's voice and the hard pressure of his arms across her back. *By heaven, I'll chase you to the ends of the earth, if I have to.* Would she now be obliged to tell him the reason why she could not marry him? And if Caterina was taken back to Buxton, where would that leave *her*?

With so many questions to be answered, it was only to be expected that the meeting at Sydney Place the next morning would be an acrimonious and heated one from which even Dorna did not escape unscathed. Amelie heard some details from Lord Elyot, though not as many as she would have liked, when he found her in the rain-lashed garden at the back of the house with a trug full of seed-heads in one hand and scissors in the other.

'What in the devil's name are you doing out here in this wind?' he called, dodging the hair-grabbing tendrils hanging from the pergola.

'Good morning to you too, my lord,' she said. 'No need to ask how the meeting with your sister went, then? Are you the only one remaining standing?'

The gale-force wind whipped the shawl off her shoulder like a spinnaker, and thunder cracked across the distant hills, echoing eerily round the valley. 'Come inside,' he said, 'and offer me some tea like a civilised woman.' His eyes supported his criticism, for she looked ravishing with her hair everywhere and her gown clinging damply to her body, a far cry from the drawing-room image.

'Heaven forbid that I should be thought uncivilised,' she murmured, leading the way back to the house. In the parlour, a fire burned in an iron grate surrounded by a polished oak chimneypiece, and the warm apricot-and-white walls and furnishings, the oak floor, and Amelie's peach, cream and mauve gown and shawl made it appear that she had dressed on purpose to match the room. Again, she had the pleasure of seeing how he reacted to her taste, how his appraisal of the sparkling glass, silver and paintings held his eyes and stayed his tongue. 'Well, my lord,' she said, giving a tug of the bell-rope. 'Will you be seated, or are you in pacing mode?'

'Hmm,' he said. 'How is the patient? Recovering?'

'Very much so,' she said. 'She slept well, had a good breakfast in bed and is now playing the piano upstairs. Subdued, of course, but not upset.'

'So she's none the worse for her escapade?'

'Worse, my lord? Well, she's certainly worse for something, though I'm more inclined to put that down to a bruised heart than anything else. I feel very sad and guilty that she felt obliged to take the wrong remedy for it.'

'Is there one?' he said.

To avoid his face, she looked out into the storm-ravaged garden. 'I don't know,' she said. 'I suppose there is, but it's not one Caterina will have access to, unfortunately. She will have to make use of time as a healer.'

Mr Killigrew knocked and entered.

'Some tea for Lord Elyot,' Amelie said, 'and chocolate for me, if you please, and some muffins. I think we have need of muffins.'

Mr Killigrew bowed and disappeared.

'Please do sit down, my lord, and tell me what happened. Did Tam have an explanation to offer?'

'I'm afraid our definitions of that word are very much at odds. He offered the *excuse* that all his friends take laudanum, he's been taking it for over a year, apparently; he didn't think it would do Miss Chester any harm, and so on. He seems to have no conception of the damage it can do to young people, females in particular. He's the most irresponsible niff-naff I've ever come across. I suppose there has to be at least one in every family, but personally I think he should be made to wear a warning round his neck.' He sat down at last, flipping up the tails of his grey coat and crossing his long, strong legs with a grace that was quite unstudied. His hands drooped over the rounded chair-arms while, with his middle finger, he caressed the grooves in the carved wood. 'And before you ask,' he continued, 'I've packed him off home to his father, who ought never to have foisted him upon Dorna in the first place. He agreed to send him away for a while, but he didn't tell me it was to be with my sister. Dorna has enough to do with two children of her own.'

'So you don't believe Tam set out to harm Caterina, to get back at Seton?'

'That kind of revenge would be beyond young Elwick. He doesn't have the brains to think along those lines.'

'Stephen thinks so.'

'He doesn't know the lad as I do. Anyway, that's a father's reaction. I would probably kill any man who harmed a child of mine.'

'Would you, my lord?'

'Certainly I would. Don't forget that Chester's been through something similar before when his brother died in his arms. In the circumstances, I think he showed great restraint towards Tam. More than Seton did.'

'What did Stephen say to him?'

'Quite a lot. If Dorna and Hannah had not been there, he would probably have said much more.'

'So has Hannah gone back home with her brother?'

'No, she refused. The problem was not hers.'

Amelie blinked in surprise. 'She'll want to stay with the children.'

'Ye…es,' said Lord Elyot, unconvinced. 'I suppose so. So why *did* you come to Bath? To escape?' From beneath lowered brows, his look was severe, but not enough to daunt Amelie.

'Last night you were determined to think so, despite my telling you about Caterina's singing engagement. Following the maestro to Bath was the obvious thing to do, but if you prefer to think we came for some other purpose, don't let me deter you. After all, we can both rush off whenever we feel like it without a word of explanation, can we not? Guessing each other's whereabouts is so interesting.'

'Amelie, you were *asleep*. I was not going to wake you when I'd hardly allowed you to sleep all night.'

She blushed, but would not let it go. 'Ah, I see. So you didn't know you were going until that moment. And you could not have left a note.'

'Something came up at the ball. Unexpected.'

'Yes, I saw them. They were unexpected for me, too. Did you enjoy yourselves in London?'

'I didn't go for enjoyment, I went to see my parents as a matter of some urgency. No one else. After that night we spent together, how could you *possibly* think otherwise? Have I made you feel so insecure, Amelie?'

Something trembled in her chest, catching at her lungs as a word fell out, headlong. 'Yes.' She shook, waiting for her breathing to catch up. 'And don't try to put me in the wrong, my lord. What am I *supposed* to think when there is so much unsaid between us? We cannot go on like this.'

Leaning forward, he touched her hand with one forefinger. 'I went to make some enquiries into your background,' he said, softly. 'That's all.'

She leapt to her feet as if she had been scalded. 'Hurst!' she said, going to stand behind her chair.

'You saw his letter, didn't you? Your brother…
he…?'

'Yes, he brought news of it to me in London, but
my investigations had nothing to do with Hurst's
letter. I didn't even go to see him. If we leave him
alone, he'll have enough rope to hang himself eventually, and I have more important matters to attend
to than the silly ravings of that lunatic. Did you think
I'd swallow it, sweetheart?'

'Your brother probably did.'

'Well, I've explained it to him, and now he
understands.'

'So you don't believe what the letter said?'

'Sit down.' He led her back to her chair, easing her
into it. 'Of course I didn't. I know full well he's
never been your lover.'

'*How* do you know that?'

Passing a hand over his eyes, he groaned. 'Heaven
help me, woman. Give me *some* credit, I beg you.'

'What?'

'There are ways of telling.'

'What ways?'

'Another time. Tell me why your brother-in-law
came to Bath.'

'Didn't you ask him?'

'I did, but he told me to mind my own business. I
suspect he'd been waiting for the chance to say that.'

'Then I don't see how I can tell you either. I shall

suggest returning to Richmond with him and Caterina either tomorrow or the day after.'

'You'll do no such thing.'

'She can't stay in Bath with Lord Rayne here. That would be too unkind. And I'm not sending them away on their own.'

'Nor would you wish to sacrifice Mr Chester's company by sending him back to Derbshire after his long gallop to see you. No, I can quite understand that. There must be an alternative.'

The impending argument was curtailed by the arrival of Mr Killigrew and a tray of refreshments, the distribution of which gave them time to cool down while they munched hot muffins and caught dripping butter off their chins like ravenous children.

Lord Elyot spoke with his mouth full. 'In fact, there is a perfectly good alternative. Seton wants to talk to her. He believes, as I do, that it would be best to explain matters to her. She's a woman, and she deserves to be treated like one. Seton will soon be joining his regiment and he may be away for years. He would still like them to be friends, but—'

'But she's too young for him and not his type. Wouldn't the truth do just as well?'

Wiping his mouth with the napkin, he took issue with her unhelpful sarcasm. 'Amelie, would you prefer it if Seton just went back home without a word, or allowed *her* to go? Would you not give her

the chance to see him, alone, to make her own
decision? Or are you so set on making *all* the
Chesters' decisions for them?'

'Making…? What on earth do you mean by that,
pray? Stephen put Caterina in my charge with that
intention. He's not complained about my decision-
making, has he?'

'Not to me. But now he's here, by some marvellous
coincidence, so you can safely leave it to him, can't
you? And he believes that Seton should be allowed to
speak to her, too. May I have some more tea, please?'

'I don't want him to upset her.'

'He won't. And even if she is upset, she still has a
right to know.'

'The right to know. Yes. Then perhaps you could
tell me about the investigations into my background
you made in London, if you please.' She was unable
to tell from his infuriating calmness whether he'd
been about to refuse or tell her, for as she handed him
a second cup of tea, the door opened to admit Mr
Stephen Chester looking more wind-blown than ever
and trying to smooth the wayward strands of hair.

Amelie caught Mr Killigrew's enquiring eye and
nodded. 'Stephen! You'll take some tea and muffins,
won't you? Good.'

Having been a widower for several years and
somewhat out of the habit of consulting anyone

about anything much, least of all on topics of con-versation, Stephen Chester launched into a detailed account of the toils and tribulations of the last two days, showing them both quite clearly that his plumage had been considerably ruffled by more than the gale outside. He was today more petulant than Amelie had ever seen him.

There was more to it than he was saying. For one thing, he had not expected Lord Elyot to be so con-spicuously and unfairly good looking, or younger than him, or so outspoken in his claim to Amelie. That had come as something of a shock. Nor had he been prepared for the concern shown to himself and Caterina by Lord Elyot and his brother, or for the fury at young Tam Elwick's behaviour. He would have preferred to find Caterina himself, after all his efforts, and now he felt redundant and unwanted even by Amelie, whom he had *not* expected to find eating muffins and cosily chatting to one of the most notorious rakes in the country.

As if that was not enough, Lord Rayne was now asking to speak with his daughter, forcing Stephen to see her for the first time as an intelligent and sensitive young woman rather than as a silly mixed-up girl, as he had been doing. It was a pity, he thought, that the young blade didn't want to make an offer for her.

But it was Lady Dorna Elwick who surprised Amelie most by her flimsy excuses for not being available to help in the search for Caterina. She had been out all day with a friend, Stephen told her, filling in the gaps left open by Lord Elyot. Dorna had remained silent about which friend and where, but had left Tam and Hannah in charge of the house and told Tam not to leave it for any reason. He had obeyed her to the letter, knowing that if he did not, he would be back where he started. Dorna had known that Amelie and Caterina would be unavailable all day, so it was not until she arrived home at dinner time that she was told of Caterina's disappearance, by which time she was sure she would have turned up. It apparently did not occur to her to send to Lansdown Crescent to find out.

'Imagine her astonishment,' Stephen told Amelie, 'when she found her two brothers and a total stranger in her breakfast room this morning with faces like thunder.'

Amelie was thinking of another face she had seen beside Dorna, coming out of the abbey and walking away quickly without a word of explanation. Was he the mysterious companion of yesterday, too?

Hoping perhaps to redeem herself, Dorna had sent an invitation for them to join her at Sydney Place for dinner tomorrow before the concert at the Assembly Rooms.

'Tomorrow?' said Amelie, turning a pained look upon Lord Elyot. 'Why didn't you say?'

'How much notice do you need to dress for dinner?' he replied.

This Stephen thought discourteous and could not for the life of him understand why Amelie accepted it so meekly. Obviously, the man had a very strong hold over her or she would not be behaving as if they were already married. He would like to have known exactly what it was.

Amelie would rather have continued her private discussion with Lord Elyot, but Stephen's woes had put a damper on the conversation that had crackled and sparked so provocatively before his arrival. It was the kind of discourse she had never experienced with Josiah, part-scolding, part-loving, like a duel where losing was as enjoyable as winning. The thought that she would have to live the rest of her life without him clutched at her heart like the icy hand of winter. What *had* he discovered about her background? And why, if he had found it out, was he still insisting on making her his wife?

The meeting between Caterina and Lord Rayne took place later that morning while both were sitting on the piano stool, but with no music to ease the gentle flow of words. Caterina remembered nothing of her rescue, nor did Seton tell her how he and his brother had carried her home in their arms, which would have embarrassed her greatly. But exactly what passed between them remained private, and afterwards he took her on his arm into the town to be seen in the Pump Room and on South Parade, calling at Sally Lunn's bake shop like comfortable old friends.

What pain the young lady held in her heart, however, was not hidden from Amelie that same day when they drove in the phaeton, at Caterina's request, up to the top of Lansdown Hill. Then, while Caterina vowed she would never weep for a man again, her eyes welled as she told how kind and courteous Lord Rayne had been, not in the least censorious, but insisting that the fault lay entirely with him for allowing her to hope for something that could never be. More details she did not give, nor did Amelie press her, but Caterina's dread of some future date, when he would appear with a lovelier older woman on his arm, was the hardest to bear. All the more so for its resemblance to Amelie's very similar fear.

Meanwhile, Caterina begged to be allowed to stay in Bath for a few more days, having no wish to martyr herself by dashing off home as if she could not bear his company. Her voice was quiet, low and heavy with emotion, her bearing more like a swan than a cygnet, though when they removed their bonnets and let the wind comb through their hair, she became a young goddess with the world at her feet and a small wound in her heart.

* * *

It was Aunt Amelie, however, who received the censure for driving her phaeton up the very steep hill and down again with only Riley on the back. 'What in hell's name could *he* do?' Lord Elyot barked at her. 'He couldn't have held it if it had rolled back, and nor could either of you. S'truth, woman! Do you have a death wish?'

'Oh, don't be so *dramatic*!' she yelped, brushing past him. 'I've been driving my phaeton up hills steeper than that all my life without the slightest mishap. What's the fuss about?'

'Really, my lord,' said Stephen. 'That's no way to speak to Lady Chester. I *do* think—'

'Good for you,' snapped Lord Elyot, following Amelie upstairs two at a time. 'Keep it up.' Steering her quite forcibly into her workroom, he closed the door.

Prepared for more scolding, she tried to get her word in first, but was stopped by his hard embrace and the determined pressure of his mouth over hers; by the time he had drunk deeply from her lips, her words had been stolen. It was some time before either of them spoke, their need for each other having almost reached desperation, and it was clear to Amelie that his rebuke about the phaeton was no more than an excuse to haul her off and relieve his craving.

'You are like a drug, woman,' he whispered, lapping softly at the side of her throat. 'The more I have of you, the more I want. How are we going to get rid of him? Eh?'

'Who…Stephen?'

'Yes. I want to take you to bed.'

'Can you wait?'

'No. How long?' He lifted a strand of her hair and placed his lips where it had been.

'Tonight? We really *do* have to talk, you know. Things cannot go on as they are. You must see that.'

'It's not talking I have in mind, sweetheart. But, yes, we do have to talk. My parents are back in Richmond and I shall take you to meet them as soon as we get home.'

'No…no! That's the problem that must be resolved. You've changed the original plan. It was not meant to be like that. You know it wasn't.'

'You're mistaken. It was *always* meant to be like that.'

'By you, perhaps. But my lord…listen to me… please.' Backed against the piano, she was captured inside his braced arms with her palms pressing the lapels of his coat, trying to keep hold of what she had to say.

'Yes,' he said. 'I will listen to you tonight, but meanwhile we shall carry on as we have been doing, to your brother-in-law's great annoyance.'

'He *was* good to me, my lord.'

'And I shall be even better.'

'He was never in my bed, if that's what you think.'

His wide mobile mouth moved, and there was some slight crinkling at the corner of his eyes. 'No, I'm sure he was not.'

'Not that he didn't want to be, I think.'

'I doubt there's a man anywhere in the world who would not want to be.' His hands had strayed on to her hips, and there was another delay as her body responded, and ached, and allowed itself to be fondled, intimately.

The afternoon was still wild, but not wet enough to prevent them from visiting the King's Baths to watch the bathers, walking through the abbey, plundering the shops and buying extra tickets for the following night's concert at the Assembly Rooms which was to be conducted by none other than Signor Rauzzini. That evening, Amelie, Dorna and her sister-in-law joined the men at the White Hart Inn for dinner, which might have been another ordeal for Stephen Chester had not Miss Hannah Elwick sat next to him to tend his needs like a mother and her favourite child.

If it had been part of Amelie's strategy to use the hapless Stephen as a possible second string to her bow, she now had no option but to let it go when he and Hannah stuck together like glue all evening. But it was beneficial in another way, for as the two brothers escorted Amelie and Caterina back to Lansdown, Stephen escorted the other two ladies back to Sydney Place and so missed Lord Rayne's solo return to the White Hart.

Amelie had been unusually quiet that evening, though Dorna's gaiety bubbled over the meal and no one noticed except Lord Elyot, whose hand stole more than once across to Amelie's lap, as if he knew instinctively which of her concerns was uppermost in her mind.

Later, behind the white bedcurtains that kept out the wind's buffeting roar, she lay in his arms feeling that this might be for the last time, wondering how to reconcile what she knew with what he had discovered and whether, or indeed how, he would accept it. But the time for accusations had passed, and now their starving bodies came together and fused along every surface to assuage the long week of emptiness.

The time away from each other, marred for Amelie by doubts, gave her an edge of anger that she could not suppress, as if to make him aware of every discomfort he had imposed upon her, wittingly or not. Aroused and kindled to white heat, she still refused him access, biting, fending him off while leading him on, fighting him, telling him *no* when every fibre cried out *yes*. He played along with it until she was too tired to contest him any longer, then, holding her flailing arms into the pillow, he met her lifting thighs with a fierceness that matched her own, subduing her in an instant. There were no words, not even endearments, but the breath-shattering beat of his body against hers said all she needed to know about his desire and commitment. How could she ever have doubted him?

Although his need of her had burned in him so long without release, he was a careful and unselfish lover who knew well how to give pleasure through all the ebbing and flowing tides, how to bring her to the height of the wave, to wait, then to crash down with rapturous cries of delight after an eternity of suspense.

Limp and satiated, she lay sprawled across him, savouring every inch of the moist warm contact and wondering if what they had just done would bring on the monthly event which, this time, had failed her when she needed it most.

Consequently, when he said, very quietly, 'I believe you have something to tell me, sweetheart,' she was lost for an answer. Was he able to read her mind?

She hesitated, and he prompted her. 'Do you want to tell me how a widow manages to remain a virgin? It is rather unusual, you have to admit. Was Chester impotent? Is that the reason?'

She felt the prickling sensation at the base of her neck. 'No,' she whispered. 'He was not.'

'So what happened? Can you tell me?'

She smoothed a hand over his powerful chest,

calming the expected storm. 'I've always maintained that I cannot marry you,' she said, 'for a very good reason. I have no natural parents. No ancestry. My parents, the Carrs, adopted me a few days after I was born. Sons of marquesses, my lord, don't marry foundlings. Even though you may wish to, your father would not allow it. You know that. You may say that he need not know, but *I* know, and I couldn't let it happen. No man should be so deceived.'

'That's…*very*…interesting,' he murmured, drowsily, 'but it hardly accounts for you holding on to your virginity after you were married, does it? Unless Sir Josiah discovered your birth and felt cheated. Was that what happened? Had you better start from the beginning, sweetheart?'

'You were not supposed to know that I was a virgin. How did you find it out? Was it guesswork?'

He sighed and rolled on to an elbow to see the dark fearful eyes in the candlelight. 'No, not guesswork. A man can tell, you see. Unless he's blind drunk. And I wasn't.' He smiled, tracing a tender line down her nose with a finger.

'Can he?'

'Yes. Believe me. Now, can we get back to your marriage?'

'When Stephen lost his wife, he wanted me to take her place, but he was the second son, you see. Josiah was the first, the wealthy baronet, and he offered for me too. My mother had huge ambitions for me and I was their only daughter, dutiful and obedient, and although I didn't love either of the brothers, Josiah was fatherly and kind, and I thought I could make him a good wife. I didn't particularly want to step into Stephen's first wife's shoes. My mother insisted I accept Josiah, and my father went along with it, intending to keep the details of the adoption secret. I believe it was not too difficult. They had spent months in Switzerland before they took me in, so she could have pretended that she was pregnant during that time. But this is what I fear Ruben Hurst may have discovered, according to his letter.'

'I think that's highly unlikely. But go on.'

'As I said, my mother would have told nobody, not even Josiah, but my father took a different view and, on the night before our wedding, he was struck by conscience. He told us both how I'd been rescued from the Manchester Foundling Hospital, and said that Josiah should not be deceived into thinking that he was marrying a woman of good ancestry when he—that is, my father—had no idea who my parents were. He and my mother had felt it best not to ask for details, and I think at that time they were not keeping proper records as they do in London. In Manchester, the children were left with some little item belonging to one of the parents, in case they wanted to reclaim it.'

'Did you have anything?'

'No, I think not. Nothing. I think, you see, that my father wanted to give Josiah the chance to call the marriage off before it was too late. He deeply respected Josiah. They had been friends for years.'

'But he preferred to go ahead with it. Did he love you too much?'

'There's more, my lord. When my father left us, Josiah was very upset, and eventually he confessed to me that the choice would be mine. He'd had an affair with his mother's maid when he was twenty-three and, to cut a long story short, to save the maid's job he'd taken the newborn child, a girl, to the same Foundling Hospital in Manchester, only a few days before I was rescued from there by the Carrs. He was quite sure about the date. And because of that, and because I had the maid's looks by then, Josiah believed there was a strong chance I could be his daughter. Perhaps that explained his love for me. I don't know.'

'What was the maid's name? Did he say?'

'No, it would have been nice if I'd known my mother's name, but Josiah thought it best not to say. We agonised about the problem for a long time, and Josiah would have released me, but I wouldn't let him call it off. I knew that, if we said nothing, no one except ourselves would know.'

'But couldn't he have verified it, somehow?'

'The wedding was the next day. It was to be the greatest day of my mother's life, and Josiah's too. I couldn't...I simply *couldn't* pull out at that late stage. It would have been the end of my mother, I think. There was no time for him to enquire before the wedding, and even if he'd postponed it, he may have been proved correct, after all that, raising a lot of questions he didn't want to answer about his lover and her identity, a terrible scandal and a daughter he didn't want. He was forty-three, highly respected with an expanding business and a solid reputation, and I couldn't bear to think of the consequences, so I was the one to decide it was best not to know. But that also meant we could never consummate our marriage, in case it was true.'

'Yes, I see. But that was a great sacrifice for you.'

'It was my choice, Nick. I was a dutiful daughter, and the thought of hurting such a good man was more than I could have borne. I knew he adored me, you see, and I didn't know anything about lovemaking, and I didn't know what I was missing except the chance to have a family of my own.' Her voice wavered and dropped a pitch. 'That's all I missed.' She turned her head away and, when he brought it back to face him, he saw how her eyes were filling with tears, her lovely features contorted with anguish. 'It was my duty, Nick,' she whispered, 'and he was offering me so much with the chance to please my ageing parents.'

She had carried that burden for four years, two as a married woman and two as a widow and now, having spoken it out loud for the first time, the significance of it swamped her with deep despair, exposing a grief for her childlessness and for what she saw as failure in every direction she took. 'Nick…Nick,' she sobbed, hiding her face in him, 'you must know…before you…you go…that I…love you. You must know that.'

Pushing her damp hair away, he rocked her in his arms and mopped her tears. 'Sweetheart, hush now. What are you talking about? I'm not going anywhere. And I know you love me. Why, I have only to look into your eyes to see that. There now…hush…I'm not leaving you. It's *you* who cares most about your parentage, not me, sweetheart. I've found the woman I love, the one I'm going to marry and have children with, and I don't care a damn who her parents are. As it happens, I believe your kindly Josiah may have withheld some of the truth, even from you, to protect your mother's good name. Come now, lass, dry these tears. You'll not get away from me on that kind of excuse. Tell me you love me again.'

'I love you, Nick…dear heart,' she gulped. 'I love you, and I can't bear the thought of losing you.'

'Sweetheart, you're not going to. I told you at the start that this relationship was not going to fail. Didn't I?'

'You say you've found the woman you love. Is it true?'

'Quite true. Do you know that I almost threw myself at your feet in Rundell's that day we first met? Dearest love, there hasn't been a single moment when I've *not* been desperately in love with you, and I would have used every trick in the book to get you, unwilling widow. Everybody knows how in love with you I am, little goose, so it's no good dragging up your dodgy parentage to hold me off.'

'But everybody also knows how bloodlines matter more than anything to the aristocracy, Nick. Your father would not accept it, if he knew, and I could not so deceive a man. And your mother doesn't tolerate scandal. You told me that yourself, didn't you?'

When he rolled off the bed, Amelie took it as a sign that he was debating the reply, but in the next moment she was being wrapped in the counterpane and carried over to the hearth where the low fire was resurrected into a dancing blaze. Holding her within the circle of his arms, he pretended to have mislaid the question.

'You were saying, m'lady?' He smiled, behind her head.

'Well, *that* was a fudge, wasn't it, *my lord*? My informant reliably tells me that the scandalous doings of your mother would make the Chesters' saga look almost respectable. How *could* you have used such an excuse to get me into your bed?'

'I admit it,' he said, nuzzling into her neck. 'I did

it to make you beholden to me. And it was not just my bed where I wanted you, either. If this is the prize, a little trickery is allowable. Forgive me, my sweet, but I had to hold you somehow, and you were so determined not to let me near you. Am I forgiven?'

Like a cat, she rubbed her head against his neck, hardly able to believe that this was happening to her. 'Wicked man,' she whispered. 'Is it any wonder I tried to avoid you after what I found out of your reputation? But for Caterina, I would never have given in to your disgraceful demands, my lord. It was quite the most shocking way to behave towards a lady. But now I'm not quite what I seem, am I? Who knows what or who I am? Did you really make any discoveries in London, or was that all fudge, too?'

His fingers roamed over her face, lifting a stray tear off her eyelashes and taking it to his lips. 'Oh, dear. Am I in danger of losing all my credibility now? I hope not, because I did find something that may fit in rather neatly with your foundling story, sweetheart. It looks as if Sir Josiah Chester may have been trying to protect the identity of his early love when he told you she was his mother's maid. That's not quite how it looks. It began with that portrait of you by Lawrence that hangs in your bedroom; it reminded me so strongly of someone I saw at Sheen Court. I was a child of about six or seven and she was an exquisitely beautiful creature. She made a big impression on me, and I suppose that was the first time I ever fell in love. Even at six. When I saw your portrait, I realised that there *must* be some kind of connection, so when I saw Lord Dysart again at Lady Sergeant's ball, I went to have a chat with him while you were dancing with Seton.'

'That was when you vanished, and I thought…oh, never mind. Go on, if you please.'

'Well, I asked Dysart what he knew about your late husband and about your family, but he didn't know the Carrs personally except that they were big mill owners, and all he could tell me about Chester's early years was that he'd sown a few wild oats before he settled down into business. What Dysart was *more* interested in was you. Like me, he was reminded of someone he'd once known in the late 1770s, a society beauty formerly known as Fanny Scales. Her real name was Francesca, and she'd been married to Viscount Winterbourne, who was fighting abroad for the first year of their marriage, like many others. And that's all Dysart could tell me.'

'What then?' said Amelie, holding his hand to her cheek.

'Then I went to see my mother in London. I knew that she'd known the Winterbournes well. She'd been friends with Fanny even before her marriage. The interesting part is that Fanny's parents lived in Manchester and, while her new husband was with his regiment, she spent the best part of a year up there in the north with them. According to my mother, this would have been in about 1780. She returned to London, but later confided to my mother, her closest friend, that she'd had an affair with a wonderful man and borne a child. She never said who the father was, but the babe had been taken immediately to the Foundling Hospital in Manchester. Viscount Winterbourne would never have accepted another man's child. My mother said she was always racked with guilt about having to abandon it.'

'Did she mention any dates?' said Amelie, suddenly breathless.

'She believed it was about springtime in 1781.'

'April. That's when the Carrs adopted me. My father told us he wanted a boy so that he could inherit instead of his nephew, but there was me, a girl child, and my mother clung to me and thought I was most likely to grow up looking like their natural child. But what happened to Fanny? Is she still in London?'

'This is the sad part. She died giving birth to her second son, and they both died in infancy too. Winterbourne returned to his regiment, but he was killed in action soon afterwards.'

'Oh,' she said, clinging to his hand. 'That is a sad, *sad* story. That is so…so…oh, Nick…how could she do it? A child…a tiny babe? Could she not have found a family who would have taken it, and loved it? To give it away like that.' Her words ended in a whisper, and hot tears dripped on to his hand, and he knew without a doubt that here was the reason for her passion for waifs and strays, for abandoned pregnant women and lost souls. Naturally compassionate, she had channelled all her latent mothering instincts into caring for unfortunates, perhaps to give back what she had been given, though the inevitable deceit was a great price to pay. Young Fanny Scales would not have been the only one to let her child go, for the sake of respectability.

'Don't weep,' he said. 'It happens. It always will. You've been doing what you could to help, sweetheart, and no one is going to object to that, even if it was unorthodox. But what about Lady Fanny's story? Do you think it ties up with yours somehow? Was Sir Josiah right, after all?'

'It does look as if he knew more than he told me, and perhaps he *would* have told me one day if he'd not died so suddenly. But why did you think Lady Fanny's story might be relevant, Nick darling? You were not to have known that I was adopted.'

'Your portrait and my childhood memory, and you saying that there was yet another skeleton in your closet. And Dysart's memory too. He'd made the same link as me.'

'But Thomas Lawrence didn't.'

'No, she was before his time, sweetheart. But you

see what this means, don't you? That your ancestry is as good as it gets, adopted or not. Better even than the Carrs. Mrs Carr would surely have known the lovely Fanny, Viscountess Winterbourne. She'd have approved of that. Just think.'

She had to smile at the irony. 'I can scarcely believe it, dearest. Are we going to have to tell your parents about it? We should, you know.'

'I don't see why. It's important to you, but I think we can safely say that your last skeleton is released, and you have no more to worry about. Yes?'

'Doesn't it make any difference to you, either?'

'Not in the least. And I think we've been engaged long enough now. It's time it was officially announced, and a date set. You and I should be made respectable.'

Certainly, there was another reason for urgency now, though she could not tell him of it until she was more sure. But the solving of so many of Amelie's problems made a difference to their loving that extended their experience of each other even further, marking the beginning of a deeper phase in their unusual wooing. That night was for Amelie the start of a new life also, not just as the daughter of aristocrats, but as the untroubled future wife of the man she had come to adore, the one around whom she had erected so many obstacles. Paradoxically, if she had not come this far with him, she would never have discovered the answer to the one problem that had lain like a dark menace at the roots of her life; the question of her birth and abandonment.

After dinner with Dorna at Sydney Place, her guests were convinced that the concert at the Assembly Rooms would be something of an anticlimax, for the meal had been riotous, even without the extrovert Tam. The mood had lightened, the two brothers were in good form, even Stephen had rallied with the aid of a suddenly animated Hannah, and Dorna had excelled with a meal so varied and novel that each dish was a topic for discussion and some absurd guesswork.

She had invited her mysterious friend to join them, a very presentable Captain Ben Rankin who, once he had adapted to the banter and irreverence between them, showed an attractive wit and a wicked sense of humour. He was also, Amelie and Nick agreed, a risk-taker to step so boldly into Sir Chad's slippers, for they had little doubt that that was what he was doing here in Bath. Nevertheless, they could well understand what attractions the captain held for Dorna after the unresponsive Sir Chad, and they took to him easily.

In glittering silver and white, swathes of feathery shawls, plumes and pearls, Amelie and Caterina won a large slice of the attention from the concert-goers that evening as they glided through the columned passages to the soft shush of feet and the rustle of silk and lace, the fluttering of fans, the whispers of guests with their printed programmes and lorgnettes poised to pick out names and unctuous introductions: '*Mr Taylor...earnestly felicits the attention of the Nobility and Gentry...and trusts that his exertions will...*'

'Exertions?' Caterina whispered to Lord Rayne. 'For pity's sake.'

'Sounds as if he's offering to do press-ups,' he replied, with disdain.

'Heaven forbid. Look...oh, look...here's Signor Rauzzini.'

'Don't wave.'

'Thank you. I wasn't going to. He's smiling at me.'

'Then you may smile back, but not too much or he may ask you to sing.'

'You are *so* disagreeable. I don't know why I came with you.'

'Shh! He's taking the rostrum. Stop fidgeting.'

The musicians' tuning-up had drowned out the bickering, which in turn was a cover for something much more affectionate and which fooled none of their companions except dear Hannah, who could not understand it. Amelie's hand reached across Nick's lap to squeeze her niece's arm with an exchange of smiles and, after a last fleeting glance at the festoon of gleaming chandeliers below the white-vaulted

ceiling and the assembled line of artistes, she settled
into her velvet-covered gilded chair.

The maestro introduced the vocalists, the musicians, the programme, its sponsors and their aspira-
tions, but it was soon evident that the popular
mezzo-soprano was far from well, though she struggled valiantly in a duet by Handel, then in a quartet
composed by Rauzzini himself. By the interval, the
audience had begun to wonder if she would have to
retire and if they would have to forfeit what many of
them had looked forward to, her solo.

With a cup of tea in her hand, Amelie was discussing the situation when she caught sight of Signor
Rauzzini threading his way towards her, though she
felt both privileged and slightly alarmed by a premo-
nition of his intent. Even in late maturity, the Italian
was still the handsome man he had been in his youth
when women had clamoured to become his mistress
and men had envied his popularity and success. His
renowned castrato singing voice was now well past
its best, but his charm was as potent as ever.

'Lady Chester…my lord…pray forgive the inter-
ruption,' he said, smiling so broadly that they would
have forgiven him anything, 'but we have a slight
problem…no, I lie, it's more than slight, it's a catas-
trophe.' And as if they had not noticed, he explained
that the mature Mrs D'Oliveira was suffering a crisis.
Her voice had gone. Throwing up his hands, he flut-

tered his fingers like wings. 'And I wondered, dear lady, if your niece has recovered enough to help us out for the second act. I saw her here with you. Do you think…am I asking the impossible? I *know* she can do it. A solo, and our duet, perhaps an encore? That's all.'

Caterina was sought, and asked. 'Signor, I am honoured,' she said. 'But do I know the music?'

'Sing whatever you wish, Miss Chester. The musicians will know it. The duet you and I will perform as we were to have done at my house, only here we shall have the applause afterwards. There is no one else I would ask to do it.'

His standards were of the highest, his reputation also. As brave as an Amazon, Caterina grasped at the chance. 'I can do it,' she said. 'Of course I can.'

'Are you sure, my dear?' Amelie whispered. 'You need not feel obliged.'

'I'm not about to forgo a chance like this,' said Caterina. 'This is what we came to Bath for, and now Father can hear me. Lead on, *signor*.'

The word went round: the maestro had found a replacement. The audience settled down once more; necks craned as the introduction was made and Caterina was led on to the small dais to polite and sympathetic applause. She was a stunner, they murmured, but would she be able to match Mrs D'Oliveira?

But from the first haunting notes, the air became electric with intense concentration as it had not been previously, and the young goddess who stood so confidently before them without a sheet of music in her hand held every one of them enthralled by the pure unaffected richness that poured from her in tones of honeyed gold. Bent to their instruments, the musicians watched and followed her, awed by her beauty of expression, the phrasing, the nuances of colour, the control, for this was a poignant love song they had assumed to be beyond her experience to tell convincingly.

Yet there were some who listened, knowing that it was her own experience of which she sang, of the one she loved and was losing, and how she would recover and be merry with others, while always returning to the minor key that gave the lie to her bravado. It was heartbreaking, piquant, alternating between optimism and melancholy, and when she sang of how this love would hold her heart for ever imprisoned, there was not one in the hall who disbelieved her, especially not the one to whom she was singing. As the last long sad note floated softly around the hall, soaring upwards, every ear straining to hold it back, the silence that followed was like a wait for an echo until Caterina moved and tipped her head a little to one side, looking directly at Lord Rayne.

To his credit, he was the first to stand and blow her

a kiss, followed immediately by the whole audience, whose applause was the loudest and most prolonged of the evening, both tearful and ecstatic. Even this did not unsettle her, Signor Cantoni having briefed her how every moment on stage was part of the act, the applause their thanks to be accepted graciously. When Signor Rauzzini joined her for their duet, the audience had never before sat down so quickly.

This too was a performance that set Bath society talking for months afterwards, for the maestro's voice, though changed, was still beautiful and in the same range as Caterina's, but of a different timbre. And though they had never sung together before, she took her cues from him, held his hand, and sang with him a love duet of quite a different kind, sweet and full of promise. For a great artiste at the end of his career and a young woman at the beginning of hers, it had a significance that no one could miss. Once again, the applause rattled the chandeliers.

Wisely, she left them wanting more, modestly offering the excuse that the other singers still had a programme to finish, resuming her place with her family, whose emotional greetings lifted those spirits which, only days before, had been at rock-bottom. The rest of the concert, though enjoyable, could not match Caterina's brilliance, and by the end it was she who had assumed the status of celebrity. But it was to Amelie she remarked, when they were alone, that she had found it both exhilarating and consoling to sing in public about a wounded pride rather than weep about it, and that if it helped her to understand love songs, the heart's pain must have its uses.

Chapter Ten

There were several reasons why Amelie must return to Richmond sooner than she had intended, most of which concerned others more than herself. Caterina and her father were keen to return to their family at Buxton, while Nick and Seton were anxious not to keep their parents waiting at Sheen Court where they were preparing to send Seton off in style and to celebrate their eldest son's engagement. The only one of their company who was not inclined to leave the freedom of Bath was Dorna, who was enjoying herself too much, confident that her husband would miss her less than Captain Rankin. Duty came first, however, and family celebrations were much to her taste.

So for the remaining few days of their stay, they indulged in every opportunity for enjoyment that Bath had to offer, using each morning, noon and night to parade, to ride and walk to the surrounding beauty spots, to games of bowls, shopping sprees, assemblies, dinner parties, country dances and, on the Friday to come, a formal dress ball. One of their visits was to Perrydown, where Signor Rauzzini had a beautiful cottage and where he entertained them lavishly. Here the maestro did his utmost to convince Stephen that he must take his daughter's talent seriously, but Amelie and Nick, discussing the event later, agreed that it was Caterina herself who had been largely responsible for her own success with only a little steering in the right direction from them.

The ball at the New Assembly Rooms was intended to mark their last night before their return home and, for this, Lise and Millie spent hours preparing gowns, stockings and pumps, gloves and fans, and in arranging hair entwined with plaits, braids and pearls. An evening gown of cream lace for Amelie and a flower-sprigged white muslin for Caterina put the two of them once again in a class of their own, and Lord Rayne's admiration that had once been only for the aunt was this time for the niece. It was enough for her to see how his eyes lingered, without straying.

Still on cloud nine since the banishment of her cares, Amelie gave herself generously to every moment in Nick's company, able for the first time to indulge in those small signs of affection she had never quite been able to show before: squeezing his hand, pressing close to him, whispering intimate secrets, laughing at nothing, the talk of lovers. When he led her into the enormous pale green and white ballroom lined with Corinthian columns into a blaze of light from no less than nine cut-glass chandeliers, there was nothing that could have diminished her joy at being by his side as his beloved final partner. It was during the supper interval in the tea room where an incident took place that came very close to removing her joy forever, and which brought their last evening in Bath to a more abrupt end than they had expected.

As the crowds jostled around the groaning supper tables, Amelie, Hannah and Dorna carried plates of food to a table in one corner to await the men, who had offered to bring tea and wine. Raising their eyebrows at the level of noise as guests clamoured for food, the three women paid little attention to a burst of shouting over by the door to the octogon, a central room that led directly into all the others. Assuming that the rowdiness would soon be dealt with by Mr King, the Master of Ceremonies, they continued to chatter and nibble until Dorna suddenly stopped, sat up very straight, and frowned severely at someone standing close behind Amelie's chair.

At that same moment, Amelie felt the touch of a hand beneath her elbow and, sure that it must be Nick, half-turned with a smile at the ready. But by that time Dorna had leapt to her feet, enraged by the stranger's effrontery. 'Sir!' she scolded. 'Take your hand away from Lady Chester this *minute*. How dare you come in here dressed like that?'

Suspecting that Dorna was overreacting, Amelie turned fully from her conversation with Hannah and saw that instead of the regulation knee-breeches and white stockings, the man standing too close to her was wearing dirty riding boots and a brown coat she had last seen in her Richmond workroom, though now it was shabby and stained with food. His face had suffered too, showing a desperation and hollow-eyed gauntness that the last few weeks in London's gambling hells had inflicted on him. Ruben Hurst.

In the next moment she was on her feet, desperate to put a distance between them, knowing that his mission would not be a peaceful one after her refusal to communicate. He reeked of danger and spirits, and yet again he had found her unprotected and vulnerable. Knocking his hand away and using her arm as a barrier, she searched the room for Mr King, whose white wig was easy to spot, pushing his way towards them, dodging hand-held plates and ladies' trains. 'You!' she snarled at Hurst. 'Get out of here…get *out*!' Where were Nick and Stephen when she needed them?

But Ruben Hurst had not traipsed all this way only to be thrown out before concluding his business with the woman who obsessed him. This time he did not mean to leave empty-handed as he had done on two previous occasions. This time, she would go with him.

Nauseated by his heavy sour breath, Amelie grappled with him, doing her best to evade him, but eventually being pinned back to the wall by the table on one side and her chair on the other, and all so fast that no man had realised what was happening until it was too late. Catching at her wrist, he pulled it hard across her throat and held her with her back to him, helplessly off-balance and rasped along her cheek by his disgusting stubble. Twisting her head away, she caught sight of the long cold length of a duelling pistol like an extension of his arm, levelled directly at Mr King's white head, stopping him in his tracks.

Through the hubbub, Dorna's hunting-field cry cut like a knife. 'Nick! Ben! Stephen…Seton!'

Someone screamed. A plate crashed to the floor, and a mist of silence descended as the crowds pressed backwards, the men open-armed to shield their women, herding them away, hovering on the edge of the place where Amelie stood linked to Hurst. Three tall men pushed their way through to stand in front of Mr King: Nick, Seton and Captain Rankin. Stephen was nowhere to be seen.

'Hurst!' called Nick. 'Listen to me. Let Lady Chester go. We can talk…settle this outside.

Whatever you prefer. Now…let her go, man, or you get even deeper into trouble.'

For the first time, Hurst spoke, slurring his words and sounding even more like a Manchester man than he had before. 'Oh, no,' he said. 'Oh, no, my lord. This business is already settled, in my favour, this time. The lady is with me now, and that's where she'll stay. Don't you think I've waited long enough, sweeting?' His mouth came close to her ear, dripping flecks of foam on to her bare shoulder. 'Ready to come now, are ye? One shot for you and one for me. You'll not feel a thing.'

'Mr Hurst…please,' Amelie whispered, half-strangled by his arm. 'Let's talk about this, sensibly. This is not the way…' But he was impatient, jerking his arm and holding her head in the crook of his elbow. She caught sight of Dorna's terrified face, and Hannah with a hand over her mouth, and she said a silent prayer of thanks that Caterina was not in the tea room. She looked along his arm at the gleam of brass with one finger hooked round the trigger ready to squeeze, and she froze in horror as it swung slowly round to point at Nick, swamped with a fear greater than any she had ever known at this appalling threat. She had found real love at last, the fulfilment of her dearest wishes with the man she wanted above all else, his child in her womb. And this half-crazed vindictive creature was about to put an end to all she had ever yearned for, to satisfy his own corrupt infatuation. He had blighted her life once and was now about to do it again, even to end it. 'Nick,' she whispered, watching the shaking weapon. 'Nick…I love you…I love you.'

'Sweetheart…hold on,' he called back. 'We can still talk, Hurst. Come, man. Put the weapon down. You cannot get away with this.' He held out a hand across the space. 'Will you—?'

'No!' Hurst yelled, almost frantic now. 'I held on too, thinking she'd come to me. I shot Chester and I'll shoot you…the lot of you… hypocrites! Then it'll be just you and me, lady. Just you and me.'

From the other side of the room, a voice called, loud and raw with fury, turning all heads, including Hurst's. 'And *me*!' he bellowed. 'Over here, Hurst. Over here, man! It's *me* you have to deal with now.'

For an interval between heartbeats, Amelie felt Hurst hesitate as the sound of Stephen's voice searched for a niche in his memory, and the mean, sleek, shining pistol swung slowly away from Nick's head towards the voice her captor was struggling to remember, and to find among the throng.

'Let me go, Ruben,' Amelie whispered. Using the name she had not spoken for years, she hoped to distract him further. 'I'll go with you. We can go away from here…together…just you and me…lower the pistol…please.' And as she pleaded, Nick watched and understood what she was saying, nodding to her to keep talking, to promise the dreadful man anything while he and Seton could sidle round the wall and out of her line of vision.

'Who's that man?' Hurst stammered. 'Who called to me?'

'I don't know. Let's just get away from these people, Ruben.'

'Where? Where is he? *Damn* you!' he yelled into the crowd. 'Show yourself!'

The gun wavered again and Amelie closed her eyes at the pressure across her neck and back, and she said another prayer of thanks that Caterina was not present to hear her father's challenge. What on earth was Stephen thinking of to goad the man so?

When she opened her eyes, the scene was changing again, for now the crowd had opened up a corridor that widened as she watched, revealing the solitary figure of Stephen Chester with a duelling pistol in his hand, pointing it at the floor. His face was whiter than Amelie had ever seen it, twisted with the effort of control, his usual kindly voice hardly recognisable as he screamed at Ruben Hurst, 'Here, you *bastard*! I'm here! And now it's *your* turn. Put Amelie aside and face me as you once faced my good brother, if you dare.'

Again, a woman's scream cut through the horrified silence. 'Stephen…*no!*' It was Hannah. Dorna grabbed her, holding a hand over her mouth.

The pistol in Hurst's hand swung again, but the earsplitting explosion synchronised with the brutal grasp of a hand that wrenched his wrist and twisted it upwards towards the ceiling, sending down a shower of white plaster upon the heads below. At the same moment, while Amelie's ears still buzzed with the retort, she went crashing down backwards to land on top of Hurst with his arm still about her neck until it was prised away, and she found that, beside her on the floor, he was being roughly manhandled by three very competent men, one of whom sat on his shoulders to pull his hands together behind his back.

Undignified that fall may have been, but Amelie had taken worse ones from her horse, and she was prone neither to histrionics nor fainting. Nevertheless, she could not prevent herself from shaking as relief overwhelmed her, not only for her own deliverance from the menace of Ruben Hurst, but for everyone else's too. The strong arms that lifted her and drew her into their safe haven belonged to Nick, who had risked his life to throw himself at Hurst's weapon.

'Nick, darling,' she whispered. 'Hold me…just hold me.'

'Sweetheart, did he hurt you?'

'No, not really. Bruised a bit, that's all. Oh, my love. He's mad. I'm sure he's mad. Has he gone now, for good?'

'Mad as a hatter, sweetheart,' he agreed, kissing her. 'Very bad form to walk in here looking like that.

Deserves to be locked up.' He looked round at the hasty attempts to right the overturned tables and to collect the heap of plaster, and at Hurst being hauled away by Mr King's burly stewards. 'I put a cup of tea down for you somewhere,' he said, laconically.

Amelie made a snuffling sound into his waistcoat. 'I must go to Stephen,' she said. 'He was quite wonderful, but he's very upset.'

In the less crowded octogon, they sat to recover themselves while sipping fresh tea. Emotionally, Stephen was in a worse plight than Amelie, having come so close to fulfilling the ambition he had waited two years for, to revenge himself on his brother's killer. But for Amelie being in his way, he would certainly have shot him. With Hannah and Caterina beside him, he explained, tearfully, how he came to have a duelling pistol with him at a dress ball.

'It's the one Josiah used when he died,' he said. 'I kept it, carried in a hidden pocket every single day, and at night under my pillow, waiting for a sight of that…sorry…' he gulped, then whispered '…that bastard. He knew Josiah was better with swords, but he was challenged, and he chose pistols. Well, I could have done better than Josiah, but he insisted on doing it himself. I could have got him…him then…instead of…'

'Hush now, dear one,' said Hannah, holding his hand. 'Hush.'

'Hurst was drunk,' said Seton. 'That wouldn't do, old chap.'

'I'd still have killed him, drunk or sober. Scum like that deserve—' and here he broke down again while Caterina and Hannah held him between them and looked sadly at each other over his head.

'He'll be dealt with,' said Nick. 'It's best this way, my friend.'

'But for Stephen,' Amelie said, 'I would not be here. I've never seen anything so courageous as when you drew his fire towards you. Truly, you're my hero.'

'Really?' said Stephen, brightening a little.

'Yes, really. It was a remarkable thing to do, wasn't it, Nick?'

'Indeed it was. Truly remarkable. I have Chester to thank for my future wife's life. That lunatic would certainly have done some terrible damage without your prompt action.'

Stephen blew his nose and smoothed his hair. 'Oh…really, it was nothing,' he murmured. But Hannah and Caterina, catching each other's eyes behind his shoulders, had just arrived at a mutual, if unspoken, decision to make Hannah's presence in Buxton essential. Stephen Chester, they seemed to agree, needed someone more like Hannah than Aunt Amelie, who got herself into situations rather too easily, these days.

Staring wistfully into the tea room where the hum

of gossip was warming to its newest subject, Dorna remarked quietly to Amelie that she had done her a favour, if only she knew it.

'Done you a favour?' whispered Amelie. 'Whatever can you mean?'

'I mean, dear heart, that no one is now going to think anything of my attending the ball with Captain Rankin after that débâcle, are they? And as for you wondering about the scandal, well, why worry? You'll be halfway home by this time tomorrow, darling. Even Mother could not have timed it better. And when you and Nick return next year, half will have forgotten and the other half will envy you.'

'Dorna...' Amelie laughed. 'You're impossible.'

'Maybe, but I know what I'm talking about.'

They finished the evening at the White Hart Inn round a blazing fire, eating a supper that surpassed the one they had missed at the New Assembly Rooms and deciding, among other absurdities, that the ballroom guests should be asked to pay extra for the impromptu entertainment. Until they remembered the damaged ceiling that they themselves would be expected to pay for.

Though traumatic in many respects, the evening marked yet another milestone in Amelie's relationship with Nick, now that Hurst could do no more damage. From the White Hart, the mood of relief continued into Amelie's bedroom, for now she had shared the dread secret, and with credentials like that, Nick told her, she was worthy to join the scandalous ranks of his family with her head held high. Being a northerner with trade connections could only add a touch of spice, he said.

That night, their loving was unhurried and very tender, both of them having recognised, in a very dramatic manner, the true depth of their love for each other, after having come close to the prospect of losing everything they lived for. It had scared Nick as much as Amelie, his dive at Hurst being, he admitted, not so much an act of heroism but fear of losing her. It was a vision he never wanted to see again.

Over and again, they assured each other of their everlasting, profound and unconditional love as they had not thought needful before. They had never been guilty of taking it lightly, but now the telling of it held a new significance they were unlikely to forget, and their night in Amelie's bed was made all the sweeter by the most beauteous words of love either of them had ever used or heard. She told him of his rare ability to listen to a woman, to look at her as if she mattered to him, and he used new words to describe her luscious body, her compassion, courage and independence, her grace and flawless taste, her devotion to her relatives' needs, which went, he said, well beyond most women's loyalty.

'Well, my lord,' she whispered, nestling closer, 'you tested *that* to the limit, did you not? Never has a woman been faced with such a terrible dilemma. It was truly outrageous.'

'Was it so very wicked of me?'

'No,' she said, smiling at his tone of contrition, 'it wasn't. It was shocking, but I was not as insulted as all that. I wanted you, you see.'

'*Did* you, wench?' he drawled, sliding his hand into deep places. 'Is that what made you link your name with mine so easily?'

'No, you were simply the first name that sprang to mind, my lord.'

'Really? And all that protesting, then?'

'Was to slow you down, brute.' She caught at his hand. 'You were all for leaping into my bed there and then, and I was determined to make you wait.'

Rolling himself on top of her, he sensed her body's response to him. 'And who won, my beauty? Eh? Who was it needed a new experience to add to her growing list? That was a bonus I certainly didn't expect.'

She could have continued the verbal fencing, but the quest of his hands was already luring her mind away along a different course, and the story of what she had heard in the jeweller's shop would have to wait for another night, as would her growing certainty of a new Elyot within her.

* * *

Their sedate and good-humoured progress from Bath in several carriages was a far cry from their individual journeys in the opposite direction which, with the exception of Dorna, had been undertaken with some degree of anxiety. After an overnight stay at Marlborough, which taxed the poor innkeeper's resources to the limit, they came to Richmond in a kind of convoy that caught the Sunday citizens unawares. Full of curiosity, they lined the roadway on their way to evening church, waving and welcoming, setting the tone for the next bright phase of Amelie's life.

She discovered a few changes to her house on Paradise Road, the most important being the instalment of the new laundry-woman and her baby Emily from the workhouse. Even better was the attention the two were receiving from her young gardener Fenn, who liked to see nature reproduce itself and who had helped to make the mother and child's settling-in so comfortable.

Losing not a moment, Nick arrived just after breakfast on Monday morning to take Amelie, Caterina and her father to Sheen Court to meet his parents, an event that no longer filled her with trepidation as it once had. She was able to see how, in his fifties, the handsome Marquess of Sheen resembled his son in manner and speech as well as in looks, controlled, intelligent and unstintingly appreciative, thoughtful, yet quite droll in his attitude to his sons, whom he treated like younger brothers. White-haired and still athletic, he and Stephen Chester put on a display of fencing in the great hall as if they had known each other for years.

Nor was Amelie disappointed with Lady Sheen's reaction to her, for the chattery Dorna had already regaled her mother with an account of events at the ball and so, by the time they came face to face, Amelie's reputation had gone before her. To have had men fight over her *twice* by the age of twenty-four was more than even the Marchioness could boast of, but no wonder when she was such a beauty, she said, generously.

'No…oh, no, my lady,' said Amelie, glancing at Nick to obtain some backing. 'It was not quite like that.'

In front of the heavy gilded mirror, Nick was tweaking at his cravat with a frown of concentration on his face. 'Nonsense,' said his mother. 'Any other reason would be too sordid and not worth repeating. This is a *lovely* bit of scandal, my dear. But tell me, having family connections with Manchester, could you be…by any chance…related to the Scales family? Fanny Scales was a friend of mine. Such an unusual beauty. You have her look about you.'

'Viscountess Winterbourne *was* related,' Amelie said, 'on my mother's side, I believe.'

'I thought as much,' said the Marchioness. 'They were a lovely family. I was so very fond of her. Dear Fanny. You must allow Lawrence to paint you, you know.'

'He already has, Mother,' said Nick, turning away from his reflection with a sigh.

'Good heavens. Lawrence has a waiting list as long as my arm these days,' said the Marchioness. 'Now, about this dinner party on Wednesday. Come and look at the guest list, both of you.'

By the time she left that day, Amelie and Lady Sheen were close friends with more in common than ever she could have imagined, their concern for unfortunate women not the least of it. To her delight, Nick's father invited her to become a member of Richmond's Vestry, which she promptly accepted, thinking that, if Nick had mentioned her interest in parish concerns, he must have concentrated on the more positive aspects rather than the unorthodox ones.

As the doyen of Richmond society, the Marchioness was delighted by the prospect of taking a beauty like Miss Chester under her graceful wing and, turning her this way and that, declared that no door would be closed to her by the end of next season. It was all Stephen Chester could have hoped for and all Caterina had dreamed of, though she was never to discover the full story behind the success.

Before the all-important dinner party, which would be a farewell to Seton and a celebration of Amelie and Nick's future, Nick walked Amelie through the village one evening just as dark was falling. The lamplighter was doing his rounds with his ladder and torch, the green in the middle of Richmond was emptying of children playing conkers and chasing hoops, and a horse and cart rumbled past on its way home from the brewery on Water Lane with the aroma of roasted hops.

'Where are we going now?' Amelie said, as they turned into Paradise Road. 'You're being very mysterious, my lord.'

'Will you sit a while?'

'What, here? On the church wall? Why, my lord?'

'Because it's probably the nearest we're going to get to where the paradise garden used to be at the eastern end of the old friary. It's not quite as romantic as that, I'm afraid,' he said, peering over the wall at the outline of tombstones, 'but it seems to be a tradition our family has that proposals take place as near to the paradise as one can get, sweetheart. Will this do, d'ye think?'

'For a proposal of marriage, my love? Oh, I think so. Just here? You were not intending to take me by surprise, then?'

'Yes, but I muffed it, didn't I?' He sat beside her, pulled up one tail of his dark blue coat and fumbled in its lining for the small pocket. 'Ah, there it is. Now, is this going to fit, I wonder?'

'Er…is this as romantic as it gets, my lord?'

'Well…er, no. But I hesitate to kneel on this muddy pavement in my best pants. I will if you wish it, but… I've never done this before,' he said, plaintively.

'I'm delighted to hear it. If you must know, that was one of the conditions of my acceptance. I would not like such a proposal to be second-hand, you see. A proposal to be your *mistress* at second-hand would be different, of course, because then I might be number twenty-seven, or eight, and one must accept that…'

'Will you shut up, woman,' he said, 'and let me get a word in edgeways? Good grief, I can just about live with the blackcurrant juice in the decanter, but this is getting ridiculous. Now, what was I saying?'

'A proposal?'

'A what?'

'Stop teasing. What's that in your hand?'

'This? Blessed if I know. Let's have a look. Can't see properly in this light.'

'Then let me look. Oh…oh, Nick! That is….so beautiful.'

'What is it?'

'A ring, idiot.'

'Is that an acceptance, then?' His arms went round

her before she could reply, and it was several moments before either of them could remember at which point they should resume negotiations.

Leaning against him, Amelie stretched out a hand, twisting it under the light from the parish lamp to catch the gleam of the magnificent fire-opal surrounded by blue flashing diamonds. 'Thank you,' she whispered. 'And since you ask, yes, I will marry you.'

'It's just for the ring, isn't it?' he teased. 'And my perch-phaeton.'

'Well…er…they might be two good reasons. The house would be another—the name—the lovemaking too, that's quite good. Then there's—'

'Enough, woman. The real reason, if you please.'

'A certain condition? Does that qualify?'

He stared at her, his face a picture of sheer delight. 'Amelie?'

She nodded. 'It's a bit early to be sure, but I think it's possible.'

All teasing ended, he drew her again into his arms, holding her to him as if he would never release her, lost for words, swaying gently. 'My darling…sweetheart…my beautiful fruitful woman…my adored one. I am the happiest of men.'

'My lord,' she whispered. 'My dearest lord.'

It was not quite the done thing for adults, in love or not, to walk with their arms around each other, hip to hip, past the very elegant and proper Georgian houses lining Paradise Road. But these two did, too lost in each other to care about propriety and too much in love with their future together to dwell any longer on the problems of the past.

Epilogue

By anybody's standards, the dinner party held by the Marquess and Marchioness of Sheen for their sons was a splendidly successful event that was not an ordeal for either Amelie or Caterina, knowing so many of the guests. The betrothal of Lord Nicholas Elyot to Lady Chester was announced, after which he presented his brother Seton with four handsome horses to take with him next week when he joined the Prince of Wales's own regiment, the 10th Light Dragoons. Only the two brothers knew the true significance of this generosity. Seton's farewell to Caterina was, at her own devising, the same as that to everyone else, a kiss, a handshake, a smile and a blessing. Anything else, she said, would be superfluous.

But now the romantic focus had shifted slightly towards Miss Chester's father for, when they departed for Buxton the next day, Miss Hannah Elwick travelled with them, expecting to stay quite some time. When Caterina returned to Richmond just after Christmas, however, Hannah did not accompany her.

Nor was Tam Elwick expected to return for at least two years from his tour of Europe with a scholarly family friend, but no one seemed to mind that as much as they missed his sister.

Amelie's hopes of their becoming parents were fulfilled the next summer when she gave birth to a lusty young Elyot with a healthy pair of lungs who was given one of the family names of Adrian. But it would be inaccurate to say that the parents were in paradise, because by that time, Number 18 Paradise Road had been taken over by Stephen Chester and his growing family, while Amelie had gone to live at Sheen Court.

For the sake of the story, a slight inaccuracy exists in the dates given for Lady Nelson's residency in Bath, where Amelie met her. It was not until November that Viscountess Nelson went to stay in Sydney Place and almost immediately heard of the death of her husband, Admiral Lord Nelson, at Trafalgar on October 21st. News travelled very slowly. The sad story of the second of Lady Hamilton's twin daughters, however, is unfortunately a fact.

The escapades of Lady Adorna Pickering and Sir

Nicholas Rayne in Elizabethan Richmond mentioned by Lady Dorna Elwick in Chapter Eight, are fully recounted in *One Night in Paradise*.

Coming soon is a continuation of Miss Caterina Chester's story.

HISTORICAL ROMANCE™

LARGE PRINT

INNOCENCE AND IMPROPRIETY
Diane Gaston

Jameson Flynn is a man with a mission. Nothing will
knock him off course. Until one summer's evening in
Vauxhall Gardens, when a woman's song reminds him of
the world he left behind. Rose O'Keefe's beautiful voice
and earthy sensuality have made her a sensation. In such
dissolute company, how long can it be before her virtue
is compromised…?

ROGUE'S WIDOW, GENTLEMAN'S WIFE
Helen Dickson

Amanda O'Connell is in a scrape. If she doesn't find a
husband while she is in America, her father will marry her
off against her will. Then Christopher Claybourne – a dark,
mysterious rogue sentenced to death for murder – inspires
a plan. She'll marry him secretly and return home a widow.
But sometimes even the best laid plans fall apart…

HIGH SEAS TO HIGH SOCIETY
Sophia James

Asher Wellingham, Duke of Carisbrook, was captivated
by her! He had happened upon Lady Emma Seaton
swimming naked and, beyond her beauty, had seen the
deep curling scar on her thigh –a wound that could only
be the mark of a sword. Who was this woman? And what
lay behind her refined mask? High-born lady or artful
courtesan, Asher wanted to possess both!

MILLS & BOON®
Live the emotion

HIST0707 LP

HISTORICAL ROMANCE™

LARGE PRINT

A MOST UNCONVENTIONAL COURTSHIP
Louise Allen

Benedict Casper Chancellor, Earl of Blakeney, is the kind of elegantly conservative English lord that Alessa despises. The maddening man seems determined to wrest her away from her life in beautiful Corfu. But the Earl hasn't anticipated Alessa's propensity to get herself into a scrape. Now, in order to rescue her, this highly conventional Englishman will have to turn pirate!

A WORTHY GENTLEMAN
Anne Herries

Miss Sarah Hunter was delighted at the prospect of a season in London – and at the opportunity to spend time with the man who'd once saved her life! But Mr Elworthy was much changed. Rumours and secrets tarnished his honourable name, and the *ton* had began to wonder where the truth lay. He found a staunch champion in Sarah – but as she defended him she was inexorably drawn into the mystery…

SOLD AND SEDUCED
Michelle Styles

Lydia Veratia made one mistake – and now her freedom is forfeit to the man who all Rome knows as the Sea Wolf. Sold into marriage, the one thing over which she still has control is her own desire. So when Fabius Aro offers her a wager – if she doesn't plead for his kisses in the next seven days, she can have her independence – Lydia thinks it will be easily won. But Aro is a dangerously attractive man…

MILLS & BOON®

Live the emotion

HIST0807 LP